SUPERHERO SYNDROME

CARYN LARRINAGA

Cover Design by Night Witch Illustrations
www.nightwitchery.com

ISBN: 0-9990200-0-5
ISBN-13: 978-0-9990200-0-5

A Twisted Tree Press Publication
Salt Lake City, UT
www.TwistedTreePress.com

For Kelly, my every-day superhero.

Tess vs. Grouchy Goose

I wish I'd been with the people I loved on the day the world changed. Then again, if someone had said, "Hey Tess, reality as you know it is about to be turned upside-down. You should probably witness this moment with someone you care about. Anybody fit that bill?" I would've barked out a bitter laugh and told them I'd rather be alone. Which, as it turns out, I was.

The meteor shower was all over the news. CNN covered it nonstop in the hours before it was visible, bringing on astronomers and astrophysicists to explain why it was such a big deal for a meteor shower of this size to be happening in the middle of January. Apparently, our scientists were supposed to be able to predict this kind of thing. The fact that one had snuck up on our collective set of observatories and satellites was—to quote one NASA representative— "extraordinary."

I didn't care if it was unprecedented. I didn't care if people around the world were calling it a sign or a portent of the Second Coming or whatever. I just knew it was beautiful, and I wanted to see one more beautiful thing before I died.

The trick was explaining that to the floor nurse.

"Miss McBray, please go back to your room." Nurse Davies crossed her beefy arms over her chest and planted her white-sneakered feet to the floor. "We've been over this before. You're in no condition to leave."

"How do you know?" I growled. "Nobody here can even tell me what my condition *is*."

I shifted the weight of my duffle bag on my shoulder and leaned to the left, craning my neck to gauge the distance between Davies and the elevators. Only a few dozen yards. Sure, she towered over me. Sure, in the month I'd been in the hospital my body had wasted away to little more than a skin-wrapped skeleton. But I might be able to make a run for it.

Davies shook her head. "Do you think you're going to find the answers out there?"

"Maybe. I don't really care."

She glared at me, and I knew exactly what she was thinking. It was the same thing she'd spat at me every time I'd fought against the IV, or questioned the contents of the murky soup they forced me to eat, or requested—and then repeatedly demanded—to have my comic book collection brought into the hospital. And just when I began to worry she'd disappoint me by refusing to lean on her catchphrase, she said it.

"Stop being so melodramatic."

I actually grinned, and Davies flushed. I'd started drawing a comic book two weeks ago. It was sort of a play on the classic cat vs. mouse theme where an adorable blonde mouse outsmarted an angry old goose dressed in polka-dot scrubs. I taped the sketches up all over my room, and the orderlies liked to come in and read about the latest adventures of *Grouchy Goose and Melodrama Mouse.*

Davies was not a fan.

"You're being ridiculous. You had the good sense to check yourself in here," she said. "Now please have the sense to stay."

"You know what, Davies? You're right." I straightened up. This old hag had been bossing me around for so long, I'd forgotten who was really in charge here. "I came here on my own."

She lifted one eyebrow, but her frown—so ever-present it could've been tattooed on—deepened. "And?"

"And I'm an adult. I checked myself in here, and I'm not contagious. Now, I'd like to check myself out."

"Miss McBray, Dr. Fredericks feels he's quite close to a breakthrough. He's been working with the team at the CDC. If you'd just let him run some more tests—"

"No. I'm done with tests." Pulling my shoulders back, I raised my voice, projecting all the way across the waiting room that sat on the other side of Davies' desk. "I'd like to check myself out, please."

Several people turned their heads to cast curious glances in our direction. *That's it*, I thought. *Enjoy the show.*

Davies stared at me, her jaw set into a hard line. I stared right back. Minutes ticked by, while news coverage of the meteor shower played on the televisions in the waiting room. My eyes began to water, but I refused to surrender.

She gave in first, blinking and huffing out through her nose. "I can't stop you, Tess."

My eyes widened. She'd never addressed me by my first name before. More than anything else, it felt like a concession. In that moment, I'd stopped being her patient.

"I can leave?"

Davies nodded. "You can leave. You'll just have to sign these forms first, acknowledging that you're leaving against medical advice and releasing the hospital of any liability if—or should I say *when*—your condition worsens."

"Fine by me."

In the end, the process of checking myself out was stunningly easy. I'd pictured making a mad dash for the elevators, bashing the Close Door button repeatedly while Davies bore down on me in her pink scrubs, only just managing to escape her clutches. Signing a few papers and then calmly walking through the waiting room felt... well, a bit anticlimactic. I pressed the button to go down and waited for an elevator to come carry me to freedom, however short-lived—in the most literal sense—it might end up being.

"Wait!" Davies called from behind me.

This is it, I thought, tensing my shoulders and turning around. *She's not going to let me leave after all.*

The heavyset older woman puffed across the waiting room, her arms full of something large, brown, and hairy.

A dog? I stepped back, my shoulders brushing against the cool metal of the closed elevator doors. Of course they'd use a dog to stop me. They knew how I felt about those damn things.

But as she slowed to a stop, I saw it wasn't an animal in her arms. It was a heavy wool blanket, and she handed it to me along with a bottle of water.

"Here," she said. "You're going to watch the meteor shower, right? Go to Thatcher Park. It'll be a good spot to see it, but it'll be cold."

"Thanks." I shifted the bundle of scratchy fabric so it rested under one arm and held up the water bottle. "And this?"

"Oh, honey. I can't send you with an IV, so it's the best I can do. Keep hydrated, or else..."

She didn't need to finish. We both knew what could happen. What was *going to* happen.

Davies sniffed and let out a low cooing sound.

"Um... are you... *crying?*" I couldn't believe it. Davies ran this hospital floor like a drill sergeant, marching around with a steel rod for a spine and a matching metallic stick up her butt.

In response, she reached out and gathered me into a hug,

pulling my head into her expansive chest. "You take care of yourself, child," she muttered into my hair.

"I'm not a child," I protested. "I'm twenty-one."

My words were so muffled by her body that I doubt she heard me. If she did, she didn't care to argue. She squeezed me one last time then released me just as the elevator doors slid open. I stepped inside and pressed the button for the main lobby.

"Goodbye, Tess." Davies crossed her arms over her chest again, but the façade of the foreboding floor matron was gone, forever banished by the kind woman who'd only bothered to reveal herself when I finally left.

"Bye, Davies." I lifted a hand in a wave as the doors slid shut.

When they opened moments later, I caught a view of the dusky Albany sky through the hospital's main entrance. Outside of this building, I could survive for maybe a day. But there was no guarantee I'd live much longer than that in here, anyway. They had to bump up my fluids every day, and I still burned through everything they could pump into me. At first, I'd been peeing every half hour, but now I hadn't needed to pee in three days. It would come to a point soon where the IV wouldn't be able to keep pace with my own metabolism and I'd just... fry.

And if I was going to burn up, I didn't want to do it alone in that damn hospital room, surrounded by bleak white walls and breathing filtered air—not when a million bits of space rock were about to burn up in our atmosphere and light up the night sky. It felt poetic. It felt appropriate.

It felt like fate.

I strode across the lobby and pushed open the hospital doors, breathing in the crisp air as I passed into the dying light of day.

2
Tess vs. Stunning Celestial Objects

My 1985 Ford Escort was waiting for me in the back corner of the hospital's open lot, just where I'd left it. By the time I hiked back to the car after checking myself out, I was seriously concerned I might croak before the end of the forty-minute drive to Thatcher Park. When I'd checked into the hospital last month I hadn't yet felt like a BBQ riblet that'd sat on the grill for twenty-seven straight days, so the walk downhill from my parking spot to the registration desk hadn't felt quite so epic.

Exhausted, I tossed my duffle bag on the passenger seat and rested my head on the ripped leather steering wheel. I sat there for a while and wheezed. Then I fumbled in my bag for my key, slid it into the ignition, and turned it.

The car made a sickly *click-rwwrrr-rwwrrr-rwrrr* sound and refused to start.

"Oh, no."

This was a possibility I hadn't bothered to consider.

"No, no, no, no, no." I thumped my forehead against the steering wheel in time with my protests. "You can't do this to me. Not today. Just turn over one more time and then I promise you can rest."

Crossing the fingers on my left hand, I tried the key again with my right. *Rwwrr-rwwrr-rwwrr-rwwrr.*

"Shit!"

I banged my fists on the wheel, accidentally honking the horn. The sound startled me, and I glanced around sheepishly, hoping nobody was watching me fail at the simple task of starting my car. This entire corner of the lot was empty; nobody else was crazy enough to park a mile away from the hospital, up a hill.

Up a hill. I might not be out of luck, after all.

"This better work," I muttered to the dashboard.

If it didn't, I'd have to try to hitchhike to the park. Who would pick up a bony, stringy-haired girl with skin as gray as the winter sky and huge bags under her eyes? I wouldn't. I'd probably say something really generous like, "Get a job, druggie," and speed past her.

The alternative to hitching a ride was giving up on this mad scheme and going back inside the hospital.

Unacceptable.

Gritting my teeth, I shifted into reverse, turned the ignition back to "on," and released the emergency brake. The car rolled backward, picking up speed. I crossed the fingers on both my hands and held my breath as I popped the clutch.

The engine sputtered to life, and I let out a whoop of joy. I wouldn't miss the meteor shower. The last thing I saw wouldn't be the view from my hospital room. I wrestled with the stubborn stick shift until it agreed to go into first gear and headed out of the parking lot.

The drive to Thatcher Park took me straight through the Albany suburbs, and I flipped off the telemarketing call center where I'd last worked as I passed it. I'd been lucky enough to land that job just under a year before I got sick, which meant no FMLA protection. I was only two weeks shy of being eligible, and HR could've worked with me, but holding my job and continuing my benefits wouldn't have been cost-effective. So they canned me.

If I said my impending hospital bills didn't factor into my decision to just give up and die already, I'd be lying.

My apartment was in the opposite direction, but I didn't feel the need to stop there for anything. Couldn't take it with me where I was headed, anyway.

The thought of my cell phone, stuffed into the bottom of my duffle bag, tugged at my conscience. If I was lucky, I had a few more hours left on this planet. As I pulled onto the highway, I considered calling my sister. It'd been so long though. I tried to count the months, and stopped when I had to start counting years. Too long. Too long for me to call her out of the blue like this. *Hey, sis. Just wanted to let you know I'll be dead by morning. But don't worry about that. How's your prick husband?*

Or I could call my parents. I chewed my lip. Imagining the conversation made my chest ache. I hadn't been able to bring myself to tell them when I'd checked into Hudson. I didn't have any answers for them, and they couldn't do anything to help from Palm Bay. They'd just worry. I figured I'd give them the good news when I was cured.

So much for that.

Leaving my cell phone in my bag, I switched on the radio and listened to NPR interview yet another scientist about the meteor shower. "This will be unlike anything we've ever seen," the newscaster said. "Don't miss this once-in-a-lifetime event. Visit our website for a list of dark-sky spots near you.

"In other news, a spokesperson for the Centers for Disease Control reiterated today that while they're still not sure of the root cause for the mysterious and deadly wasting disease that's striking individuals across the globe, they've ruled out the possibility of viral or bacterial contagion. The disease, now dubbed 'Solstice Syndrome,' has been reported on every continent, including Antarctica, where a research assistant succumbed to the illness last weekend. At least four hundred deaths worldwide have been attributed to Solstice Syndrome in the last month, and hospitals in the United States alone report over 6000 active cases."

"Make that 5999," I muttered.

"Despite the large number of individuals stricken with the

disease, there has been zero evidence of the illness passing from person to person, and it doesn't appear to stem from an infection. Each patient appears to have begun exhibiting symptoms—which can include high fever, aching joints, and severe dehydration—last month, on or around December twenty-first. CDC officials warn that while the majority of patients suffer no more than a mild flu-like illness lasting seven to ten days, approximately ten percent of those who develop symptoms are at high risk of persistent dehydration and muscle loss. For these individuals, without medical intervention and IV fluids the chances of surviving the disease are severely reduced. If you or someone you know has Solstice Syndrome, please report to—"

I flicked off the radio. She wasn't telling me anything I didn't already know—or anything most everyone in the country didn't already know. Aside from the meteor shower, Solstice Syndrome was the big news item of the month, getting even more coverage than Zika or Ebola had. I'd heard enough about it. Everyone had the same facts, but I seemed to be the only person willing to face the truth. The CDC couldn't find a cause, which meant they couldn't find a cure. And since my body was a textbook overachiever, it hadn't been content with the mild version. I had the full-blown syndrome, and the prognosis was grim: IV fluids as long as my kidneys could handle it and dialysis after that.

The thought made my stomach turn. As I passed New Salem, the trees on either side of the road began to thicken into a dense forest. I thought back to my sterile hospital room and knew I'd made the right choice. This was the kind of place a girl could go to die.

Apparently, everyone in upstate New York was heeding the media's advice to see the meteor shower, and the entrance to Thatcher State Park was congested with cars and tour busses. I pulled off to the side of the road, parking between a Volkswagen camper van and an old station wagon. Around me, people piled out of their cars carrying folding chairs and coolers. I dug my sketchbook and pencils out of my duffle, grabbed Davies' blanket, and rubbed the car's cracked vinyl dashboard.

"So long, baby," I whispered. "You were good to me."

I left my keyring on the dashboard. Someone who needed a ride could drive the Escort home after the shower, and they could have my laptop and cell phone as well. Climbing out of the car, I followed a large family who was ducking into the forest at a nearby trailhead. Many other feet had walked this trail in the hours before us, packing down the snow and making a wide path. I struggled to move my atrophied legs fast enough to keep up and eventually allowed myself to lag a bit behind the family. There was only one path, and I didn't want an audience to my wheezing.

Just as I started to worry that I'd drop dead before reaching a good spot to watch the shower, the trees opened into a wide clearing. Someone had taken the time to stamp down the snow so the ground was flat and hard, and hundreds of people were setting up chairs and laying down blankets in preparation for the big show. I chose a small gap between a few clusters of people, folded Davies' blanket in half a couple of times for extra insulation, and wiggled my way under the top layer. I pulled the blanket in tight around me, wrapping myself in it like a cocoon.

I felt someone's eyes on me but ignored them. I knew what I looked like. I knew how my hazel eyes had started to look too big for their sockets and how my swollen joints looked wildly out of proportion with my thin limbs. I snuggled into the blankets and pulled out my sketch pad, drawing the people around me to keep my fingers warm. In front of me, a short woman with poofy red curls was digging around in a picnic basket, handing sandwiches to the two small children who sat beside her. To my right, a middle-aged guy with glasses was cringing as he tried to pop the cork on a champagne bottle. I flinched when he finally succeeded. The cork shot off into the trees, and the people around him laughed nervously, probably as happy as I was that they hadn't lost an eye.

A lump formed in my throat, and I gripped my pencil tighter as I sketched. Everyone here had a future. They had something to look forward to tomorrow... and the day after that. Once the meteor shower was over, they'd go home to warm kitchens and cups of hot cocoa and talk about how perfect and beautiful the night had been.

And I... well, I'd be here until someone found me, I supposed.

The sky above us was rapidly darkening. Millions of stars

shone, and everyone in the clearing stared upward waiting for the show to begin.

The universe did not disappoint.

Sometime around midnight, a streak of light appeared above me. I gasped as it bolted partway across my field of vision before vanishing. A few minutes later, another appeared. Then another. It was unlike any meteor shower I'd ever seen, and from the gasps and oohs around me, I could tell I wasn't alone in my awe.

I tasted salt. *When did I start crying?*

The cold seeped through my jacket and Davies' blanket, stinging my skin, but it didn't bother me. My tears could freeze right on my face for all I cared. I could melt into the ground beneath me and not even feel it. There was no looking away; I was riveted by the magic above me.

Three lights appeared in the sky at once. They were much brighter than the streaks that had preceded them, and they tore through the stars like soldiers rushing into battle. My eyes went wide. I knew it had to be an optical illusion, but they appeared to be coming right at me.

As the meteors sped toward the clearing, a rushing sound filled my ears, growing louder with each breath. A wave of nausea hit me, and I realized I was about to pass out. It'd been happening a lot lately. The edges of my vision fuzzed into blackness, but the cluster of meteors shone in the center, still appearing to speed directly at me.

This is it, I thought.

This was no ordinary fainting spell. It was different; I

could feel it. The skin from the top of my head down to the soles of my feet began to tingle and burn, and my heart pounded in my ears.

These were my last moments.

A face, so much like my own, swam in front of my eyes. My sister smiled at me, but her eyes were filled with sadness.

"Goodbye, Bethany," I whispered.

And the world went dark.

Tess vs. The White Light

Holy shit, *there really is a white light.*

The brightness shone through my closed eyelids, which fluttered open, trying to see what would be waiting for me on the other side. Grandma McBray? My hamster, Scampers? The light was too glaring; I couldn't see anything.

But boy, oh boy, could I feel. My body was on fire, burning and tingling, and my face was like a freezer-burned popsicle.

The light shifted, moving above my head.

"Miss?" a gruff voice asked.

The world around me came into clearer view. Next to the source of light, a bearded man in a green hat hovered over me. At least eight other faces of varying sizes and colors ringed his, and every pair of eyes was fixed on me. I recognized none of them as dead relatives or beloved pets, but I did recognize the green leaf emblem stitched onto the bearded man's hat; he was a New York State Park Ranger, and he was shining a flashlight right at me.

"Miss?" he said again.

I groaned in response. The onlookers leaning over me breathed a collective sigh of relief, and one older woman blessed herself.

"All right, everybody, give her some room." The park ranger raised a hand, warding off the crowd. He leaned down and rested a hand on my forehead; I guessed he was checking my temperature.

If I could've managed anything more coherent than a groan, I could've saved him the trouble. That ever-present fever was one of many reasons I'd been looking forward to death... to an end to the pain and discomfort of my wasted body, and the constant shivering...

"Well, you don't have a fever," he announced.

The connection between my brain and mouth was suddenly reestablished. "What?"

The park ranger raised his voice. "I said, 'You don't have a fever.' Did you get enough to eat today? Enough to drink? Do you have a history of seizures?"

"Seizures? I—no." I struggled against my blanket, in which I'd somehow become tangled. "I've never had one of those. I just... yeah. I didn't get much to eat today, that's all."

"She doesn't look like she gets enough to eat, ever," the old woman who'd blessed herself muttered to the man beside her.

Stop looking at me! I wanted to scream.

If these people decided I was unwell, they might call an ambulance or something, and back to the hospital I'd go. The thought galvanized my stringy muscles into action, and I managed to squirm out of my blanket and lift myself to my knees. The park ranger helped me to my feet and held a hand on either side of me as though waiting for me to fall over.

"I'm fine." Then, as an afterthought, "Thank you. Thank you all for your concern. But I'm fine, I swear."

I realized the truth of the words as I spoke them. The tingling burn that had coursed through my skin when I'd first woken up had dissipated, and I felt no lingering dizziness from losing consciousness. For the first time in weeks, I had zero nausea. I sucked in a deep breath of crisp, cold air and grinned. I wasn't even wheezing. I raised my hands and patted my face. It still felt skeletal and thin on the outside, but on the inside... everything just felt *right*. I'd forgotten what it felt like to not live in constant pain. I could flex my fingers without my joints screaming in protest. I could even raise my arms above my head and bend in every direction at my waist, and *nothing hurt*. I laughed as tears streamed down my face.

"Miss?" The park ranger reached out and touched my shoulder. "Are you sure you're all right?"

"I'm great." I smiled at him and nodded to the onlookers. "Thanks again for checking on me. Really."

With that, I gathered up the brown blanket and headed down the path as quickly as my legs would carry me. They were still weak and little more than skin on bone, but I no longer felt like they were going to give out from underneath me. Instead, it reminded me of pushing myself during gym in high school, trying to improve my mile time for a chance to win an Amazon gift card. It didn't feel good, necessarily, but my body didn't really seem to mind the extra effort.

A feeling I never thought I'd have again began to stir awake inside of me. *Hope.* I was alive. More than that, I was better. I didn't even feel the urge to go to a doctor to confirm it; I just knew. The syndrome had left my body. Somehow... I'd survived.

"Suck it, Dr. Frederickson!" I shouted. My words echoed off the trees around me, and I let out a whoop. I'd never need to see or hear from him again.

Except...

"Dammit!" I came to a halt beside my car as a thought struck me. I'd certainly be hearing from him again. Or at least I'd be hearing from the hospital when they billed me for my inpatient stay. I didn't dare guess how much it would cost. No matter the amount, it'd be too much for me to pay.

Sliding behind the wheel of my car, where my keys were thankfully still resting on the dash, I felt all the hope and joy from the last few moments seep out of me. I was alive, but what kind of life did I have? I was broke, unemployed, and nobody in the world cared about me.

That's not true. She *probably still does.*

I saw my sister's face for the second time that evening. I'd been surprised when hers was the image my brain drudged up to show me in my last moments. I don't know what I'd been expecting to see exactly, but it hadn't been Bethany.

And why would it have been? I hadn't seen her in years. We hadn't spoken since I'd left home. I was sure the divide was her fault.

Probably, anyway.

For all I knew, she'd left Weyland after I had. Maybe she'd followed my parents to Florida or finally made good on her dream to move to Paris to work in the fashion industry. But if I had any money for betting, I would've put it all on the odds that she was still living in Weyland, still married to that walking liquor bottle, and still working at the cosmetics store in the mall.

Thoughts of her tugged at my mind, and as I sat in my car staring out at the dark woods, pieces of a plan snapped together in my head like a dollar-store jigsaw puzzle. Enough bits were missing that I couldn't make out the whole picture, but even partially completed it made more sense than staying in Albany. Weyland was cheap. Weyland had jobs. And Weyland had my sister, who'd spent her childhood cooking colcannon and Shepherd's pie beside my mom and who might be willing to have me over for dinner four or five times a week.

My empty stomach gurgled and squeaked, and a few more pieces popped into place—enough to convince me to do something I never thought I'd be crazy enough to do.

It was time to go home.

Tess vs. The Sidewalk

I've made a huge mistake.

Downtown Weyland surrounded me. Commercial high rises blocked out the sky except for what was directly above me, and the stench of auto exhaust and bus fumes hammered my sinuses as the frigid January air bit at my cheeks.

What on earth had possessed me to come back here? I'd turned what little life I'd built in Albany completely upside down in the past week, breaking the lease on my apartment and even selling my car to fund this nutty scheme. I'd spent eight brutal hours on a bus cruising down the East coast at a miserable sixty miles an hour... for *this*?

"Hey lady, you comin' or goin'?" A burly man in a pinstriped suit waved a briefcase at me. "Some of us wanna get home by dinner."

"Sorry." I stepped into the doorway of the diner behind

me and tried to find my bearings. It'd been three years since I'd been in this city. Even then, I'd spent most of my time in the suburb where we lived and only came downtown for concerts or school events.

I admitted defeat and ducked into the diner, where the hostess was kind enough to give me directions to the nearest train station.

As I trudged down Keel Avenue in the direction she'd pointed me, I flirted with the idea of calling my parents to tell them I'd come back to Weyland, but ditched the notion almost immediately. I wasn't ready for my mother to shriek, "I told you so!" She'd hated the idea of me moving out of state in the first place—never mind the fact that she and my dad bolted from Weyland the instant I was out of the house.

Her words from our last telephone conversation before I'd checked into the hospital still rang in my ears. *It's probably food poisoning, Tess. You know you should be more careful about what you eat. And how much you eat. Are you watching your weight? You know you tend to carry a little extra pudge in your tummy.*

If only she could see me now. In the days since the meteor shower, I'd had the appetite of a thirteen-year-old boy. I ate out at restaurants every single meal and never skipped appetizers or dessert. This new "Eat Everything!" diet was doing my stringy limbs some good, and I was starting to feel less like a newborn deer.

My credit card company had already texted me four times to make sure the charges were legit. I normally only splurged at Shelton's Comic Chalet on some Wednesdays—okay, *every* Wednesday—especially if an alternate cover issue was being released.

My phone buzzed in my pocket. I had to unzip my long, puffy black jacket to fish it out of my jeans. Bethany's face grinned at me from the display.

"Are you in town? How was the trip? When are you coming over?" My sister rattled off questions like bullets, and she was as loud as gunfire to boot.

Wincing, I held the phone away from my ear. "I literally just got off the bus. I have to drop my bag off at my apartment first."

"Where are you living?"

"I found a place off Triton." I weaved through the crowd of office drones who were marching toward the train station with me. "My stuff is supposed to be waiting for me."

Silence from the other end of the phone.

"Hello? Bethany? Are you still there?"

She exhaled into her mouthpiece. "Triton? That's in the Trident."

"Yeah, I know. How else do you think I could afford it?"

"I don't like it. It's not safe there."

"As opposed to your neighborhood? By the docks?"

"You think the docks are dangerous?" Bethany said with a snort. "Watch the news, Tess. There've been a lot of kidnappings. Girls our age. Jim Jenkins says it's a human trafficking ring."

"Don't tell me that old vampire is still doing the news."

"Every night at five. Listen, I'm not kidding around. At least ten girls have gone missing in the last month alone, and four of them were last seen in the Trident. Promise me you'll be careful."

"Hey, you know me. Careful is my mid—"

"I *mean* it, Tess." Her voice was firm.

"You sound like Grandma."

"Good. She was the only person in the whole family with any sense. Now promise me."

"For God's sake, settle down. I'll be careful. I swear."

"Okay. Do you remember how to get here? Dinner's tomorrow at six."

"Yeah, I'll take the Fishbone to Portside, right?"

"Right." Bethany giggled into the phone, sounding more like a little girl than my older sister. "Aw, you've always loved those trains. I wish I was there to see your wittle face when you get to ride them again."

"I do *not* love the train. It's gross and smells like fish, just like the rest of this godforsaken place."

A tall woman in a cream-colored pea-coat shot me a dirty look. I raised my eyebrows at her.

"If you don't like what I have to say," I told her, "don't eavesdrop."

The woman wrinkled her nose and picked up her pace, quickly outstripping me with her long legs. I glared at her back as she went. *Weylanders,* I thought. *Bunch of jerks.*

"What was that?" Bethany asked in my ear.

"Nothing. I'm coming up on the station. I'll see you soon, okay?"

I hung up the phone and shoved it back into my pocket. The throng of commuters into which I'd managed to insert myself had reached the wide staircase that led to the elevated train platform, and I wanted both hands free in case I had to shove my way onto a train car. I managed to hustle my way in front of a few people to board the train and slid down into a plastic yellow seat with a sigh.

As far as I was concerned, Weyland was a stinking bucket of fish guts. I hated almost everything about this town. Not the trains, though. Bethany was right; I loved them. The steady *click-click-clack-clack* as the railcars sped away from downtown was comforting, like laying my head on my mom's chest and hearing her breathe when I was little. I'd been riding these trains my whole life, and everything about them —the elevated tracks, the screeching of the brakes, even the ever-present discarded coffee cups and fast-food wrappers from the hordes of commuters—reminded me I was home.

Back in the early 1940's, Weyland had tried to re-invent itself as the premier cultural center of the Atlantic coast. The city council went on a spending spree, authorizing millions to build up infrastructure. The crown jewel was the WART. That's right, WART. Weyland Area Rapid Transit.

Did I mention yet what a well-thought-out place my hometown is?

The elevated commuter rail system was modeled after Chicago's famous L trains, and the city council hoped to bring in new businesses and young working-class couples who would fill in the new subdivisions around the shipyards. They even dared to dream that families with new money would build summer homes along the coastline. The strategy worked, bringing in people like my grandparents, who'd imagined kissing their children goodbye and then reading the paper on the train as it carried them from their tidy bungalows near the docks to the new downtown high-rises. The blue-collar workers in the canneries and factories near the docks gave the main rail line and its splintering sub-lines a more fitting name: the Fishbone.

I leaned my head against the glass for a moment before pulling a pencil and my trusty sketchbook out of my backpack and beginning to draw. I'd missed this view, the way the crowded skyscrapers gave way to five- and six-story mixed-use developments, growing older and more rundown as we left downtown. My hand drifted across the thick, rough paper as I sketched the skyline until we passed into the Trident.

On either side of the tracks, three long blocks of identical brown apartment buildings marched between downtown and the suburbs like dominoes. They weren't pretty. They weren't exciting. They were the city's response to an over-population problem, and most taxpayers didn't give a crap if low-income folks had to live in the architectural equivalents of oversized and overcooked toaster waffles. Somewhere in the sea of postage-stamp-sized balconies was my new home.

The train coasted to a stop at the station on Triton

Avenue, and I hoisted my bag up onto my shoulder. The doors slid open, and the frowning face of Jim Jenkins greeted me from an advertisement over the platform's benches. The serious-faced anchor had been whipping the residents of Weyland into panicked frenzies over everything from tropical storms ("Watch out for looters, folks! They'll be using power outages to their advantage!") to NBA finals ("No matter which team wins, there'll be riots in the streets! You can count on that!"). In all likelihood, the "human trafficking ring" Bethany was fretting over was nothing more than a few runaways hyped up by a paranoid old newsman.

I descended the concrete steps from the platform to the dim street below. As the sun began to set, all natural light disappeared beyond the towering apartment complexes around me. In the ritzier parts of Weyland, the city's elite built homes high up on the hillsides to enjoy the sunset over the mountains to the west and the sunrise over the ocean to the east. Here in the Trident, the residents at street level had to live with artificially shorter days.

The ground floor of each building was taken up by shops, fruit stands, and payday loan centers. I glanced into the windows of a few fast food joints as I passed them, my stomach growling. I was ravenous after surviving on chips and soda for the whole trip. I suddenly felt exhausted, and all I wanted to do was find my apartment and collapse onto the floor with a bucket of French fries.

As I walked down Triton toward my new building, the street lamps dotting the sidewalk every fifty yards started turning on, creating pools of sickly yellow light that didn't come anywhere close to touching each other. The tiny hairs on the back of my neck twitched as I scurried from lamppost to lamppost, and I wondered if Jim Jenkins could be a broken clock, finally right after chiming midnight all day. My sister's warning rang in my ears, and a tiny pang of fear prickled in my chest. My hand slipped into the depths of my bag, curling around the tiny canister that rested at the bottom. Despite my tough talk to Bethany, I was just a teensy bit nervous about moving to this area... nervous enough to grab some Mace from a rest stop on the way down from Albany. With my defensive strategy in hand, I scanned the businesses around me for somewhere to duck into for a cheap meal and a little sanctuary from the dark street.

Just as I was about to make a decision between a greasy fast food chain and a cheap sandwich place, a tall man in a hooded sweatshirt stepped out from the covered doorway of a pawn shop and fell into step a few paces behind me.

Is he following me?

Only one way to find out. I rounded the corner onto Palaemon Street—a narrow offshoot mainly filled with boarded-up businesses—and he made the same turn a second later.

It didn't feel like a coincidence. Sure, he could live near me. Hundreds of people lived on each of these city blocks; he could easily be one of them. But would that explain why his strides exactly matched mine? Why he slowed when I slowed, and kept up with me when I quickened my pace to a light trot?

Chancing a glance over my left shoulder, I confirmed that the man was still behind me. His hands were tucked into the wide pocket at the front of his dark hoodie. We locked eyes, and fear stabbed my chest again. He dropped back a few paces, but when I turned my face forward again, I could still feel his stare boring into the back of my head. No. This wasn't coincidence. He was following me.

My breath caught. I tightened my grip on the can of Mace, visualizing pulling it out of my bag, spinning around, and blasting it into his eyes. Was it even possible, or would I just spray wide, somehow managing to blind myself in the process?

Thin tendrils of panic began to creep around my organs. There was no way I'd be able to fight him off when he grabbed for me, and it had become a definite *when* in my mind. I wanted to walk more quickly, but I was terrified he'd realize I was onto him, and that would spark him into making his move. Ahead of me, the white-and-blue banner of Helena's Place glowed comfortingly in the twilight from the other end of the block. I knew that sign from the internet search I'd done while looking for an apartment. Safety lay just over that diner.

Don't run, I cautioned myself. *Act normal.*

The word echoed in my mind. Normal. Normal. Normal. In an instant, it lost all meaning. There was no normal. There was just me, a tiny girl who was literally just skin and bones.

And then there was him, this hulking monster with some-thing in his hoodie pocket.

What's he hiding in there?

I imagined a chloroform-soaked rag, a switchblade, or even a gun, and picked up my pace, nearly sprinting toward my building. I didn't want to look behind me; I was sure if I did, I'd see his face inches from my own and feel his hand close around my wrist. But when I was within a few yards of my building, I knew I had to check again.

If he's still following me, I decided, *I'll duck into the diner for help.*

Eyes wide, I turned my head to look over my shoulder once more. He was still there, but he'd allowed the distance between us to grow so he trailed me by half a block. The tension in my chest loosened, and a sigh escaped my lungs.

And then the toe of my beat-up sneaker caught the edge of an upraised section of sidewalk, and I pitched forward. By instinct, my hands rushed upward to protect my face, and the rough concrete shredded my palms as I dove into it. My canister of Mace went flying, and I heard a faint *clink* as it landed in the street.

Footsteps thundered toward me from behind. I twisted my neck to see the man who'd been following me, now sprinting toward my prone body.

Tess vs. The Neighbors

My stalker skidded to a halt beside me and grabbed my shoulder. I was completely defenseless, and he knew it. I couldn't help it; I screamed, letting out a high-pitched yelp that echoed off the brick facades of the buildings around us. My shoulder burned where the stranger gripped me, and then I felt it.

A pulse—like an electric shock—raced from my fingertips, up my arms, and down my spine. My body convulsed, every muscle twitching together like they were part of a choreographed flash mob.

"Whoa!" a deep voice said, and the pressure on my shoulder released. "Are you okay, lady?"

"Don't touch me!" I shouted, rolling away from him. The sidewalk scratched my face, but I didn't care. I ended up on the large welcome mat in front of the restaurant with the blue-lit sign and only stopped moving when I bumped into someone's legs. Scrambling to my feet, I raised my hands and held them in front of me in a defensive pose.

The hooded man mirrored my stance, raising his hands in front of him. "Hey, it's okay. I'm not trying to hurt you." With one hand, he pulled back his hood and revealed a lean face and chin-length, sandy blond hair. "I'm not trying to hurt her," he repeated in a louder voice, looking past me.

I turned my head to peer into the restaurant. I'd attracted the attention of everyone inside, and several people had left their tables to stand in the entrance and get a better look. I searched their eyes; they looked curious and a little frightened. The woman whose legs I'd rolled into stepped backward, closer to the knot of other diners.

That's when I realized nobody was looking at the hooded guy. They were all staring at *me*, the Skeletor-impersonator in the puffy coat. They had the same expressions on their faces as the other patients in the hospital, and the strangers at the meteor shower, and the park ranger.

Pity mixed with disgust.

Only one person looked truly concerned. A tall woman with long, dark curls pushed her way through the crowd. Deep lines creased her forehead, giving her a serious appearance, but her brown eyes were warm.

"Are you all right?" she asked.

I glanced back at the blond guy who'd been following me. His eyes were wide, and he looked genuinely surprised to be suddenly faced with a knot of onlookers. He met my gaze and raised his hands a little higher.

"I swear," he said. "I was just trying to help."

The woman nodded to him. "Okay, then. Why don't you move along?"

He dipped his head in a quick nod of his own and hurried along the sidewalk, walking in the same direction I'd been heading and ducking into a record store a few doors farther down the street. My shoulders fell. All that fuss, and he was just a regular guy shopping for some music.

"Show's over, everybody," the woman called to her patrons.

They shuffled back to their seats, murmuring to one another. I distinctly heard the word "crazy," and the knot in my chest tensed up again.

"Thank you," I told the older woman.

She looked down at me, the lines of her face deepening as she frowned. She had a motherly demeanor, and I got the sense she was trying to decide whether to call the cops or give me a hot meal. Then her expression softened, and the crease between her eyebrows let up.

"You still haven't answered me," she said. "Are you all right?"

"Yeah." I turned my hands over, assessing the damage. The flesh on my palms was raw and red, and bits of gravel had cut angry little swaths into my skin before lodging themselves into the meaty parts above my wrists. But they didn't hurt as much as my pride. I gazed around at the restaurant patrons, who continued to stare at me from their seats. "I just feel stupid."

She shrugged. "Yesterday, I dropped an entire tray of enchiladas on the ground while I was serving a table. I'm still waiting for the dry-cleaning bill from the customer they landed on. We all have those moments."

"Seriously? You're not just making it up to make me feel better?"

She grinned. "I wouldn't make up something that embarrassing. Good thing I own this place, or I could've gotten fired."

It was funny, but I was still too shaken up from my fall to give anything more than a weak chuckle. "Well, thanks again. I appreciate it."

"Want a cup of coffee? It's on the house."

My stomach growled, but all I wanted was to get into my apartment, away from the judgmental eyes of the diner's patrons. I shook my head. "I'd better not."

She shrugged and picked up a tray from an empty table. "Offer stands, any time. Good luck out there."

I wanted to tell her I didn't need it, but as I stepped out of the diner and cast a nervous glance up and down the block, I suddenly felt like I could use all the luck I could get. I stared at the spot on the sidewalk where I'd convulsed just moments before and shuddered. I honestly didn't know what was worse: that I'd beefed up my hands or that I'd had an audience while I'd done it.

Either way, so far Weyland didn't seem any happier to see me than I was to see it.

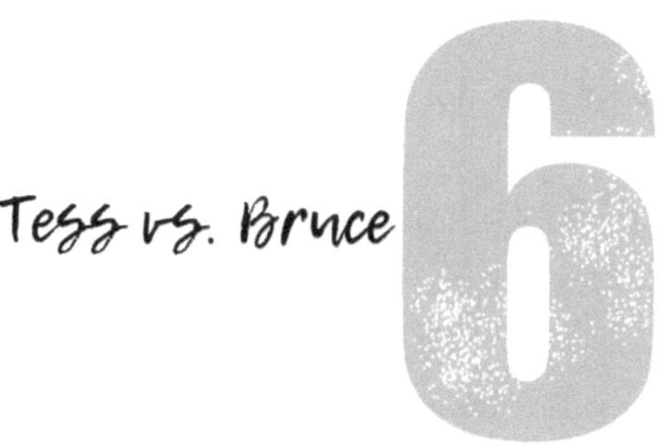

Tess vs. Bruce

Bethany's hands shook. Steam billowed up from the tea as she poured it into the china cup in front of me, and I shivered. We had no business sitting on her screened porch in January. Even though I sat within the reach of the small electric heater, cold air pricked at my face. Every gust of wind from the ocean managed to scream its way through the neighborhood and race down the back of my shirt. Grateful for my mittens, I wrapped one end of my long scarf around my neck and pulled up the hood on my puffy black jacket.

She sat across the coffee table from me, cradling her cup in her hands, and just *stared* at me. I stared back, trying to figure out her expression. She didn't look angry. She didn't look sad. She just looked like she was trying to figure out where in the hell I'd come from. It was like looking into a very confused mirror.

I cleared my throat. "So... I'm back."

"You're back," she said.

I could only nod. I didn't like it. When I'd texted her that I was moving back, she'd seemed excited. And yesterday on the phone, she'd sounded happy I was in town. I'd dared to hope she'd forgotten why we'd stopped talking, and maybe we could just slip back into the easy friendship we'd always shared.

But from the way she was gazing at me, half in wonder and half in disbelief, I got the feeling something very awkward was coming.

And I was right.

"So, what was it that finally brought you back?" she asked. "I thought it'd take the apocalypse to ever bring you home."

"What gave you that idea?"

"Oh, I don't know. Maybe because you said, 'I'm leaving and I'm never coming back.'" She took a sip of her tea. "Right after you called me a stupid bitch."

Heat raced up the back of my neck. So this had been a trap. She'd been all nice to me on the phone yesterday just so she could lure me here and confront me? What a bi—

But just as I was about to think it, the memory of that day came back. It was my eighteenth birthday. We'd been standing in the living room at my parents' house drinking champagne (hey, I was the guest of honor—of course I had some) and celebrating, and then *he'd* waltzed into the room, made a joke about how I was "legal" now, smacked Bethany on her ass, and burped like a foghorn.

Maybe I'd been emboldened by the champagne. Maybe there was something magical about being an adult on paper that made me think I could talk to other adults however I wanted. Whatever the reason, I'd suddenly been brave enough to call him a drunken waste of space.

The room had fallen silent.

Then, for some inexplicable reason, everyone in the room started yelling at *me*. Like I was the bad guy. Like *I* was the one who'd treated Bethany like shit for years and given my parents zero respect ever. Yep, my parents, my aunts and uncles, and even my cousins had glared at me, mouths hanging open after asking things like, "How dare you?"

And Bethany? She was the worst of all. She burst into tears and demanded an apology. When I refused, she called me an ungrateful brat and stomped off to comfort her husband.

Cue the "stupid bitch" remark, the claim that I'd never set foot in Weyland or see any of them again, and a flurry of online job applications to anywhere and everywhere far away from here.

Bethany was still staring at me as little wisps of steam rose up from her teacup and curled around the tip of her narrow nose. I was struck again by the fact that her eyes weren't angry... She really just looked curious. I wondered if she'd already forgiven me. Was it even possible? I'd never even apologized.

So I did.

"I'm sorry," I said.

She blinked, nodded, and gestured toward my cup. "Milk or sugar?" she asked.

I frowned at my sister. Could it really be that easy? I wasn't in any hurry to discuss the past, so I rolled with it. "Since when have you used either one? What is this, *Downton Abbey*?"

She cringed. "Okay. You got me. I've been marathoning it all week."

"And now you're suddenly British?"

"I just want to try it. They're always doctoring their tea just like it's coffee." She pushed a sugar bowl toward me. "Come on, Tess. Let's give it a go."

I picked up the bowl and set it on a side table, effectively exiling it from my presence. "Ew, no. Milk and sugar in peppermint tea? You're a monster."

We grinned at each other. I hadn't realized how much I'd missed teasing her. Mom used to call it "poking the bear" when I was little, because Bethany would get so flustered that she'd freak out and start throwing around insults. They never stung, though. The angrier she got, the funnier I thought it was, and I'd laugh until I puked.

She didn't disappoint. "*I'm* the monster? You're the one wearing sweatpants outside your house."

I burst out laughing. It was like a spell was broken. Bethany doubled over and giggled, and all the awkwardness and tension in the air fizzled out, carried away from us by the winter breeze. And I had to admit she was right. She was chic as always in a pair of high-waisted pants and a cream-colored Burberry coat. Meanwhile, the stuffing was poking out of my jacket, and I had a mustard stain on my gray sweatpants.

"Hey, give me a break. The rest of my clothes haven't gotten here yet." I nodded toward her outfit. "Once I can unpack, I'll look all fancy, too."

Bethany tucked her blonde hair behind her ears. "If you think comic book T-shirts and baggy jeans are 'fancy,' then—"

"What the hell is that?" I interrupted.

A sliver of purple glared at me from her cheekbone. She'd done a good job covering most of the bruise with makeup, but now that her long hair no longer masked the left side of her face, one of the edges shone through.

She brought a hand up and touched the mark. "Oh... I-I walked into an open cupboard." She laughed, but it sounded forced. "It was a silly mistake, but you know how clumsy I am."

"Yeah. Funny how you went from being as graceful as a swan to a total klutz right when you married Bruce." I cringed when his name left my mouth. Just when we'd gotten past our last ugly conversation, *he* had to come up again.

Bethany's eyes hardened. "He had nothing to do with this."

I leaned forward and studied her face. She was three years older than me, but most people wouldn't know it. She looked like she could be my twin. We shared the same slender build and fair complexion, and even had the exact same hazel eyes. I'd taken to cutting my hair into a short page-boy, but Bethany loved to keep her golden locks long and flowing. She'd always looked like a fairytale princess. I saw now that behind her clever use of cosmetics, her face looked gaunt. Her eyes looked too large in their sockets, and her cheeks were hollow.

She looked... unhealthy. Which made her look more like me than ever.

"When I texted you last week, you said Bruce was doing well." I reached out and touched the bruise with a gloved hand. "You said things were good."

"They *are* good, Tess." She leaned away from me and crossed her arms over her chest. "God, I haven't seen you in three years, and I want to see you, okay? But if you're going to be here... you need to *let this go.*"

We glared at each other across the coffee table for a moment. There were so many things I wanted to say. Each one vied for position in the place between my brain and my mouth, pushing and shoving to be the first to come out. I wanted to yell at her for lying to me, for letting Bruce continue to treat her like a punching bag. I wanted to beg her to come with me. My apartment was a one-bedroom, but we'd shared before. We could share again.

But I hadn't come here to fight. I'd come here because out of everyone in the world, it'd been *her* face that'd popped into my head while I'd thought I was dying. And I'd just barely avoided an argument. *Can we just have a normal conversation?* I wanted to scream. *Now isn't the time for this.*

"You're right," I said. "I don't want to fight with you. Just... promise you'll come to me if you need help?"

Her shoulders relaxed, and she let her hands fall back into her lap. "You don't need to worry about me. I'm the big sister. I get to worry about you."

I stopped myself from telling her I wouldn't have to worry about her anymore if she'd just cut that asshole Bruce out of her life. It wouldn't be productive, and I didn't want this visit to end in a shouting match. So instead, I sipped my tea in silence and waited for her to make the next move.

She took a deep breath and smiled at me. "So, you didn't answer me. What brought you back? The Big Apple wasn't exciting enough for you, Tess McBray?"

"I think you're picturing *Sex and the City* or something. You know I wasn't in Manhattan, right? I was in Albany. Totally different vibe."

She waved a hand. "Whatever. You were in New York, right?"

I didn't want to drag out my last three years of failing at being an adult and lay it all on the coffee table for Bethany to see. She didn't need to know about my string of part-time and dead-end jobs, each more unbearable than the last. And she certainly didn't need to know I'd had the Solstice Syndrome.

"It's not an exciting story or anything. I lost my job." That was technically true. I glossed over the rest with a shrug. "Figured if I was starting over, might as well do it back here."

"Liar. You came back because you missed me."

She was kidding; I could tell. But she didn't realize how close to the truth she was getting.

"So, are you sad about leaving anything behind in New York? Like... any guys?" Bethany batted her eyelashes and puckered her lips. It was the same face she'd made when she caught me kissing our next-door neighbor, Anatolya, behind our dad's toolshed when I was seven.

I snorted. "Yeah, right. Trust me, there wasn't anybody who cried when I left. Maybe the guy who ran the comic book shop by my office. I don't know how he'll put his kids through college without me around."

"Well, that's one thing I can help with."

"Putting Mr. Shelton's kids through college?" I said with a grin.

"No, you dork. Finding you a guy who would be sad to see you go." She straightened her spine and bowed, twirling her hand toward the ground. "Bethany Fabiano, matchmaker extraordinaire. I'll find you a guy lickety-split."

"Oh, please don't." I couldn't imagine who she'd dig up to take me out on a date. One of Bruce's drunk friends, no doubt. Gee whiz, that'd be great.

"I mean it," she said. "I'll admit, I don't know many single guys. Er... any single guys, actually. But I'll help you out however I can. We can set you up with one of those online profiles—I see commercials for them all the time! And oooooooh!" She clapped her hands together. "I can give you a makeover. You'll love it, I promise."

I pursed my lips. When Bethany was excited about something, there was no talking her out of it, as evidenced by the fact that she'd married Bruce in the first place. If she was determined to find me a boyfriend, it was a sure part of my future. I decided to let her set me up on exactly one date, show her I was willing to play ball, and then I would shut the whole endeavor down.

Sipping at my tea, I marveled at her across the table. I'd left in a blaze of profanity and drama and hadn't bothered to send her a single note or Christmas card the entire time I'd been gone. If somebody did that to me, I'd write them off. But here she was, fussing over tea and biscuits and worrying about my love life. I was a lousy sister. I didn't deserve her, and she didn't deserve to be left in the dark about the important things in my life.

I set my teacup down on the table and took a deep breath. It was time to tell her about my illness.

Just then, the back door burst open. Our peaceful afternoon tea was over. Bruce was home.

Bethany's husband strode onto the porch, baring his teeth in a wide grin. For the most part, he still looked like the popular wide receiver from our high school football team—tall, wavy haired, and blue eyed. But he'd put on a lot of weight in the years since I'd seen him. His hair was beginning to thin, and his once-handsome face was marred by a dense network of spidery blood vessels.

My shock at seeing him age fifteen years in a fifth of that time was mingled with a little bit of satisfaction. He'd always thought he was hot shit, and I'd once overheard him telling another guy, "It's not cheating when you look this good." It was nice to see somebody in this world get a little come-uppance.

Bethany jumped to her feet. In an instant, her entire manner shifted. Her shoulders hunched, and she looked several inches shorter than she had a moment ago. Even her voice changed. It went up in pitch, making her sound like a little girl.

"Oh! You're home early, sweetheart," she squeaked.

"Dinner ready yet, Beth?" he boomed.

I raised an eyebrow. She'd always hated that nickname, preferring the full version. When we were kids, she told me the more syllables your name had, the classier it sounded. It'd been a not-so-subtle criticism of my decision to go by Tess rather than Teresa.

"N-no, I'm so sorry," Bethany stammered. "We weren't expecting you till five."

"Don't worry about it. Just get movin'." Bruce stomped over to Bethany's chair, favoring his left leg. He sat down, propped his feet up on a wicker ottoman, and lit a cigarette. "And bring me a cold one, would ya?"

Bethany scurried into the house, returning a moment later with a can of beer. She handed it to her husband and ducked back inside. I heard pots and pans being shuffled around through the kitchen window behind me.

Bruce cracked open his beer, took a long swig, and grinned at me. "So you're back. Beth told me you couldn't hack it in the big city. Ahh-hahahaha!"

I cringed. I'd forgotten about Bruce's ear-splitting cackle. I reminded myself not to make any attempt to be funny. It wouldn't be hard. I had no desire to impress this guy by making him laugh.

"Yep. Here I am." I slumped into my chair and tried to invent a plausible reason to get out of staying for dinner. I couldn't handle the thought of sharing a meal with this guy. I'd thought I could forgive Bruce for the way he'd treated Bethany in the early years of their marriage, but that was when I'd still believed her lies about him changing his ways. The man who sat before me now bore no signs of improvement, and Bethany's bruise spoke volumes.

Bruce stretched his arms up over his head and cast a satisfied gaze over his backyard. Their house sat partway down the forested slope to the seaport, and their screened porch offered a view of the smokestacks from the factories and fish packing plants that surrounded the harbor.

"You made the right call," he said between sips of his beer. "Weyland's a good place to be. Treated us good, anyhow."

"Are you still working at the fish processing plant?" I asked, more out of politeness than genuine interest.

He nodded. "Got promoted last year. Floor supervisor now. We was thinking of moving down to Florida before that. Be closer to your parents. Sunshine, man. But they put the old golden handcuffs on me. Couldn't turn down that dough."

Something twisted in my stomach. Bruce was somebody's

supervisor? He was in charge of hiring and firing people? I almost wanted to meet the idiot who'd decided to promote him, because I wouldn't trust Bruce to supervise a houseplant. Especially not since he was drinking again.

"Once we decided we was here for good, we even got a dog." Bruce put two fingers into his mouth and whistled shrilly. Before the sound had finished echoing through the nearby trees, a lean Doberman came crashing out of the house and ran up to Bruce, who let the dog lick his fingers.

I tensed. This was a large animal, sleek and muscular, and despite the fact that he was currently lapping at his master's hand, he looked vicious. The muscle in my left thigh twinged, and I winced at the memory of my aunt Catherine's shiba inu's tiny, sharp teeth sinking into my leg when I was eight. I drew back into my chair, almost unconsciously trying to put some distance between myself and Bruce's attack dog.

Bruce saw the motion and grinned at me. "Still hate dogs, huh?"

"I don't hate them." I eyed the large animal. "They just make me nervous, that's all."

"You don't need to be scared of this one. He's a good boy, ain't ya, Bear?" he crooned. "Say hello to our guest."

The dog leapt away from Bruce and lunged toward me. With a small shriek, I tried to pivot away from him, but he'd already planted his front legs on my lap and began sniffing my face. I stiffened, not sure what to do. I must have smelled good enough to eat because he started licking me vigorously. When I opened my mouth to shout at him to get down, his slimy tongue slipped inside like a slobbery French kiss.

The shock of that indignity was enough to make my arms move on their own, and I shoved the dog away from me and jumped up out of my chair.

"Ack!" I coughed and spat onto the ground. "Dog breath! Gross!"

"Ahh-hahahaha!" Laughter consumed Bruce, and he doubled over in his chair. "Don't complain too much, Tess. Bet that's the most action you've had in years!"

Shaking with anger, I stormed into the house, leaving Bruce to cackle away on the porch behind me. Bethany was in the kitchen putting a casserole into the oven.

Her delicate eyebrows knitted together when she saw me. "What's wrong?"

"Nothing," I lied. "Listen, I'm not feeling well. Can I take a raincheck on dinner? My place next time."

Disappointment welled up in her eyes, but it wasn't enough to keep me there. Wishing I had the guts to drag Bethany out with me, I grabbed my backpack off a kitchen chair, left the house, and headed for the Fishbone. It would've been pointless to try to get her to leave. She'd have dug her heels into the ground and fought me all the way down the block. Bruce had some kind of hold on her that was impossible to break.

This is why I'm single, I thought, watching my breath puff into the air in front of me. *There aren't enough good guys in the world, and there are way too many Bruces.*

Tess vs. The Wall

My head throbbed and my stomach churned as I stomped down the sidewalk away from Bethany's house. Anger and sadness, and yeah, maybe even a little bit of shame roiled inside of me. I suddenly felt sick, and I clenched and unclenched my fists in time with my footsteps.

I reached the run-down station on Portside Avenue just as a train arrived. The doors stuck, and for a moment I debated sprinting down the platform to try the next car. Just as I leaned to the side to start running, the stubborn door finally slid open with a wet *thunk* and I stepped inside.

The train sped me toward the city, and I scowled out the window. I couldn't get Bruce's stupid bloated face out of my head. Over and over, he brayed about his damn dog licking the inside of my mouth. The image skipped and froze in my mind until it was more like a panel in a comic book than a real memory, and anger simmered in my belly.

By the time I reached my stop, that simmering mass had become a rolling boil, and I realized I wasn't just *angry* at Bruce. I hated him. I hated him even more than I hated being sick, and I thought that'd hold the high score forever. I stomped down Triton and Palaemon in a haze, trusting my feet to carry me through the red-tinged miasma of my own emotions. Before I knew it, I was back in my near-empty apartment.

The glow from the sign above Helena's Place cast the tiny living room in blue light. It felt like a little aquarium. The entire apartment was roughly the size of my bedroom when I'd been growing up at home, but the small space felt airy and roomy compared to my hospital room. Maybe it was because it was so bare. Four large cardboard boxes sat squarely in the center of the room, but my furniture was apparently coming to Weyland from Albany by way of Moscow. I sunk down into a corner of my living room and pulled off my coat and mittens.

My hands were still tender from the scrapes I'd gotten the day before. I rested them on my thighs, palms facing up toward the high plaster ceiling, and I wondered how long they'd take to heal.

"Unpacking while injured," I grumbled to myself. "Thanks a lot, jerk."

Men. I didn't know if they were awful everywhere or just in Weyland. Literally every man I'd encountered since coming back was a raging prick, from the guy in the hoodie to Bruce.

And there was his face again, laughing at me from the empty white canvas of my living room wall. I clenched my fists and winced. They were too tender for that—so tender I didn't dare unclench them. But I wished they weren't. I wished I could go back to Bethany's house and drag Bruce out through the back door, then beat his face in. I'd give him more than the bruises he'd given my sister, but that was only fair. This wasn't something he'd started doing yesterday. He had years of abuse to pay for.

Years you weren't even around for.

"Dammit!" As the word burst from my mouth, my left hand shot out and collided with the wall beside me. Plaster exploded around my arm, and my fist sailed clear through the wall until I sagged limply in the corner with my arm in a hole.

Startled, I yanked my arm back and stared at the mess I'd made. My landlord was going to kill me. I hadn't just dented the plaster—I'd punched clean through the wall and could see my empty bedroom on the other side.

I raised my left hand up to my face. My fingers were still curled into a tight fist, but other than that, my skin didn't look the way I expected. It was no longer red. It still looked like it'd been torn up a bit, but in the blue light from the sign outside, it looked even unhealthier than usual. It looked... gray. Like the little bits of broken plaster all over my floor.

"What the..." I murmured, bringing both of my hands closer to my face.

They stung like a rug burn, but beneath the pain, there was something else—a warmth, almost like I was hovering my hands over an invisible fire. It was such a strange feeling. I focused on it, trying to figure out where it was coming from, and tried to open my fists. I wanted to rub my palms together to see if that would intensify the warmth.

My fingers wouldn't budge.

My two fists rubbed against one another, knuckles to knuckles. But I felt nothing. And instead of the soft, dry sound of skin rubbing against skin, I heard a rough scraping like two stones grinding into each other.

Frowning, I pulled my hands apart. I stood and bumped on the light switch with my fist, sure it was a trick of the light, but the bright yellow glow only made the truth clearer.

My hands were covered in hard, dry plaster.

I'll admit it. I screamed.

Heart racing, I stumbled across the living room, tripping over a cardboard box and spilling its contents on the floor. Ordinarily, the thought of one of the fragile comic books sliding out of a slipcover would've terrified me, but there was no room in my brain except for a single, shrill question: *What is this?*

The fluorescent bulb above my bathroom sink flickered and buzzed when I hit the switch. My hands were stiff, robbed of all dexterity by the hard shell that had somehow encased them, but I managed to bump the left faucet handle and send a stream of water into the basin. I thrust my hands under the flow. Before long, the water was steaming, but I felt nothing. Neither wetness nor warmth managed to penetrate the stone gloves.

Panicked sobs rose up in my chest. I sank to the floor, leaving my hands in the sink. Would I be stuck like this forever? Would my hands wither away inside the plaster?

I'll never draw again.

Determination surged through me. I had no idea what in the hell was going on, but I wasn't going down without a fight. I didn't survive Solstice Syndrome just to let myself get beaten down by some freaky thing like this. I'd figure out a way to get this stuff off even if I had to smash it away bit by bit in a back alley.

I stood up to turn off the water and felt something.

Warmth.

Then... pain.

The skin on my hands tingled and burned. It was like standing up on a dead leg after sitting for too long in an odd position. Pins and needles pricked at me, and the water streaming from my faucet was near-boiling. I jerked my hands out from the sink and stared at them. They were a deep shade of red. There wasn't a spec of stone to be seen. My skin looked... new. Uninjured but raw, like the fresh skin beneath a scab.

My wounds had healed.

I don't know how to handle this, my brain informed me. Then it stepped out for a cup of coffee to mull things over, leaving me to black out and smash my face into my bathroom counter.

Tess vs. Social Graces

For the second time in as many days, I made an embarrassingly public entrance into Helena's Place. Blood ran down the side of my face, and I cupped a hand over my right eye to keep it clear. Pain radiated from my forehead, so sharp and intense I couldn't stop picturing a piece of my bathroom countertop sticking out of my skull.

Unlike the last time I'd come into the diner looking for help, everybody in the place leapt out of their booths and dashed to my side. A hundred voices seemed to speak at once.

"Oh, my goodness!"

"Your face!"

"Quick, somebody get Helena!"

Someone helped me into a booth and tipped my head back slightly. I allowed my eyes to close and heard a familiar voice a moment later. It was the same woman who'd helped me the day before.

"What happened?"

"I fainted," I whispered. I hadn't meant to speak so softly; I'd wanted normal, but my voice box opted for church mouse.

I opened my eyes, and Helena's round, concerned face filled my vision. It reminded me a bit of an owl—a big, fluffy brown owl with walnuts for eyes—and I wondered if she could turn her head all the way around. Wouldn't that be nice? I could see behind me all the time. Never get snuck up on. No need for rearview mirrors. Maybe I could look down and check out my own butt... *hey, I look pretty good in these sweatpants.*

"Stay with me now."

My eyes flew open. How long had they been closed?

Helena patted my cheek. "No sleeping. Now let me see. You've got to move your hand."

She tugged at my fingers, and I allowed her to lift them away from my wound. Pain immediately stabbed into me again. I cried out, and she pressed something warm against my forehead.

"It's all right," she said. "It's not very deep."

"But the blood..." Thin rivulets of it ran down my arm and dripped onto my jeans. I focused on Helena's face so I wouldn't have to see the deep red streams.

"Head wounds just bleed more. Nothing to worry about. Now relax. My daughter is bringing the car around. We'll get you to the hospital and—"

"No!" I struggled against her, but she gripped my shoulders too tightly for me to get away.

"Honey, you need stitches. There's no two ways about it. Here's Angie with the car."

Two men with thick, shaggy beards appeared at Helena's side and helped me out of the booth. They gingerly walked me to the curb, where an old green station wagon was waiting, and buckled me into the passenger seat. Before I could thank them, the door was closed, and I was being sped down Palaemon Street.

"How far is it?" I asked, trying to turn my head to look at the girl beside me. Pain jolted through me, and I decided maybe I should just stick with facing forward. Her head remained a fuzzy blob in my peripheral vision.

"Not far," she said. "Just a couple minutes. You need to stay awake, okay? Do you need the radio on?"

"I'll be fine."

I focused on the white lines in the road as we drove, forcing my eyes to stay open until they began to feel dry. Then I blinked, slowly, making sure my eyes opened again. Angie kept up a steady stream of conversation, but most of it flowed over and around me without actually making it into my ears.

"That used to be a great little bookstore... You're from around here right... Remember the St. Patrick's Day parade... my mom always used to... Here we are."

The station wagon screeched to a halt in front of the emergency room doors, and a man dressed in teal scrubs helped me out of the car and into a wheelchair. Angie scurried along on at my left side, jabbering to the guy as he wheeled me through the blessedly empty waiting room.

And then there was pain. Doctors leaned over me, poking around in my head wound. They draped something large and white over my face, and I watched the light filter through the cloth as they poured water into the gash on my forehead to clean it out. Then, the pain stopped. A few stitches later, and Angie and I were left alone in the exam room. The pounding in my head had subsided, and I could hear my own thoughts again.

This sucks.

My irritation at the whole situation burned inside my chest. I'd been in Weyland less than forty-eight hours, and I was already at South Weyland General. Hadn't I spent enough time in hospitals over the last month? At least the research facility in New York had been pretty new, and they'd made an effort to make it a pleasant place to be, painting the walls in gentle pastels and flooding each room with as much natural light as possible. Whoever designed North Weyland had apparently never even heard of a window, and their favorite color was a too-bright pea-soup green that managed to clash brilliantly with everything from the bold colors in the abstract-patterned carpet to my faded hospital gown.

Silence hung in the air around us, and I vacillated between struggling to find something to talk about and wishing Angie would just go away. She just sat there, digging around in her spaceship-shaped backpack, not looking up at me as I stared at her. She looked a lot like her mom—dark skin, brown curls, and deep-set brown eyes. I didn't know what to say to her. I hated that a stranger had driven me to the hospital, that she'd probably watched while the doctors sewed me up. I would've preferred to endure that indignity privately, and I'd have liked some time to try to figure out what in the hell had happened with my hands. The business with the plaster around them had been real. And aside from looking slightly more pink than usual, they were completely healed from my fall in the streets. I'd only ever heard of something so weird happening in comic books, and I wasn't ready to go down that line of thinking yet... wasn't ready to think words like "mutation" or "powers."

I shivered. I wanted to be alone. I wanted to poke at my hands and see if I could get whatever had happened to happen again, but Angie had repeatedly said she would stay with me until they let me go home. So here I sat, trying to imagine what someone with good social skills might say right now.

Angie pulled a bottle of lotion out of her bag, squirted some into her hands, and saved me the trouble of coming up with something to say by breaking the silence herself. "How are you feeling?"

I shrugged. "Not too shabby, now that they've given me the Frankenstein treatment."

She cracked a smile. "Atta girl."

"Thanks, by the way. For driving me."

We fell into another awkward silence that lasted until a

short, thin woman stuck her head through the door. "Miss McBray? Do you have a moment?"

"Uh... I guess so."

"Great! I just need to get some financial information from you." Her high, chipper voice felt completely at odds with everything about the current situation. She bounced to my side and held a pen over a clipboard. "Employment status?"

"Um..." I glanced over at Angie.

"Do you want me to step out?" she asked.

After a few moments of thought, I shook my head. It didn't really matter. She'd seen my naked skull. We were past shame now. "Unemployed," I told Mrs. Clipboard.

She scribbled something on the sheet of paper. "Do you have medical insurance?"

"No."

More scribbles, plus a brief frown from Angie.

Clipboard asked me a few more questions before thanking me and turning to leave.

"Wait!" I called. "Did they say how much longer I'll have to stay?"

She glanced down at her papers. "They want to do a CT scan. Someone should be in shortly to take you to Radiology."

"A CT scan? Why?"

"You blacked out in the diner for about a minute," Angie put in. "I guess after a head wound that's not a super great thing. They want to check for any swelling or bleeding in your brain."

My stomach twisted and hugged itself. Swelling? Internal

bleeding? *Great.* The hospital employee slipped out of the room, leaving me alone with Angie and my fears.

"Hey, don't stress out." Angie cast her gaze around the room. "Umm... oh! Here. Let's watch some TV. Distract you a little bit, okay?"

I shrugged. I doubted anything on television would be able to overpower the voice in my head that was screaming about concussions and how I might die in my sleep if I closed my eyes, but at least I wouldn't have to make any more small talk.

Angie grabbed the remote control on the tray beside me and turned on the television. The end credits from some sitcom were rolling across a black screen. Then, the opening sequence of the nightly news began, and a tsunami-sized wave of nostalgia crashed into me.

The same face that had manned the news desk since I was a kid stared at me from the television. Jim Jenkins' jet black hair and severe widow's peak gave him an ominous look. When I was five, I'd thought he was a vampire. I figured he'd taken a job as a nighttime news broadcaster because it was the only thing he could find where he didn't work while the sun was out. I hadn't understood until I was much older why my mother insisted on telling everyone she met—literally every single person—about my theory, and why everyone seemed to think it was hysterical.

"Good evening, Weyland," he began in a deep, sonorous voice. His sentence ended on a faint tremble, and I realized with a start that he had to be in his sixties now.

How much does he pay his hairdresser to keep quiet about his dye jobs? I wondered.

Mean-spirited questions aside, I relaxed against my pillow at the sound of his voice. I loved the news, but I'd been so engrossed in dismantling my life in Albany and moving back to Weyland that I hadn't listened to or watched anything since my drive to Thatcher Park. I hadn't even bothered to read anything online. Watching a broadcast made me feel just a little bit normal.

"Good idea," I told Angie. "Thanks."

"Our top story tonight: another young woman has gone missing from the Trident." A photograph of a thin black girl about my age faded in beside his face. "Chelsea Thomas was last seen leaving her family's apartment on Athens Avenue earlier this evening. When she failed to meet a friend at a coffee shop near her home, her mother initiated a search. Miss Thomas' purse and one of her winter boots was found beside a dumpster at the corner of Palaemon and Triton, but there has been no other sign of her in the area."

A pulse shot through my body, and my heart stopped. An age passed as a terrifying thought formed in my brain, and then my heart began to beat once more.

Palaemon and Triton. That's the corner I turn down to get home from the station. Did I pass her?

And then the question I hated to ask: *Did I pass whoever took her?*

I doubted I'd have noticed anything suspicious. I'd been too wrapped up in thinking about Bruce. I crossed my arms, digging my fingernails into my biceps and leaving tiny half-moons in my skin.

That guy... I wouldn't be here right now if not for him. I could be at home, reading comics and maybe drinking a nice hot cup of tea before bed. But nope! I'm here instead, waiting to get wheeled into a radiology bay.

From her chair beside my bed, Angie murmured something and made the sign of the cross. It occurred to me that she might know the missing girl.

"Friend of yours?" I asked.

"No. We've been lucky. Nobody we know has been taken. But still... it's heartbreaking. I hope they're all okay."

I was about to ask how many other missing girls there were when a knock sounded at the door. A man in pale khaki scrubs entered, head bent over yet another clipboard as he walked toward my bed. At first, all I saw was a mess of sandy blond hair. Then he lifted his head and stared at me, brown eyes going wide in his lean, too-familiar face. He looked as stunned to see me as I was to see him.

It was my stalker from the day before.

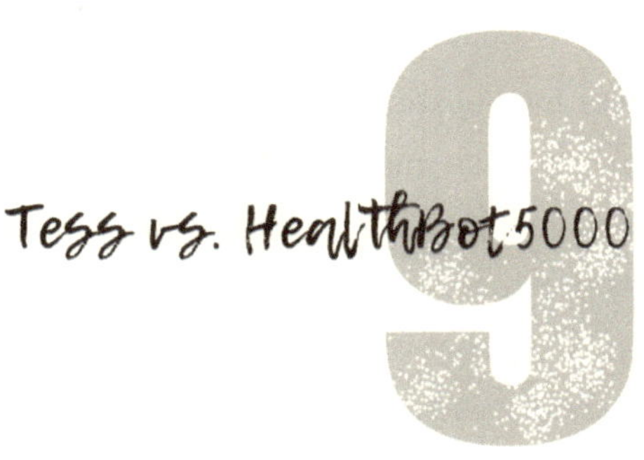

Tess vs. HealthBot 5000

The words shot out of my mouth before I had any hope of stopping them. "You've got to be kidding me."

My stalker's expression darkened, and his mouth twisted into a deep frown. "What's that supposed to mean?"

Angie stared back and forth between us, but I didn't feel like taking the time to fill her in. I preferred to leap into an argument.

"You're the guy who was following me yesterday!"

"I wasn't—!" He huffed out through his nose and gripped the clipboard, knuckles whitening around the flimsy plastic. He glanced at Angie, but she just frowned and shrugged. He stepped forward and lowered his voice. "You don't seriously think I was following you, do you?"

I didn't, but I also didn't know how else to classify him in my brain. 'Guy who wasn't following me and was probably really trying to help me up' didn't have the same ring to it as 'Stalker Jerk.'

A tiny hum of pain skittered across my forehead, and I was reminded of what I was doing here in the first place. I elected to answer his question with one of my own.

"Are you here to take me to the CT scan?"

He stared at me for a moment, eyes narrowed as he seemed to consider his next move. I was giving him an out, and I crossed my fingers at my side and hoped he'd take it and let me just pretend I wasn't being an irrational freak.

A moment later, he nodded. "My name is Reed. I'm a radiology technician, and I'm here to take you for your CT scan."

His voice was cold and flat. All the heat and defensiveness from a moment before were gone, as though he'd flipped a switch and become HealthBot5000. He set his clipboard down on my legs and raised the sides of my bed before wheeling me out into the hallway, leaving Angie behind us. If someone had asked me two minutes before, I'd have been certain I wouldn't want her to come with me for the scan. Now, however...

Reed pushed my bed down a long hallway lined with exam rooms. I resisted the urge to peek into any of them. Before my stint at Hudson, I'd had a bit of morbid curiosity about what other people were being seen for. But after seeing the curious looks on the faces of people who passed my room day after day, I'd lost the taste for speculation.

That is, I'd lost it for speculating about strangers. When it came to making wild guesses about my own condition, my brain was in fine form this evening. By the time we reached the room with the radiology equipment, I'd swung entirely the other direction on whether or not the plaster around my hands had been real. It became obvious to me that the Solstice Syndrome was back, and it'd brought a new friend: hallucinations! Hooray!

When we reached the room with the radiology machinery, Reed bent over to help me stand. He gently grabbed my right arm and an electric pulse ran through me, just as it had in Palaemon Street. This time, however, only the muscles in my arm twitched. I stared down at it, my eyes wide.

Reed noticed and frowned. "Do you have any history of convulsions? Epilepsy? Tourette's?"

"No."

"Hmm." He picked up his clipboard and flicked through a few pages, then stopped and stared at something. His dark eyes widened, and something tightened in his cheek. At last, he looked back up at me. "You're a Solstice Syndrome survivor."

I didn't like the way he said it. It wasn't a question. He wasn't looking for confirmation. His tone was almost accusatory, like I'd done something wrong just by being alive. I shrank back in the bed, my defensive walls snapping up around me.

"Says who?"

"Says you, when you filled out your medical history."

"Is that a problem?" I asked, trying to keep my voice calm. I failed; the last word came out in a squeak.

Reed's expression softened. "No. I mean, it shouldn't be. I assume you haven't had any symptoms since the meteor shower?"

I hadn't, but it seemed like a big assumption to make. "How'd you know?"

"It's been all over the news. Everyone who was hospitalized for it just suddenly got better the night of the shower."

"Oh."

For some reason, my response made him smile. He held up a single finger and, very slowly and deliberately, brought it toward my arm again. I braced myself for the jolt. This time, it was a minuscule spark, barely more than being touched by someone who was rubbing their feet on a rug to build up static electricity. I met Reed's eyes, and we both shrugged in unison then laughed at the same time.

"Well," he said, "You might be part electric eel, but we've still got to scan you. Come on."

He helped me stand and guided me over to the CT machine. I eyed it warily; this wasn't my first time in one of these things. I'd been scanned more times than a barcode at the research hospital. At least this was just a CT scan, and I wouldn't have to spend an hour getting shrieked at and deafened by an MRI. But the whole process still felt sickeningly familiar, and I hardly needed Reed's instructions as he completed the process.

Something occurred to me as he was pushing me back to

my room.

"Did you guys have any Solstice Syndrome patients here?" I asked.

He shook his head. "No, and I'm glad. A hospital in Chicago had four patients, and somebody there leaked it to the press. A few days after the meteor shower, when the patients were released, reporters and cameras were all over them. I'd hate for that to happen to anyone here."

The thought of getting caught in a media frenzy just when I'd finally gotten out of the hospital made me sick to my stomach. If I hadn't left Hudson when I did, would the same thing have happened to me?

Reed pushed open the door to my room and wheeled me inside. Angie was gone, and I wondered for a moment if she'd left me before realizing she'd probably just gone to the bathroom. Reed eyed her empty chair then turned to me.

"Your doctor should be in with your results in a little while. And..." He paused, then sucked in his lower lip. "I'm sorry about yesterday. I didn't mean to freak you out, I swear."

He looked so genuinely contrite that I felt a little guilty for how much vitriol I'd mentally hurled at him over the last day.

"Thanks," I said. "I'm uh... I'm sorry for assuming you were trying to attack me or something."

Reed shrugged and said, "Better paranoid than dead."

On that upbeat note, he left me alone to wait for the doctor.

10

Tess vs. Office Furniture

"Your scar is looking less gnarly," Angie told me. "Your hard work is paying off."

In the two weeks since my emergency room visit, I'd been regularly and obsessively caking anti-scar ointment on the little gash over my right eye. In the right light, it looked almost like a second eyebrow. But I'd take it, because it was literally the only thing currently wrong with me. My CT scan had been clear, my stitches came out without incident, and not a single Solstice symptom had come calling.

That hadn't been the only good news. My shipment of furniture had shown up, so I'd been able to unpack and sleep on a proper mattress again. On top of that, Angie had put in a good word for me with her supervisor at the car rental call center where she worked when she wasn't helping her mom at the restaurant, and I'd landed a job. The work was repetitive—I mean, there's only so many times you can help someone reserve a car at Weyland International Airport before you could probably automate it with a series of recordings of yourself—but the hours were consistent. And I even got to sit right across the aisle from Angie. I was surprised how nice it was, having a friend at work.

Today we'd turned around in our chairs so we could toss a miniature Nerf football back and forth between phone calls.

"Hey, do you have plans tonight?" Angie asked. "I've got this new deck-building card game, and a few of my friends are coming over to try it out. Want to join us?"

"That sounds super fun." It didn't; I loved a lot of things about Angie but couldn't figure out why she was so obsessed with card games. "But as it happens, I have plans."

"A date?"

I had to suppress a bitter laugh. "Yeah, right. No, I'm meeting my sister at some place called Tavern for a drink."

Angie wrinkled her nose. "Tavern? Isn't that the yupster joint downtown?"

"I'm not sure. She picked it out."

She pouted a bit, but I'd learned she never stayed down too long about any one thing. By the time her face had arranged itself into a sad expression, she was already over it. She tossed the football back to me. It went wide, sailing over my head and landing in the next row of cubicles.

"Man, that was a crap catch," she said. "Go get it."

Before I could stand, the phone on my desk began to jingle. "Ah, would if I could. Guess you'll have to fetch it while I handle this important grownup stuff."

Grumbling, she heaved herself out of her chair while I talked someone into paying for a GPS upgrade in their rental car. The caller was the type of indecisive person who feels like choosing between a compact and a sub-compact to save a total of five dollars is as important as naming their firstborn child, so it took me all the way through to the end of my shift. By the time I was able to hang up, Angie had retrieved our ball and was engrossed in something on her computer.

"Hey, you on a call?" I asked.

She didn't turn around to face me. "You have to see this."

Pulling on my coat, I walked up behind her and peered at her computer monitor. She'd been reading the news, and her screen displayed a headline I never thought I'd see outside of a comic book.

Masked Vigilante Cleans up Weyland South Side.

"No way," I breathed.

"Cool, huh? Wait'll you see him."

Angie clicked a link, bringing up a security camera video. There was no sound, and the footage was choppy—a series of still images set a second or so apart—so the result was like a flipbook with most of the pages torn out or poorly done stop-motion photography. A stooped old woman wearing a heavy coat walked into the frame. A moment later, a skinny kid ran up to her and grabbed for her purse. The two of them wrestled with it for a few seconds.

"Here he comes," said Angie.

From the top of the camera's field of vision, a third figure appeared. He was clad head to foot in black and was wearing a fox mask with long, pointed ears. He raised a leg, and in the next frame, the mugger was lying in a heap and the old woman's purse was airborne. Within two more frames, the masked man had secured the mugger to a barred window and returned the bag to its owner.

Even with the choppy video footage, the masked man seemed incredibly fast. It was possible to track the movements of the mugger and his victim from frame to frame, but the guy in the costume seemed to flit from place to place, disappearing from one side of the video and reappearing on the other in an impossibly short amount of time.

It took me a moment before I could produce actual words. "What in the literal hell?"

"It's crazy, right? They're calling him The Fox. The article says he cleared out a brothel last week. When the cops went in to check it out, they found the guys who were running the place all zip-tied the same way as that mugger. And get this—there was a fox face spray painted on the wall."

I gripped the back of Angie's chair. "He's a vigilante?"

"Yup. And I'll tell you something else—I don't think he's human. Did you see how fast he moved? That's not right, man." She clicked the button to replay the video, and the footage started over. "I think he might be an alien or something."

My hands began to tingle, and suddenly the rough texture of Angie's office chair seemed amplified. Every strand of thread in the fabric pressed against my palms, growing so warm it felt like it might burn me. But I couldn't let it go. My fingernails dug into the cheap padding so hard that my joints ached.

I looked down. My hands were turning the exact same shade of navy blue as the chair.

Gasping, I stuffed them into my coat pockets.

Angie turned away from her computer. "You okay?"

"Fine," I said quickly. My heart was pounding. I could feel my skin tightening, just like it had when I'd punched a hole through my wall. I needed to get out of there. "It's… just crazy, that's all. But listen, Ang, I've gotta go."

Not bothering to wait for her reply, I dashed out of the office, weaving between cubicles and pounding down the concrete steps in the back stairwell. I didn't stop running until I'd reached the faux-marble floor of the lobby.

Nodding at the security guard who manned the desk by the doors, I speed-walked to the lobby bathrooms and locked myself inside a stall. I almost didn't dare look, but I had to know. It'd been two weeks since the last time, long enough that I wasn't sure if it would ever happen again, or if it'd even really happened in the first place.

Shaking, I pulled my hands out from my pockets and lifted them to my face.

Yep. They were blue.

Not only were they the exact same color as our chairs, they had the same texture. Fat threads crisscrossed each other in a tight, square weave. My hands were covered in crappy office furniture upholstery.

Covered? I wondered. *Or...*

I curled my hands into loose fists and then released them. It was a little difficult. The fabric was thick and stubborn, but it wasn't as impossible as the plaster had been. Turning my hands over, I examined my fingernails. They were there, molded into the fabric as though they were part of the design. Squinting down at my thin fingers, I could even just barely make out little curved lines on the backs of my joints.

My hands weren't covered in the fabric. My hands were *made* of the fabric.

The thought was like a sucker punch, and I plunked down onto the toilet, heedless of the fact that I was sitting on the seat while still wearing my work slacks. I reached out a hand to steady myself, resting it on the muted pink tiles next to the toilet paper dispenser. The wall felt cool, at first. Then something wet soaked into me and I yanked my hand backward. There was some kind of liquid splashed on the wall, and I'd absorbed it with my fabric-y skin.

Bathroom water. In my skin. Not on it.

In it.

My gag reflex responded the instant I'd fully processed that thought, and I retched. Spinning around and dropping to my knees, I managed to get my face above the bowl just as my bean burrito from lunch spewed from my mouth. Heaving, I rested my hands on the seat before remembering they were made of upholstery. Could I even wash them?

"Oh, God," I croaked, and a fresh wave of nausea hit me.

It took several minutes for my stomach to settle. I rocked back on my heels, trying to balance myself so I wouldn't have to touch anything with my disgusting hands but wouldn't fall over onto the bathroom floor. I held my hands out limply in front of me, arms bent like a Tyrannosaurus Rex.

I had to calm down. The plaster hadn't lasted forever; neither would this. I tried to remember how I'd made it go away, but all I could think about was how much bacteria was in my hands right now.

Stop it! I ordered myself. *Close your eyes. Focus.*

It was impossible. In my mind's eye, I saw tiny, infectious organisms crawling all over my blue skin. My hands tingled. I could feel them! Then, abruptly, my mental image switched, and the bacteria was on my actual skin. My normal, human, fleshy skin.

As soon as I imagined my own skin, the tingling stopped. I opened my eyes. My hands were back to normal again. Unlike the last episode, they were even back to their regular shade. There was no redness.

I threw open the stall door and rushed to the sink, scrubbing my hands with vigor for several minutes. The feeling of warm water and the vaguely floral scent of the cheap powdered soap washed away the mental images of germs crawling all over me. Then I bent forward, resting my hands on my knees, breathing deeply until I was sure I wouldn't faint and bash my head again.

Emotions churned inside me as I left the building and

hurried down the block to the train station. What was happening to me? For the second time in two weeks, I'd... *absorbed* something I'd been touching—first the plaster, then the chair. It was like I'd sucked them inside of myself through my hands.

I stopped walking and approached a red newspaper box. Experimentally, I brushed my fingers across the cold metal. I raised my hand to my face, watching and waiting for my skin to change color.

Nothing happened.

Gritting my teeth, I wrapped both hands around the handle of the box, squeezing it with all my might, and waited.

Still nothing.

"Uh, Miss?" A pretty woman in a long coat touched my arm. "You have to put money into that slot to get a newspaper."

Heat flooded my face, and I released my death grip on the handle. I'd been so lost in my thoughts, I'd forgotten I was in the middle of a busy sidewalk.

"Right." I smiled at her. "Thanks."

She inclined her head and moved on, but she cast a quizzical glance over her shoulder at me once she'd put a few paces between us. She looked concerned, and I worried she might come back and try to help me get a cab or something, so I started walking again.

Despite being surrounded by hundreds of other people, I felt isolated. They were looking forward to normal things, a date at the movies maybe, or just a quiet night in with a beer.

They weren't trying to get something terrifying to happen to them again. They weren't struggling to figure out, for the second time that year, what in God's name was happening to their body.

Was this a disease? Or something different? I hadn't fallen into any giant vats of chemicals that I could recall, or been exposed to any freaky kinds of super-radiation.

At the top of the stairs to the Fishbone platform, a new piece of graffiti covered the station marker. Bright-orange paint glowed in the fading light of day. It was the unmistakable silhouette of a fox face with pointed ears and jagged cheeks.

The video of the vigilante apprehending the mugger played in my mind. I saw him leaping across the screen at impossibly high speeds. There was something off about him. As Angie had said, it wasn't normal.

He was different, too.

And I knew, instinctively, that we were different in the same way.

I wanted to find him, to grab him by the shoulders, shake him, and demand to know if he had any idea what was going on. But I didn't know how to do that. I wasn't any more tech-savvy than anybody else; I couldn't hack into the police computer system and find out what they knew about him. There was only one thing I knew how to do, one thing I was good at.

The second I got home, I rushed to my bedroom closet and dug out a battered cardboard box. The rest of my apartment was beginning to feel like home now that my comic books and collectibles filled the tall, narrow shelves in my living room, but this was one box I hadn't bothered to unpack yet.

Beneath the lid, I found my pencils, paints, and other art supplies. I hadn't felt the urge to do more than sketch since coming back to Weyland, but I was suddenly inspired. I carried the pencils and paper to the drafting table in my living room, brushing aside my mail and some empty soda bottles to make room for the large sketchpad. For the hour before I had to leave to meet Bethany, I worked in a frenzy. My hand moved across the page like it had a mind of its own, laying down lines and shapes in a rush. When I was finished, I was panting, but I felt elated. It was the high I felt any time I created something.

Before leaving for the bar, I tacked the drawing up above my drafting table and stood back to take it in. The face of an anthropomorphic fox, its eyes hidden in shadow, stared back at me from the wall. Sure, there was a chance it was an elaborate marketing campaign for some new superhero movie, or maybe it was just clickbait and the guy who made it was making a fortune off the views.

But I could feel the truth in my gut. This guy was real, and he was special. Just like me.

I wanted to start pulling comics off my shelves and pore through them. He'd leapt right out of their pages, a costumed hero come to life. And then it hit me: he was inhumanly fast.

There was definitely something weird going on there. So he wasn't just a hero.

He was a real life, honest-to-Pete, freaking *superhero*.

The more I thought about The Fox, the less terrifying my own situation felt. I stared down at my hands. They weren't diseased. I didn't need to go to a doctor to find a cure. This could be a gift. I pictured myself jumping out of windows and rolling across the sidewalk, then leaping up and punching some criminal in the face with a concrete fist.

"Holy crap," I muttered to myself.

I was tempted to cancel my plans with my sister so I could stay in and think some more about this. How would I even research it? Could I Google "superpowers" and come up with anything more applicable than a list of comic books and movies? I highly doubted scientists at MIT were studying something like this.

I gripped the pencil in my hand. There was one thing I could do. I could design my own costume, something to wear while I roamed the streets, looking for bad guys and kicking some ass.

My phone buzzed on the table. I picked it up and saw a brief message from Bethany.

Just got on the train, she wrote. *Can't wait to see you!*

She'd punctuated it with four smiley faces and three hearts.

Guilt squeezed my heart. I couldn't bail on her. Not again. Plus, there were a huge number of flaws in my plan to follow The Fox's footsteps and become a costumed crime fighter, not the least of which was that I'd never even thrown a punch in my life. Well, aside from the one I'd thrown at my living room wall. I wasn't even confident using a can of Mace. Was I crazy?

On top of that, I had no idea how to make my hands change. Zero clue if I could make more of my body change, too.

Shaking my head, I tugged on my coat. I'd been trying for weeks to get Bethany to meet me in the city. She'd kept inviting me out to her house, but I wasn't going to spoil a perfectly good get-together with my sister by risking a conversation with Bruce. She'd finally agreed to have a night out with me, she was excited to see me, and I'd been considering ditching her to spend the evening fantasizing like a little kid.

I opened the door and took a last look at the drawing of The Fox. He was amazing, but I had my own life to deal with.

11

Tess vs. The Internet

A blast of warm air greeted me as I stepped into Tavern, drying out my face. The bar was a long, narrow room with a high ceiling and white-washed walls. The structure had a classy feel, which was reflected in their cocktail prices, but their garish holiday decorations made me want to pound some cheap booze. Garlands made from paper hearts wrapped around the exposed beams above my head, and little Cupid statuettes topped every table, reminding everyone that Valentine's Day was just a couple of weeks away. I would've preferred a snug hole in the wall with a happy hour beer special, but Bethany had read that Tavern was "the place" to hang out in Weyland right now. After weeks of lobbying—unsuccessfully—to get her to come out with me, I'd just been happy there was somewhere she was willing to go.

I found her at a tall table at the back, waving to me with a martini glass in one hand. She'd ordered me a Stella—my favorite—and was bouncing up and down on her barstool.

"Can you believe this place?" she asked when I sat down.

The bar was packed with college kids, all carefully groomed to somehow look scruffy yet well-to-do at the same time. Colorful scarves, sport coats, and vintage liquor T-shirts abounded. It wasn't really my scene, but Bethany looked like she was already having the time of her life. She fit in, too; today she wore a slouchy purple beanie over her long golden hair and a brown knit dress with sleeves that covered her hands. I felt a little out of place with my loose-fit jeans, Marvel sweatshirt, and comic-themed messenger bag.

"It's great." I smiled and picked up my beer. "To more outings like this one."

I left the real toast unspoken: *To you finally being willing to ditch that mutt you're married to for one night.*

She grinned back at me and clinked her glass against my bottle. "Deal."

We each took a sip, and I contemplated the mystical ability of a Stella to drive my worries right out of my mind. Suffering from mutant hands? No idea where they came from or how they work? It's all good. Plenty of time to worry about that later. I leaned back on my stool and relaxed against the cinderblock wall.

"So how was your day?" Bethany asked.

Those five words undid the magic of the beer, and all the stress came flooding back into me. What if I told her what happened to me today? It was an absurd thought. She'd never believe me; she'd just worry I'd lost my mind. Besides, I wasn't ready to talk to anyone about it yet. It was all still a mess in my head, and I wouldn't know how to answer a single follow-up question she might have.

I cast around for anything to say. I didn't have to look far. My sketch of The Fox still loomed at the forefront of my mind.

"I saw a cool video. Did you hear about the guy who's fighting crime in a fox mask?" I asked.

Bethany laughed. "I knew you'd be excited about it. You and your comics. Most people grow out of reading the Sunday funnies." She had a mischievous glint in her eye; she knew exactly what she was doing.

"I'm not even going to dignify that with a response," I said, taking another swig of beer.

"Did you bring your computer like I asked?"

"Yep." I slung my messenger bag down off my shoulder and pulled out my laptop.

She grabbed it and powered it on, then shoved it back at me. "There's a password."

"Hold your horses."

As soon as I logged in and connected to the bar's Wi-Fi, she took over my laptop again and pulled up a web browser. In seconds, I was staring at an online dating profile. The user-name at the top read "Sexy Tessy."

I looked up at my sister. "What is this?"

"Do you like it? I had some extra time last week so I threw it together."

"Last *week*? How long has this been up?"

"Don't get mad. I just want to help you find somebody."

"I do fine on my own," I retorted.

Bethany raised an eyebrow. "Oh, really? That's so strange, because according to what you said last time I saw you, you weren't exactly queen of the dating scene back in New York."

I sat in silence. I couldn't come up with a response that wouldn't be an outright lie, yet I didn't want to admit she was right. The last time I'd been on a date, I'd been wearing a prom dress.

Bethany took my lack of an answer as an admission of loneliness. "You can't marry your comic books, you know. This site has the best reviews out of all the ones I found. Just try it."

Sighing, I pulled the laptop closer to me and began scanning the profile. *She did a good job*, I thought grudgingly. Bethany had remembered the bands I'd liked in high school, and she'd even put in that I loved comics.

My faith in her evaporated when I scrolled to the right and saw the profile picture she'd chosen. My mouth dropped open in horror. Sixteen-year-old me was grinning from the laptop screen, showing off a mouthful of braces and holding up a blue ribbon at an art fair.

"Oh, my God," I said. "You can't be serious."

"What?" Bethany leaned over and smiled down at the screen. "You look so cute! You were so proud of that painting.

Besides, it's the most recent photo I have of you where you're smiling."

I stared at her. "Okay, first of all, I think it's pretty dishonest to put up a picture that's five years old. Second, this is a *dating profile*. Do you know what kind of man would be attracted to a picture of an obviously underage girl?"

She gasped, covering her mouth with one hand. "Oh, no. I didn't even think about that."

"Yeah, clearly." I pulled out my cell phone and started flipping through my photo album. It was filled with pictures of sunrises, wildlife, and cosplayers at New York Comic Con. "There has to be a better picture in here somewhere," I muttered.

"Ooh, there's one of you." Bethany reached out to stop me from swiping past a bathroom-mirror-selfie.

"Uh, that's a 'before' photo for an acne medicine I tried last year." In the picture, my light hair was held back by a black headband. I wore a neutral expression and my face was covered in a horde of angry red pimples. "Not exactly the first thing I'd want a guy to see."

"Where's the after photo?" Bethany asked.

"The medicine didn't really work, so I didn't see the point in taking another picture."

"What?" Bethany squinted at my face. "I don't see any acne."

"It turned out to be a reaction to a moisturizer I was using. Easiest fix ever."

"Well, that's good." She kept examining me, her eyes

narrowed in concentration. Or judgement. "What's on your forehead?"

Reflexively, my right hand shot up and touched the scar above my eyebrow. I hadn't been planning to tell her about my fainting episode. My mind raced, scrambling for a lie that would explain it. *Fell asleep on my desk and my keyboard left a mark? I'm really bad at filling in my eyebrows, and this is the result? Come on, I can do better than that!*

And then it hit me. I'd been lying to her nonstop since coming back to Weyland by not telling her about my illness. I'd been lying by omission—same as her not telling me that Bruce was back to his old punch-drunk self again. I stared at her. How could I expect her to be honest with me if I wasn't honest with her? I didn't need to burden her with everything. Not right now, in the middle of this hipster joint while a mellow indie-rock ballad played over the speakers above us. But I could start somewhere. I carefully set my phone down on the table and prepared for the worst.

"I fainted in my bathroom a couple of weeks ago and hit my head."

Her eyes widened, and she went very still. "Are you okay?"

"Yeah, I'm fine. No concussion or anything like that. The doctors say I don't have anything to worry about."

She looked incredulous and opened her mouth.

"Really," I said, before she spoke. "I'm *fine,* okay?"

"Did you tell Mom and Dad?"

"Are you crazy? You know how she is," I said. "Her magic

power is finding a way to turn *everything* into a criticism. If I told her I'd gotten hurt, she wouldn't ask if I'm okay or how bad the injury was. She'd cluck and tell me, 'You should really be more careful, Tess. You know how clumsy you are.'"

I nailed my mom's high-pitched, judgmental voice. It was the only impression I'd ever been good at, and it had always cracked us up when we were kids. I grinned at Bethany, expecting her to laugh, but her eyes were glistening. I sagged down onto the table in surprise. I'd always known she was the golden child, the one my mother never seemed to find fault with, but I didn't realize the adoration went both ways.

"You don't understand. She says things like that because she worries. She loves you. A mother always loves her children." Her voice hitched and cracked. "Always."

A cocktail of guilt and sorrow squeezed my chest. I suddenly knew who Bethany was crying for. It wasn't me, and it wasn't our mother.

It was herself, and the years that had gone by without her being able to have a child.

I reached forward and covered Bethany's hand with mine. "Hey. When you have a chance to raise a kid—I mean it, *when*—you're going to be the world's best mom. Your kids are going to be so damn lucky."

She flashed me a weak smile. "Thanks, Tess."

We sat in companionable silence for a few minutes, sipping our drinks, until the melancholy threads of our conversation were muted by the effects of the alcohol. I relaxed against the wall once more and let a slow smile take over my face. This was the evening I'd been hoping to have when I'd visited Bethany during my first week back. Maybe not dredging up her heartbreaks or arguing about Mom, but all the rest was perfect. A warmth that had little to do with my Stella spread throughout my chest, and I felt like I'd stepped through a wormhole and returned to a time when I was happier, when I had friends.

Bethany spoke, pulling me back into the moment. "You know, you look pretty amazing right now."

"You're my sister," I told her. "You're sort of biased."

"I mean it. You look so relaxed and confident. The lighting in here isn't hurting either, and your scar actually looks kind of badass." She reached across the table and snatched up my cell phone. "Come on, if you hold up your drink it'll say, 'Hey, not only am I super cute, but I'm legally drinking in a bar, so pedophiles need not apply.'"

"Well, I guess that would help undo some of the damage you did with that high school mugshot. Of course, I run the risk of people thinking I'm an alcoholic or something."

"Just shut up and pose," she ordered.

Holding my beer bottle up near my chin, I grinned at the camera.

"Too many teeth. Rein it in," my photographer commanded.

I rolled my eyes, but shrunk my smile so it didn't show every tooth in my mouth. I heard the electronic shutter sound from my phone... and then heard it half a dozen more times.

"Calm down, Bethany. We only need one picture."

"One more." She grabbed me and pulled me toward her, then held the phone out at arm's length. "Say 'sisters!'"

"I'm not saying that."

But I did smile, and she snapped a selfie of us before handing the phone back to me. I leaned over the screen, scrolling through the photo album. In the shots she'd taken of me, my smile looked sweet, and the light behind me gave me an almost ethereal glow. Even our selfie was perfectly framed and looked like the kind of shot you'd see in an ad for a new smartphone or something.

"Wow. You're good at this."

Bethany waved a hand at me dismissively. "Ah, you flatterer."

I wasted no time replacing my profile pic. I also updated the username to ComicBookGurl, feeling that listing my favorite hobby was a much better way to go than shouting, "Look at me! I think I'm sexy!"

"Hey, we could take a photography class or something together," I said. "It'd be fun, and you've got a talent. Let's *develop* it. Huh?" I nudged her with my elbow.

"Har, har. You're a dork."

"I'm serious. I bet there's something at the community college we could sign up for on a weeknight or something."

Bethany shook her head. "I don't think so. Bruce likes it when I'm home in the evening." She glanced down at her watch. "Oops, speaking of which, I need to get back. If I want to beat him home, I've gotta leave for the station now."

"What? I thought we were going to hang out tonight. I

was going to introduce you to the miracle that is modern superhero cinema." She'd never seen any of the Christopher Nolan *Batman* movies, and it was my sisterly duty to educate her.

She stood from her stool and kissed my forehead. "Sorry, kiddo. Another time, maybe. But don't waste tonight. I know you're too chicken to talk to any of the cute guys all around us, so"—she tapped my laptop—"start looking through the hotties on here."

I stared after her as she left the bar. We'd made firm plans, settled on the time to meet, and she'd agreed to come see my apartment and watch a movie with some Chinese takeout. There was no question—Bruce had something to do with her sudden change of heart.

Sighing, I stared back at my laptop. *Might as well browse while I finish my beer.*

Considering I'd never had much luck meeting guys the old-fashioned way, the online route appealed to me a little bit. I'd kicked the idea around before but never created a profile. The odds of finding somebody who thought I was attractive, who was good-looking themselves, who could put up with my weirdness but whose eccentricities were also bearable... Well, it seemed statistically impossible. And yet, I didn't relish the thought of continuing my lonesome existence. In New York, I'd justified my homebody habits by telling myself I was still "settling in" to a new town. That excuse had started to wear thin after a few years in Albany; there was no way it would fly now that I was back home.

On top of all that, I needed a distraction. If I was left to my own company all evening, I'd start thinking about my hands again and drive myself crazy.

It took me a minute to figure out how to navigate the website and narrow my search. I decided to be picky at first, and searched for guys who were either my exact age—or slightly older—and lived right in Weyland. To my surprise, even my narrow search yielded a large number of results. I started at the top of the list and began working my way down, looking for anybody who struck me as being particularly interesting. There were a lot of good looking guys, but as I browsed their likes and dislikes, it struck me that I didn't seem to have anything in common with any of them.

Am I that much of an oddball? Are there really no guys on here who like anything but sports and weightlifting?

Finally, I found the profile of a guy who went by William27. He was attractive—bright blue eyes and a five o'clock shadow—and, lo and behold, we shared an interest. His bio section said he never missed Free Comic Book Day. A green circle over his profile picture told me he was online and available to chat.

After staring at his profile picture and imagining a million ways this could go horribly, terribly wrong, I chugged down the rest of my beer and decided to send him a message.

COMICBOOKGURL: Hi there. You like comic books, huh?

I struggled to decide if I should add a winky face emoticon or something, but eventually went with plain and simple. A second after I hit enter, a set of ellipses appeared at the bottom of the message window. My breath caught.

He was writing me back.

WILLIAM27: I like your profile pic. Stella = best beer ever.

COMICBOOKGURL: Hey, two things in common. What a start.

WILLIAM27: Yeah, we've already got more than just Breakfast at Tiffany's.

COMICBOOKGURL: Ha! Deep Blue Something.

WILLIAM27: You got the reference!

COMICBOOKGURL: :)

I had to hand it to Bethany—I'd literally been on the website less than an hour and had already found an interesting guy. If this went anywhere, I'd take her to every yupster joint in town.

That is, if she could stand being apart from Bruce for more than fifteen minutes at a time.

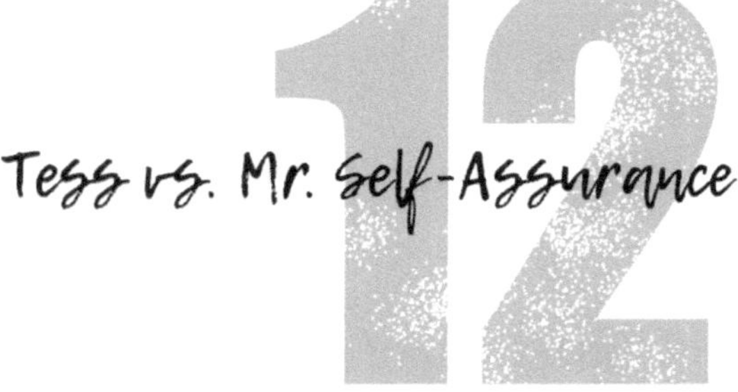

Tess vs. Mr. Self-Assurance

"Going on a date, yeah, yeah..." I sang. It was off-key, but I was in the shower. Everybody sounds good in the shower. And I liked the way my voice echoed off the tiles; it was like I was performing in a big, empty concert hall.

There was nobody around to witness it, but I blushed as I got out my razor and shaved my legs. Was it forward of me to shave them? I wasn't sure if that was like telling the universe, "Hey, I'm down for this to get physical, fast!" Because I wasn't sure if that was true. The only thing I was certain of was that if I didn't shave my legs, I'd wish I had. That was the story of my life.

My singing turned into humming as I got out of the shower and dried off. Each time I thought about my plans for the night, my pulse quickened. It was my first date in years. Bethany loaned me a colorful blouse with a daring neckline, and I had just shaved my legs. The night could go anywhere.

A hundred eyes—drawn in everything from colored pencil to charcoal to watercolor—watched me get dressed. The shadowed fox I'd drawn the Friday before had plenty of company these days. I'd been drawing him all week long, and one of my bedroom walls was now covered in that single, solitary figure in a variety of attitudes: leaping, punching, rolling, and crouching. Every news report about The Fox prompted ten new sketches. They'd taken over my entire apartment, from the wall above my couch to the front of my refrigerator.

If I was being honest with myself, I'd call it obsession. Instead, I told myself I was finally feeling inspired. Besides, drawing The Fox was the perfect way to keep from fretting about my "skin condition," as I'd been calling it in my head. I didn't know how else to think about it, since "superpower" felt... well, way too cool, for one thing. A superpower was something you could control, not a weird thing your body did on its own that you'd been completely unable to replicate, despite trying to turn into literally every single surface in your apartment or your office.

Ahem.

For the first time in over a week, however, thoughts of superpowers and The Fox were being overshadowed by something else. As I rode the train downtown and walked to the restaurant, anxiety about my date began to grow in my stomach and worried thoughts filled my mind. *Do I even remember how to flirt? Will this guy like me as much in real life as he did online?* We'd been chatting all week, just sending little messages and stupid jokes back and forth. He'd sent me a few animated gifs, which Angie assured me was the modern equivalent of passing notes in class. But I'd been able to plan, edit, obsess over, and re-write my half of each and every one of those interactions. Put on the spot, when an immediate response to a question was required, would I come off as a total weirdo?

And perhaps even scarier: *What if he thinks I'm amazing, and we fall in love, and my whole life is about to change?*

There was only one way to find out.

I pulled open the door to the Indian restaurant and looked around the waiting area. It was crowded; dinner out on a Friday night was apparently a popular idea. As I was scanning the faces of the other diners who were waiting for their table, someone tapped my shoulder from behind and stepped out in front of me.

Will's profile picture didn't begin to do him justice. He was tall and lean and smelled musky, like aftershave. The light blue sweater he was wearing clung to him just enough to show off his muscular chest, and the color made his eyes pop.

"Tess," he said.

My heart fluttered at the sound of my name being spoken in such a smooth baritone voice.

"Y-yeah," I stammered. "It's nice to meet you in person."

"Likewise."

We stood awkwardly in front of the door for a few seconds, looking into each other's eyes, until the host let us know our table was ready. I followed Will into the dining room. The walls were painted a warm cream, and deep maroon drapes hung across the ceiling. It felt warm and intimate. Our table turned out to be a cozy booth in the corner, which was partially hidden from the other diners by a set of sheer curtains.

"Wow," I told Will after the host left us with the menus. "This place is beautiful."

"Do you like Indian food?"

I nodded. "I love it. It's so flavorful and warm. I think it was a perfect suggestion."

We smiled at each other over our menus, and my heart threatened to float out of my chest and pat Will's face. My first date in ages was already going so well; I couldn't believe it. Not only was this guy totally handsome, but he seemed cultured and even a little bit nerdy.

"Do you mind if I order for us both?" Will asked. "I think we should get a couple of dishes to share."

"That sounds great." *Aw, a gentleman too!*

Our waiter, a young guy who introduced himself as Gilbert, arrived to take our orders. Will asked for the aloo ghobi, vegetable korma, garlic naan, and a bottle of something I didn't recognize. Gilbert whisked away our menus, leaving us to stare at each other over the table.

Will folded his hands beneath his chin and gazed at me. His icy blue eyes seemed to pierce my soul. I shivered slightly. What would it be like to gaze into those eyes for years to come?

"So, tell me about yourself," he said. "Your profile says you're an artist?"

"What?"

Will frowned. "I could have sworn that's what it said. You don't draw?"

Dammit, Bethany. "Well, I draw. But I wouldn't call myself an artist. Not really, anyway. I guess I should tell you my sister actually made my profile."

His frown instantly transformed into a grin, which put all of his super straight, ultra-white teeth on display. "Oh, I get that. My brother is always meddling in my love life."

Hearing him say the word 'love' made me swoon in a familiar, high-school-crush kind of way.

"So what would you call yourself, if not an artist?" he pressed.

"I don't know... I guess a doodler?"

Will burst out laughing, and heat flooded my face. *Why, oh why did I have to use a childish word? It sounds like peeing your pants or something.*

"I mean, yeah, okay. I draw. I like drawing people and putting them into costumes. Like superheroes, you know? Except, I'm not very good." *Oh, God, just shut up, Tess. Stop babbling right now. Just stop it.*

Will continued laughing and held up his hands with his palms out toward me. "Hang on," he gasped. "You're killing me."

I watched him struggle to catch his breath. The uncontrolled mirth made him even more attractive—face flushed, mouth open... it was sort of sexy.

He took a long drink of water and grinned at me once more. "So you draw comics?"

I nodded. "Not seriously or anything. I don't publish them."

"What do you do for a living, then?"

"I just got a new job in a call center." I shrugged. "It's not super interesting. What do you do?"

"I'm an attorney. It's my dream job."

"Lucky."

"Oh, it's not luck. I'm just the kind of man who knows what he wants and goes for it."

He eyed me, and the heat in my face intensified for a completely different reason. I sternly reminded myself to keep my babbling to a minimum.

Let him do the talking, I thought. *That's probably safer.*

"I'm actually glad to hear you're not in love with your career," he said. "To be perfectly honest, I'm interested in finding a woman who isn't tied to her job, so she can be a stay at home mother to our children. And drawing sounds like a great hobby to pursue on the side."

Just then, Gilbert returned with a bottle of red wine. Will's process of sniffing, peering into, and tasting the vintage before giving it his approval bought me a few moments to process his last statements. I fought to keep a frown off my face. He'd made a pile of assumptions in such a short burst, and I wasn't sure where to even begin correcting them.

My emotions sure knew where to begin, choosing the place I always started from—anger. Until the moment he called drawing a hobby, I didn't intend to pursue it as a career or let anybody else see my comics. But a fire erupted in me, and I felt a powerful urge to get a website and put my artwork out there that very night.

That'll show him, I thought.

But as Gilbert poured me a glass of wine and Will winked at me across the table, my flash of anger subsided. He'd assumed I didn't care for my job, and that I didn't take my drawing seriously. Could I blame him? I hadn't told him otherwise.

I took a deep breath. The record wasn't going to set itself straight.

"Actually, I'm not sure if I want kids," I told him. "And you're right, I'm not in love with my career. But I'm holding out hope that I can find something I *do* love to do."

"You don't want kids? Why not?"

I shrugged, feeling a prick of irritation that he'd made another assumption. "I didn't say I didn't want them. I just don't know if I do or not. I'm only twenty-one. I figure I've got time to work it all out." I smiled at him, hoping he didn't think I was being combative.

"Maybe you just haven't met the right guy—the one who makes you want to have a family." He raised his wine glass. "Here's to finding that person."

Still smiling, I clinked my glass against his. "Cheers."

The wine was delicious. It was wet and sweet and tasted faintly like blackberries.

"But I won't lie." Will emptied his glass and filled it again from the bottle. "I'm twenty-nine. I'm not looking for something casual. I'm eager to start a family. I have all the other puzzle pieces. I love my job, I have a nice little townhouse on the West side, and I'm financially secure."

I sipped at my wine in silence, unsure what I could say in response to that. This guy was so forward, but not in the physical way I'd been expecting. I didn't like the idea of just being a 'puzzle piece' and filling in this perfectly planned out little scenario. Something about what he was saying nagged at me, but I couldn't put my finger on exactly what the biggest problem was... or how to communicate that in a nice way.

He smiled at me. "I hope that wasn't too forward. I just don't really like to waste time."

I shrugged. On the one hand, I couldn't fault him for being honest. But on the other hand, I was feeling less and less attracted to him with every sentence. Our opposite situations seemed incredibly incompatible. I wasn't looking to get married. I didn't even know *what* I was looking for. Getting my sister off my back and having a good time in the process, maybe? And I definitely hadn't been expecting to be knee-deep in a conversation about our future before our food even arrived.

"So I'm on the hunt for a bride," Will continued, swirling the wine in his glass. "I've always known I want kids. Four of them. Two boys and two girls, ideally, but I understand you don't get to pick that sort of thing." He laughed.

Realization struck me, and I knew what was bothering me most about Will's life plan. He never said he was looking for a partner. It sounded like he just wanted somebody who was willing to pop out four kids and let him run the show.

"Seems like you've got it all figured out," I said.

"Yep. That's the kind of man I am, Tess. I just want to take care of somebody."

Gilbert returned with our food. He set down the dishes carefully on the table, passing his hand over each one and explaining what it was. They all looked amazing, and I couldn't wait to dig in. Maybe the business of eating would get Will to shut up for a few minutes so I could collect my thoughts.

"Here, allow me," said Will, picking up my plate and adding bits of each dish to it.

"Um, thanks." I took my plate back from him, wishing he'd given me more *aloo gobi* and less rice.

We began to eat, and the food tasted as good as it looked. Within a few seconds, however, Will's expression darkened. He stabbed at a piece of cauliflower, sniffed at it, and took a tiny bite. He tossed his fork down onto his plate.

"Son of a bitch," he said.

"What is it?"

"The cauliflower is undercooked."

I speared another piece of it on my fork and put it into

my mouth, chewing slowly. It didn't crunch; it almost melted in my mouth.

"Really?" I said after swallowing. "I think it's perfect."

"No, trust me. It's underdone."

Will spotted our waiter across the dining room, and began waving at him. "Waiter! Oh, waiter!"

"His name is Gilbert," I reminded him.

Will waved a hand. "Whatever."

Gilbert returned to our table, and Will lit into him at a volume that attracted the attention of every diner in the restaurant. I pushed myself against the upholstered back of the booth, wanting to hide my face in my hands. Where had the charming guy from the Internet gone? Who was this control freak that sat across from me now?

After Gilbert took the plate away and promised to return with a replacement immediately, Will relaxed back into his seat. His smile was smug and triumphant, like he'd just defeated someone at a game of wits.

"See? With me around, you don't have to worry about anything."

I frowned, not bothering to hide my facial expression this time. "Don't you think that was a little much? It's not Gilbert's fault the kitchen made a mistake. You didn't have to yell at him."

Will raised an eyebrow. "It's the principle of the thing. If you don't demand excellence from the people around you, they'll never give it to you."

My stomach twisted. "Excuse me," I said. "I need to use the restroom."

Afraid to meet the eyes of the other diners around me, I scurried across the carpeted floor of the restaurant with my head ducked. Once in the bathroom, I stared at my reflection in the mirror. I decided I looked very young, and it bothered me. I didn't want someone to just "take care of me." That's what Bruce had promised Bethany, but that's not the way their relationship really worked. It was the other way around, with her always worrying about *his* needs. He didn't give a crap if she was happy or satisfied. As long as dinner was ready when he got home and she was there to put a cold beer in his hand, he was good.

That wasn't the life I wanted for her, and it certainly wasn't the life I wanted for me.

How can I get out of this? I asked myself, mentally running through my options.

There was a fire alarm outside the restroom. I could pull it, and we'd all have to leave. I chewed my lip. That would cost the restaurant an entire evening's worth of revenue, and it didn't seem right to punish them just because my date was going down the toilet.

I could fake a stomachache and tell Will I had to leave. I had a feeling a guy like him wasn't used to girls using words like "diarrhea" and "farts," so I could probably stun him for a few seconds while I made my escape. The thought made me grin, and that plan dominated the "Most Tempting" list in my head until I left the bathroom and immediately struck upon an even simpler and much more satisfying one.

Just inside the alcove that hid the bathroom doors and the kitchen entrance from view of the dining tables, there was a narrow shelf filled with supplies like spare napkins, salt and pepper shakers, and to-go containers. I stood there for a moment, a plan forming in my head, until Gilbert stepped out from the kitchen with a probably-overcooked plate of *aloo ghobi*.

"Hey, can I take one of these?" I asked, pointing to the styrofoam containers.

He nodded, and I grabbed a to-go box. With our waiter on my heels, I strode back to Will's table and poured the vegetable korma into the container. After snapping the styrofoam lid into place, I snatched up my purse and coat.

"What are you doing?" Will asked.

"I'm calling it. You're an asshole."

With that, I marched out of the restaurant, leaving a stunned Will and a laughing Gilbert in my wake.

13

Tess vs. Small World Syndrome

"**W**ait!" Will chased me down the sidewalk, struggling to pull on his black pea-coat as he jogged. "Tess! Please!"

"Leave me alone, Will. We're not right for each other."

"Are you kidding me?" Panting, he caught up to me.

I cursed my short legs. Rash of kidnappings aside, I'd rather take my chances alone on the dark streets of Weyland than endure another minute with this guy.

"Here, let me carry that for you." He grabbed the takeout box from my hands before I could stop him. "Listen, do you want to come back to my place? I'm sure we can find a lot to talk about."

"You can't be serious." I snatched back my dinner. "Are you hearing me at all? We're not compatible."

That was an understatement. Dinner with this guy had left me feeling nauseated and angry. I felt like I'd gone back in time to the 1930s when a woman was just expected to manage the home and make some heirs. I was especially furious because the food had been delicious, but I didn't know if I'd ever be able to come back here. It might be haunted by the memory of the Worst Date Ever. At least Gilbert might remember me in a favorable light.

Maybe they delivered.

"I like your fire. I'll be honest. It turns me on."

Suppressing a shudder, I picked up my pace and wished he'd picked a restaurant nearer to a train station. We had several blocks to go.

"You don't know what you could have with me," he continued, matching my stride. "I'm a junior partner at my firm, and in five years I'll have my name on the sign. I'd take good care of you. Hey, you want to spend Valentine's Day in Hawaii with me?"

This guy's a nut job. I began to wonder if he was even a lawyer. Maybe he just spent his days arguing fake cases in his room at a mental hospital. I slipped my hand into my bag, then remembered I'd lost my canister of Mace my first day back in Weyland and hadn't replaced it yet.

We reached the station's turnstiles, and I let out a relieved sigh. I couldn't wait to put as much distance between myself and this guy as possible.

"Well, here I am," I said.

"Oh, no, I'll walk you up to the platform."

"You'll need a ticket."

"My company gives us unlimited passes. I don't normally

need mine, of course. I prefer to drive my Jag." He pulled a set of keys out of his pocket and jangled them an inch from my face. The Jaguar logo on his keychain was unmistakable, and my eyes widened.

He's really a lawyer? I felt sorry for anyone unlucky enough to get represented by this delusional fool.

We climbed the stairs, and I felt Will's hand on the small of my back. It was like he was afraid I'd fall backward or something. *He'd probably love it. Then he could save me and feel like I owed him my life. Ugh.*

He walked me all the way to the edge of the platform. I looked up the track, hoping we'd arrived just in time for me to hop onto the train. For the first time that evening, luck was on my side. The train was rounding the bend, and our goodbye would have to be quick. I felt my face light up. This was it. I was free.

Will looked visibly disappointed when he saw the train arriving. "Oh," he said. "I guess this is it. Well, I had a really good time, Tess. I hope we can do it again. Consider my offer, okay?"

He leaned in and closed his eyes, and I realized he was trying to kiss me. I arched backward to avoid his lips and side-stepped when my back couldn't bend any further. Will's eyes flew open, and he looked shocked to find that I wasn't in front of him anymore.

I stuck out my hand, firmly indicating that a handshake was all he was going to get. "Thanks for dinner."

Hurt flashed across Will's face, but he shook my hand,

and I stepped through the open doors and onto the train. They closed behind me, and I sagged against the stanchion, holding my leftovers in my left hand while my right gripped the cool metal pole.

First thing when I get home, I'm deleting my dating profile, I thought as the train began to move. *If this is what I can expect, I don't want anything to do with it.*

"What a romantic parting," said a voice behind me.

A tall guy in a black hoodie was sitting on the bench beside the door. His face was shadowed, and when he offered me a seat beside him, I shook my head. After just escaping Will, I wanted to stay out of anyone's reach.

"First date?" he asked.

I didn't answer. I'd just spent the last ninety minutes in the company of a creep; I wasn't about to start dealing with another one. I simply shrugged and stared out the window, intending to look very engrossed in the view.

"Is that any way to treat an old friend?"

His voice suddenly sounded familiar, and I turned to face him. My fellow train rider pulled back his hood in an all-too-familiar gesture, revealing a chiseled face, square jaw, and sandy shoulder-length hair. It was weird. He was dressed exactly the same way he'd been when I'd first seen him, but I expected to see him in scrubs. They suited him.

His name had stuck in my memory. "Hi, Reed."

He grinned, and my ears grew hot. I hoped the stinging cold I'd walked through with Will to get to the train had left my cheeks rosy enough to mask my flush of embarrassment, but the glint of laughter in Reed's brown eyes told me other-wise. Of all the tens of thousands of people in Weyland, of all the trains that ran through the city, this guy was seeing me in yet another embarrassing situation.

This night just kept getting better.

"Smells good," he said, nodding toward the leftovers in my hand. "How was your evening?"

"Fine," I said politely. "How was yours?"

Reed cocked his head to one side and narrowed his eyes. He would've looked angry if not for the wide, friendly smile on his face. "Don't ever run for office. You are the worst liar I've ever met."

"What makes you think I'm lying?"

"Because you're gripping that stanchion like it's the only thing holding you up right now."

Looking down at my hand, I saw he was right. I relaxed my grip on the tall metal post and ordered my shoulders to sit lower while I was at it.

"All right," I said. "You've got me. First date. And last. If I never see that guy again, it'll be way too soon."

Reed laughed. It was a deep, throaty sound. "I've been on a couple of those. It always feels like a bait-and-switch, you know? Like halfway through dinner I'm wondering if my date was replaced by a cyborg with a personality disorder."

"Why a cyborg? It could be a pod person, a doppel-gänger, an alien.... There are a lot of possibilities."

He frowned and rubbed his chin in mock thoughtfulness.

"Hmmm. You're right. I've been too limited in my thinking. But no matter what, the odds are good they'll assimilate me on the second date. So for safety, it's best to steer clear. You know, change my number. Go into hiding. Start wearing tinfoil hats."

Maybe it was because I was finally starting to relax after that awful date, but the image of this handsome guy wearing a pointed, shining lump of tinfoil on his head was too much to bear. I began to laugh so hard the tiny bit of *aloo gobi* I'd eaten earlier threatened to come up again. It took me a while to settle down, and I had to wipe tears from my eyes before I could look up.

"Sorry," I said. "I needed that."

"So how'd you meet Mr. Wrong?"

"Online." I winced. "My sister talked me into trying it. We're going to have words later, and my account will be history by morning."

Reed raised a heavy eyebrow. "Was this the first time you've gone out with somebody you met online?"

"Yep."

"Don't rush to delete it then. You could miss out on meeting somebody great just because you met a dud. Besides, I swear everyone I know who's gotten married lately met online."

"Really? Nobody met anyone the old-fashioned way?"

He shrugged. "Everybody has their faces in their phones all the time. How are you supposed to meet anybody anymore, unless it's through the Internet?"

They could strike up a conversation with you on the train, I wanted to say.

He grinned at me again. "It's not often you run into a pretty girl on the train, right?"

A lightning bolt struck me in the gut, and I gripped the stanchion again. The metal pole was cool beneath my fingers... then cold.

This time, I recognized what was happening in an instant.

My right hand changed color quickly, the shining gray of the steel pole bleeding into it from my fingertips down to my wrist. I released the stanchion just as my hand began to stiffen up and jammed it into my coat pocket. I glanced at Reed.

Did he see that?

No, he was distracted by his phone, tapping out something on the glass screen.

"Sorry," he said, looking back up at me and slipping his phone into his hoodie pocket. "Talk about bad timing. I'm not a hypocrite, I swear. My nose isn't always in my phone."

I needed to get off this train. Fast. What if he wanted to shake my hand? What if the metal spread, and he saw it somehow? I didn't need to know exactly what was going on with me to know it was better if other people didn't know about it.

Just then, a chime sounded, and a woman's recorded voice announced we'd reached University Avenue. It wasn't my stop, but it would do. I sidestepped to the doors, keeping my hand locked inside my pocket.

"This is my stop," I lied. "Um, nice seeing you again. Hope you have a good night."

Reed stared at me, his heavy eyebrows raised in question. He opened his mouth to say something, but I didn't give him a chance. The train had rolled to a stop, and the doors were beginning to slide open.

I hopped out of them and fled into the night.

Tess vs. Repetition

The train platform was quiet. An elderly woman waited for a downtown train on a bank of benches across from me, but otherwise I was alone.

I turned my back to her, pretending to examine a map of the transit system, and pulled my hand out of my pocket. It was pure steel, and if I squinted right, it just looked like a dark gray glove. My fingers were frozen, stuck in the fist I'd made when I stuffed my hand into my pocket.

Tentatively, I tried to uncurl my fingers. They wouldn't budge, and soon a vein in my forehead began to pulse with the effort. I wasn't strong enough to change my hand's shape. It'd become as solid as the steel bar I'd been gripping on the train.

Would it melt? I wondered. It was a grim thought, and as curious as I was about my condition, I knew that was one experiment I'd never try.

This time I didn't feel afraid. The adrenaline and nausea that had accompanied the first two episodes were nowhere to be seen. Maybe it was because compared to dinner with Will, this wasn't so bad. But more likely, it was because I knew now that this wasn't permanent. I knew exactly how to make it go away; all I had to do was imagine my normal—

Stop! An idea struck me. So far, I'd had zero luck getting this change to happen on purpose, and if I was being honest with myself... I wanted the change to come. I needed to figure out how to make it happen.

A train platform didn't feel like the best place for testing any grand theories, but I was too impatient to wait until I got home. I had to find a place to experiment. Hiding my hand in my pocket once more, I went down the stairs, heading south toward the Trident on foot. Ordinarily, I'd feel vulnerable walking the streets of Weyland alone at night, especially considering how many girls had gone missing.

But not tonight.

Tonight, I had steel knuckles.

The buzzing sign of a late-night diner caught my eye, and I dumped my leftovers into a curbside garbage can. I felt a pang of regret—the food would've warmed up nicely—but this was too important. I ducked through the door just as a group of girls exited. The smell of bacon and eggs greeted me as I surveyed the restaurant. It was crowded; the large tables at the front of the diner were packed with kids my age, laughing and making a lot of noise. I slid into a small booth at the back by the restrooms, keeping my hands in my lap and out of sight.

A lanky guy in an apron was next to my table in an instant.

"Coffee?" he asked.

"Uh, sure."

"Anything else?"

Still hungry from my non-dinner, I ordered a grilled cheese sandwich and a slice of apple pie. He returned a moment later with a bowl full of flavored creamers and a mug, then left me alone while he attended to a large group of sorority girls laughing in a corner booth. I eyed the mug's small handle with amusement, picturing myself picking up the coffee with a metal fist and trying to bring it to my mouth.

My hand was heavy in my lap. I tapped it against the bottom of the table, and it made a dull *clunk* sound. How solid was it? Was it a layer of steel over my bones and tissue, or was everything metal? I didn't see how my blood vessels could have solidified, not without me having a stroke or some-thing because of it. I raised my right hand to my cheek. The steel was cold against my skin, but my hands didn't feel cold. Not inside, anyway. Inside, they felt warm.

I sat up straight in my booth. The black vinyl squeaked beneath my coat. In my apartment, after my fall, my hands had felt warm. I remembered focusing on that warmth, and that was when...

They'd changed.

I could still feel it. The warmth coursed through my

hands like an electric current, thrumming in time with my heartbeat. Closing my eyes, I imagined I could see it, a pulsing glow beneath my skin. The color changed—none of the shades *felt* right—until I pictured a vibrant, bright red.

The color of passion.

Something in my chest tightened, not from stress, but from excitement. My pulse pounded in my veins, and the red color intensified until it engulfed the blackness behind my closed eyelids. It was all I could see, fading in and out with each heartbeat.

Smiling, I opened my eyes. I could find my way back now, make my hands change at will. I could feel it.

Looking down at my hand, I imagined it becoming normal again. As I did so, the silvery steel faded away and my skin went back to its usual color. I opened my fist and flexed my fingers; they were stiff and stubborn from being locked in the same position for so long, but other than that, they were completely ordinary. My hands were just my hands, with chipped banana-yellow nail polish and hints of blue veins beneath my skin.

I tucked them under the table. Now was the moment of truth.

After another quick glance around me to make sure my waiter was still flirting with the other patrons, I closed my eyes again. My hands felt slightly cold from the draft of winter air coming in from the thin glass window beside me. There was no sign of the earlier warmth.

Frowning, I focused harder. In my stillness, I could feel

my heart beating in my chest. I imagined a red light in each of my hands, blinking in time with my pulse. In the back of my mind, I counted them, focusing on nothing but my breathing and that thrumming red hue. Twenty-five beats later, my hands began to burn.

My eyes flashed open, and I sunk lower in my seat to watch my hands beneath the table. Just like on the train, they were changing. Morphing. Hardening.

I let out a shriek of triumph, and the chatter around me stopped.

"Oops," I muttered.

I imagined my skin going back to normal and rested my folded hands on the table. By the time the waiter had sprinted back to me, I was confident I looked completely ordinary.

"Everything okay?" he asked. He looked panicked, and I wondered what extreme things he might be worried about right now.

"Oh, yes." I scanned the table, looking for anything to explain my outburst. "I just... um... spilled coffee on myself."

He stared down at me with one raised eyebrow.

"Sorry," I added. "I overreacted."

"Do you need a refill or something?"

"No, no. Sorry. I'm fine."

"Your food will be right out."

He left me alone again, and I tried to do a better job containing my excitement. Several more times, I changed my hands back and forth. Skin, metal. Metal, skin. Each time it got a little bit easier to transition from focusing on the pulsing red warmth to imagining my normal fleshy hands and back again. By the tenth time, I didn't even actually have to picture my hands; I just thought of them as being "normal," and they were.

My food arrived, and as I wolfed down my sandwich and pie I tried to think through the implications of what I could do. It was hard; it wasn't like trying to work out the pros and cons of starting a new job or getting a different haircut. This was uncharted territory—outside of fiction, anyway. I wasn't sure what my limitations could be or how I could even test them.

I'll just have to practice.

After paying my bill, I headed home, cycling my metal hands on and off in my pockets. I grinned as I passed people having normal Friday night outings with their friends or significant others. No matter what they were doing, it wasn't as cool as what I had going on.

Back in my apartment, I sank down into my couch and stared across my living room at my drafting table. Above my cups full of colored pencils and my 12-inch tall posable wooden anatomy figure, my ever-growing collection of pictures of The Fox wallpapered my living room. I'd gotten especially good at drawing him mid-punch, his fist sinking into the faces of nameless adversaries.

He obviously knew what he was doing with his powers. I wondered if he'd had any training before, or if his gift was a sudden magical knowledge of martial arts and general asskickery. I grabbed my laptop and searched for nearby boxing gyms, thinking that might help me make the most of these metal hands.

And plaster hands, I realized.

Shoving my laptop to the side, I focused on the red heat in my hands and tried to picture them turning into the same rough stone as the first time they'd changed. When that didn't work, I pictured the fabric on the back of Angie's office chair. Again and again, I tried to conjure up any other material, but my hands would only transform back into metal.

I allowed a stream of profanity to flow from my mouth, which made me feel better about my failures.

Then an idea struck me. I leapt off my couch and grabbed my wooden anatomy figure, gripping the basic geometric shapes that made up its body. It took a couple of seconds of focusing on my heartbeat and imagining the pulsing red light again, just long enough for me to wonder if it would work, but then it happened. My skin became grainy and began to stiffen, and within the space of a breath, I had wooden hands.

Naturally, the first thing I did was knock them against my coffee table, listening to the heavy *thunks* and drumming out a steady rhythm. Then I imagined my hands returning to normal, and they did so.

When I tried to recall the metal, it was gone. Just like the cement and the fabric, it was like my hands had forgotten how to change into them. Wood was all I could do. Once I figured that out, I ran around my apartment, picking up books, pencils, drinking glasses, and pillows. I absorbed them, made my hands change, then went back to normal just long enough to pick up something else. I laughed hysterically, filled with the thrill of discovering that I could turn my hands into literally any material I tried.

Then I was finally able to say it, the word that I'd been too afraid to even think just days before. "Superpowers. I have *superpowers*."

That set off another round of laughter, and I collapsed onto my couch with tears streaming down my face. It sounded insane, but it didn't *feel* crazy. Not with all the evidence before me. Not when I could be my own sledge-hammer whenever I needed one.

But the question remained: how had this happened? It couldn't be totally random. People didn't just randomly mutate in their early twenties. Or did they? I chewed my lip, wondering if this could be like cancer, if my cells could just be going haywire. There had been a lot of cancer patients at the research hospital, undergoing experimental treatments. I'd felt a little bit envious of them while the doctors were still trying to work out how best to tackle my Solstice Syndrome. Sure, they were facing down something terrifying, but at least they knew what it was. At least the doctors had a game plan for treating them.

But it turned out I was actually lucky. I didn't have to go through chemo or radiation. The meteor shower had taken care of that.

"Holy shit," I whispered.

Solstice Syndrome. The meteor shower. One of those two

things, or maybe both of them combined—that was the cata-lyst. That's why this was happening to me.

And that meant The Fox and I had something else in common, too. We'd both had the Solstice Syndrome. Some-where, his name was on a patient list, either here or in Chicago or somewhere else.

If I could find that list, I could find The Fox.

Tess vs. Quid Pro Quo

15

Angie sat cross-legged on one end of the bright green, overstuffed sofa that dominated her tiny living room, tossing popcorn up into the air and catching it in her mouth. When I'd entered her apartment that evening, I'd thought it was a sci-fi museum. Until that moment, I hadn't realized exactly how geeky she was. She'd painted the walls of the cramped downtown studio to look like the interior of the *Enterprise*, complete with horizontal black lines and faux bulkheads. Her shelves were crowded with memorabilia from every *Star Trek* series: model starships, figurines, com badges, and even a full-sized 4-D chess set. The effect was oddly soothing; it was like walking into a place I remembered from my childhood but hadn't visited in a while.

She'd thrown on a horror movie, but I wasn't watching it. My eyes were glazed over, and I thought about the night before. I'd lain awake in bed for hours, turning my hands to the wood of my bed frame and back again until exhaustion claimed me, and I passed out. Now I flexed my fingers on top of a fleece blanket with Spock's face on it, resisting the urge to pull on that pulsing thread inside myself and change my entire body into the warm, fuzzy fabric.

"So, how was it? I want to know everything," Angie said.

"What?" Panic rose in me. How did she know about my hands? Had I accidentally changed them? I glanced down at the blanket, but my hands were their normal, pale selves atop the blue fabric.

"Your date, nerd." Angie caught another piece of popcorn in her mouth. "Is he your soulmate, or what?"

"Oh." I sagged into the couch and thought back to dinner with Will, which, compared to the rest of my night, was barely memorable. "It was... ugh. Man, it was terrible."

As Angie continued to test her ability to catch airborne snacks, I gave her a blow-by-blow of my Date from Hell. When I got to the part about Will trying to kiss me, half-chewed popcorn shot out of her mouth. I decided having dinner with Will might have been worth it, just to have a good story to tell.

"He sounds hideous," she said, picking wet popcorn off the couch cushions with a napkin.

"Yeah, but he was tricky. He kept his ugliness on the inside, under a delicious-looking candy shell. So, I just took the train home and... oh, yeah." Reed's face swam in front of my eyes. "And I sort of met someone."

"You *what*? And you didn't think to mention it until just now?"

How could I explain to her that out of everything that had happened last night, the cute guy on the train wasn't actually the most exciting part? Inwardly, I squirmed. I hate keeping secrets, and now I had this monster thing I couldn't talk to anybody about.

Angie watched me with wide, expectant eyes. For a moment, I considered just telling her about my hands. She was the world's biggest sci-fi junkie. Maybe it wouldn't seem so weird to her. And she was my best friend... but that didn't actually say much, since aside from my sister she was also my *only* friend.

Not yet, I decided. *Maybe once I have a better idea what it is.*

Instead, I stuck to the normal-ish details. "Remember that radiology tech who took me for my CT scan in the hospital?"

"I think so. Tall? Light hair?"

"That's him. Well, that was actually the second time I'd seen him... I also sort of met him outside your mom's restaurant." I left out the part about my paranoia and falling on my face. I do have *some* pride.

"And you ran into him on the train?"

"Yeah, he witnessed the awkward limbo contest that capped off my date with Will."

Angie burst out laughing. I gave her a rundown of my conversation with Reed, sparing no detail about his lean, rugged face, or about his flirtatious comment about pretty girls on trains. That's when I had to lie.

"But right then, we reached my stop," I told her. "So I had to go. But it's weird... I felt something. Like a spark, I guess? I don't know how to describe it."

"Holy crap. You have to find him somehow," Angie said. "I mean, it's like a meet-cute. If you don't chase him down, you'll miss starring in your own real-life rom com."

A montage played in my head. Reed and I on a date, eating ice cream in the park, laughing as we exit a movie theater arm-in-arm, grabbing him by the drawstrings of his ever-present black hoodie and pulling him into my bedroom...

Heat crept into my face, and I hid my redness in a pillow. "I have no idea where I'd even start," I said, my voice muffled.

"Easy. You know where he works. Just stop by the ER and ask to see him on his break."

"Sounds a little stalker-y."

"Well, what's your alternative? Take the train every night, getting on at that exact same stop at that exact same time and hope you get lucky?"

She had a point. One option seemed more likely to work than the other. And unlike spoiled Will, I didn't have an unlimited transit pass. Visiting Reed at the hospital was the most cost-effective and least creepy way to see him again.

Plus... he worked in healthcare. He might know how I could find out who else had Solstice Syndrome, or at least the cities where other severe cases like mine had been reported.

"Okay, I'll do it. But if he laughs in my face, I'm coming after you."

"He won't laugh. You're going to end up owing me a favor, and I'd like to collect on that next week."

"What? Are you stalking somebody, too?"

Angie tossed her dark curls back over her shoulders. "Hardly. My prey comes to me, kitten."

I rolled my eyes, but I knew it was true. Every guy in the office would turn to watch Angie's curvy figure pass as she walked to the break room. She had confidence oozing out of every pore.

"No, I want you to come to a rally with me next Saturday."

"Seriously? Do I have to carry a sign, or something? What's it for?"

She leaned toward me, and her eyes flashed. "It's to show support for The Fox!"

As she spoke his name, my wall of sketches popped into my head. It was growing larger by the day, spilling onto the two adjacent walls. If I was home, I was drawing him. My fingertips were perpetually gray from the pencil lead.

"He's a hero. Why does he need a rally?" I asked.

"I'll show you."

Angie picked up her TV remote and cued up a recording on her DVR. It was a news broadcast from the night before, and she fast-forwarded through highlights of yesterday's high school football game before hitting play.

"...where the undefeated Wildcats will be taking on the Spartans," the sportscaster was saying. "Back to you, Jim."

"Thanks, Ron." Jim Jenkins, his hair slicked back with so much gel it reflected the bright studio lights above him, tapped a stack of papers against the top of his desk. "And now for tonight's top story. The chief of the Weyland City Police Department announced today she's putting together a task force dedicated to the identification and capture of the vigilante known as 'The Fox.'"

Footage from an afternoon press conference appeared on screen. A slender woman stood behind a podium in front of the entrance to police headquarters. Her curly hair was cropped short around her face. Her name and title appeared at the bottom of the screen as she began speaking: KATHARINE STEELE, CHIEF OF POLICE.

"Every resource at our disposal is dedicated to determining the identity and intentions of this individual," she said. "There are many citizens and media groups who are romanticizing this vigilante's actions by giving him nicknames such as 'The Fox.' I would like to urge everyone out there to remember that this individual is a *criminal* who is acting outside of the boundaries of the law."

"Chief Steele," asked a reporter from the front row, "can you comment on the fact that this 'vigilante,' as you're calling him, has so far been able to shut down a human trafficking front and an illegal gambling establishment? We've also heard reports that he's brought in several drug dealers—how is it possible that The Fox is more effective than the police?"

The chief narrowed her eyes. "I think you're overlooking the fact that each of those criminal enterprises had been under investigation by the police for many months. Our officers were carefully gathering evidence to ensure an airtight conviction against everyone involved in each scheme. The Fox's actions, while perhaps better for headlines, destroyed our ability to collect additional information about the extent of the illegal activities that were occurring."

"But it's obvious The Fox is on your side. I mean, he's trying to bring in the bad guys, too," the reporter pressed. "Yet you're moving forward with a manhunt?"

Chief Steele pinched the bridge of her nose with her thumb and forefinger. "Again, the motives of this individual are unclear at this time. While it looks on the surface like he's trying to 'help' the police, the damage he's caused to our investigations suggests he might actually be protecting the people at the top of these criminal organizations."

Angie stopped the recording. "See? That's what the rally is for. I've met a whole bunch of other people who support The Fox. We're going to protest outside of police headquarters and try to get them to call off the manhunt."

The end of the chief's speech rang in my head. The Fox, in league with criminals? It didn't feel right. I couldn't believe it. Despite never even having met the guy, I couldn't shake the feeling he was trying to do something good for our city.

When I thought about The Fox, a fire ignited inside of me. I wanted to find out everything I could about him. I wanted to meet him more than anything, to find out if he was like me. If he was, he might know something about how this had happened to me. And if there was even the slightest chance attending this rally could bring me closer to him somehow...

"I'm in," I said.

Tess vs. Last Names

16

The smell of hospital disinfectant pricked at my nose, and I realized I was scrunching up my face in disgust. It wasn't the most attractive expression in my limited arsenal, so I rearranged my features into what I thought was a relaxed smile. I caught a glimpse of my reflection in the wide glass window behind the information desk, and my mouth wasn't curving upward by even a millimeter. Resting bitch face had struck again. Baring my teeth in a too wide, too fake grin, I tried to recreate the sweet, happy smile Bethany had managed to capture at the bar. *Reign it in,* I heard her say, and to my surprise my face settled into the kind of normal expression that probably wouldn't frighten small children.

The receptionist in front of me hung up the phone and looked up at me just as I nailed the smile.

She returned it, her voice twinkling brightly as she asked, "Can I help you?"

"Uh, yeah. I'm looking for Reed."

"Last name?"

Her fingers were poised over the keyboard, waiting to type a last name I couldn't possibly give her. Instead I stood there, open-mouthed and dumbfounded. South Weyland General was huge; it was practically the size of an airport and contained thousands of people at any given time. People scurried behind me, hurrying to an appointment in one of dozens of outpatient clinics or rushing to visit someone in one of the inpatient wings. People were born here, died here, and I expected to be able to find him by his first name alone?

"Ma'am?" The receptionist looked at me, head tilted. "I'm afraid I can't direct you to any of our patients without a last name."

"Oh! I'm not looking for a patient. I'm looking for a radiology technician. Reed... something. Does that help?"

"Are you here for test results? What's the name of your doctor?"

"No, it's not like that."

I was getting nowhere, and the receptionist's friendly demeanor was rapidly cooling. I racked my mind, trying to come up with a good reason to be here. Anything but the truth, because telling this girl I was here so I could ask out a handsome guy I barely knew... well, it just sounded stupid in my head.

Is it? I eyeballed the receptionist. She was young, probably a college student at WU. She looked naive and bubbly enough to hope for the kinds of real-life meet-cute moments Angie had been gushing about, the kind of chick who might sit on a couch watching Nora Ephron movies, holding a pillow to her chest and wishing she was kissing Tom Hanks on the Empire State Building.

I rolled the dice. "Listen, this is going to sound crazy—because it is—but I met this guy on the train and we had... a moment. Like a single, perfect, magnetic instant when lightning struck, and I just knew—*knew*—we have something. But all he told me about himself was that his name is Reed, and he's a radiology tech in this hospital. I'm here..." I took a deep breath and hoped I wasn't overdoing the twitterpated girl act I was going for. "I'm here to ask him out on a date."

She gasped and rested a hand on her chest, and I knew my gamble had paid off. "Oh. My. God. That is *so* romantic."

"Can you help me out? Please?"

"Of *course!*" She bounced up and down in her chair, looking like she wanted to jump up, grab my hand, and personally escort me around the hospital to make sure my love story had a happy ending. Instead, she turned to her computer and typed something into her keyboard. After frowning at her screen and clicking around for a few seconds, she let out an excited squeak. "Oh my God, oh my God, oh my God! There is a Reed who works in radiology, and he's on shift. Let me page him!"

She picked up her phone and dialed in a few numbers, and I expected to hear her voice calling out to Reed on the hospital's loudspeakers. They must've had something a bit fancier than that though, as nothing seemed to broadcast through the whole hospital when she said, "Reed Azeri to reception. You have a visitor."

Azeri. That was his last name? It sounded exotic.

The receptionist put her handset back into its cradle and gave me a double thumbs-up. "He should be out as soon as he has a chance. You can wait for him over here, okay?"

She pointed to a small cluster of chairs directly in front of the reception desk. I looked past them to a much larger waiting area on the other side of the lobby, then looked back at the girl. She was practically glowing, and I realized that sitting smack-dab in the middle of the busiest part of the hospital was the price I had to pay for her help. She obviously didn't want to miss the big moment when Reed and I would presumably fall into each other's arms and kiss deeply before he dropped to one knee and asked me to marry him.

When Reed reached the lobby a few minutes later, I leapt out of my chair and dropped my cell phone. So I guess that's kind of a good story for her to tell. I just hope she embellished it a bunch when she recounted it to her friends and co-workers later, because that's pretty much all she got.

He must've known I was the "visitor" he'd been paged about, because he didn't bother stopping at the desk. He came straight over to me, picked up my phone, and placed it into my hand.

"Hi," he said. "Everything okay?"

"Yeah. Shouldn't it be?"

He shrugged. "You're at the hospital, right? So either something's wrong with you, or something's wrong with someone you know."

"Oh. No, I..." I took a deep breath, and this one wasn't for the benefit of the girl behind the desk. "Is there somewhere we can talk?"

Reed raised one heavy eyebrow. "Sure. Come on."

I looked back at the receptionist as I followed Reed out of the lobby, returning her thumbs-ups with a smile. She clapped her hands and bounced in her chair until we rounded the corner, and I lost sight of her.

We rode the elevator up a few floors in silence, and then Reed led me to a cramped but empty break room at the end of a long hallway. He closed the door behind us, then turned to me with seriousness written all over his face.

"What's wrong?"

"What? I told you, nothing is wrong."

"Oh." He took a seat at the small round table in the center of the windowless room and gestured for me to sit down opposite him, which I did. "Well, what's up then?"

"Listen... this might sound kind of stupid."

He smiled, and his dark eyes twinkled with humor. "I love stupid stuff."

That didn't help me much. I stared down at my hands and reminded myself I wasn't some ordinary girl trying to ask out a way-too-hot-for-her guy she barely knew. I was a *super-powered* girl trying to ask out a way-too-hot-for her guy she barely knew. Superheroes were, at their core, badasses with questionable fashion sense. The Fox wouldn't be all limp-wristed and shy in a situation like this. He'd pin somebody up against the wall, shout at them that they should catch a movie sometime, do some karate kicks, and then backflip away down a long dark hallway.

I knew I should, at least, be able to accomplish something somewhere in the middle. I lifted my gaze, locked eyes with Reed, and went for it.

"Do you have plans tonight?" I asked, managing to almost keep my voice from wavering at all.

He shook his head and grinned. "No, I'm off work at five. Why?"

"Would you like to go with me to this rally? It's for The Fox."

The grin faded into a smile, which then disappeared completely. "Oh," he said.

Oh? I waited for something more, staring at him until the silence grew into an awkward elephant that threatened to destroy the tiny room. Yet still, he said nothing. My heart sank, and my shoulders followed suit. I'd obviously misread our conversation on the train. The spark must've been one-sided. He wasn't interested in me, after all.

"Okay then." I pushed back my chair and stood up. "Well... see you around, I guess."

"Wait."

Reed reached out and grabbed my wrist, and I felt it again. A tiny jolt of electricity ran up my forearm, zapping my elbow and making me shiver.

"It's not that I don't want to spend time with you." He stood so he once again towered over me. "It's just that rallies aren't really my thing. Can we do something else? Like dinner, maybe?"

"I'd really like that."

His shoulders relaxed. "Phew. Okay. Good to know. Can I call you next week?"

I nodded, and we programmed each other's numbers into our phones. Then he walked me back to the elevator and pushed the button for me.

"I'm really glad you came by," he said. "I've been thinking about you all week."

With that, he turned and strode off down the hall, leaving me to blush and stare after him like a preteen girl.

17

Tess vs. "Congratulations!"

"**H**old the door, please!"

My hand shot forward and hit the button to keep the doors from closing. A blonde woman stepped into the elevator with me, panting from having dashed down the hospital hallway. She lifted her head to smile at me, and her hazel eyes lit up in recognition.

It was Bethany.

"Tess! What are you doing here?"

"What are *you* doing here?"

She put a hand on her chest. "I'm still catching my breath," she wheezed. "You go first."

My mind clicked through possible explanations for my presence at the hospital. I didn't want to tell her about Reed. It was still too new. But the alternative was lying, and I was getting tired of all the skeletons I was piling up in my closet.

"I was just visiting a friend. He works here."

Bethany's eyes went wide. "*He?*"

I'd known she'd zero in on the pronoun. "He's just a friend," I said. "Seriously. Settle yourself."

"All right, all right." She was smirking in a too-knowing way that made me squirm. "I get it."

"Your turn. What are you doing here?"

Her smirk turned into a smile so genuine it infected me, and I found myself grinning with her without knowing why. Warmth and joy emanated from her, lighting up the entire elevator.

The word *radiant* popped into my head, and I knew what she was about to tell me. I had to fight to keep the smile on my face as she spoke.

"I was seeing an OB/GYN. I'm pregnant!"

She squealed and clapped her hands together, but my mouth went dry. I hadn't seen her this happy since she'd come home and told us Bruce had proposed to her at their Senior Prom. She'd been thrilled to be marrying the big football star. In her mind, their life would follow a dream path: she'd work while Bruce played football for Weyland University on a full ride, then she'd be the perfect stay-at-home mom once he went pro.

The only flaw in her plan? She set up her life to revolve around her asshole husband. The guy who'd famously developed a drinking problem at the tender age of seventeen, throwing wild parties that became South Weyland High legends. The guy who got drunk and rammed his dad's Volvo into a statue of the mayor during his second year at Weyland

U, fracturing his left leg in three places. The injury, coupled with his underage DUI, ended his football career before it even started. He was expelled and had to get a job at the fish processing plant.

I'm pretty sure that was when the beatings started. She'd shown up to my sixteenth birthday party with a black eye. My parents, bless their hearts, actually believed her bullshit story about catching a tennis ball in the face. They refused to listen to me when I told them I thought Bruce might be hurting their daughter. He was a high school hero; they'd won the State Championship with him on the team. He was the golden boy who could do no wrong. Even when he got arrested for drunk and disorderly conduct, followed by another DUI, he somehow managed to avoid going to jail.

If his boss at the plant hadn't taken an interest in Bruce and wanted to help him climb out of his hole, I doubt anything would ever have changed until Bruce killed himself —or worse, both himself and Bethany—in a drunk driving accident. Thanks to his supervisor's intervention, Bruce enrolled in an anger management program and Alcoholics Anonymous. Bethany swore up and down that the violence had been a short-lived episode in their marriage. He'd gotten better, she claimed. But as he'd shown at my eighteenth birthday, even sober Bruce was still a dick.

And I'd seen the full truth at her house weeks ago. He was still up to his old tricks, still laying his hands on her. He was clearly drinking again. And now she was pregnant. The task of trying to convince her to leave Bruce had just quadrupled in difficulty. She wouldn't want to leave the father of her child. She'd stick by his side forever, and he'd take all the stress and frustration of fatherhood out on Bethany.

And maybe even out on the kid.

The anger I'd felt the night I'd left their house boiled up again, only stronger. I tasted metal in my mouth and realized I was biting my tongue. I swallowed the blood and pasted a smile onto my face.

I'd let her have this moment. She deserved that much. Besides, he wouldn't dare lay a hand on her during her pregnancy. That bought me a little time to come up with a plan to get her out.

"That's great," I lied. God, I was getting so tired of lying, especially to her. But this one... this one was a necessity.

"I know!" She grabbed my hands and jumped up and down. Her long blonde hair bounced around her shoulders. "I'm so excited! We've been trying for so long. I can't believe this is finally happening!"

Seeing her this happy was enough to make me genuinely smile. Bethany was born to be a mother. No matter what happened with Bruce, it was going to be amazing to witness her greatest dream come true.

The elevator doors opened, and we walked out into the lobby together. I caught the eye of the receptionist who'd helped me and gave her another thumbs up, and she clapped. If Reed actually called me and we went out on a date, I owed that girl flowers.

I gathered the courage to ask Bethany the important

questions as we passed through the hospital's main doors and headed for the train.

"When are you due?"

"October seventeenth."

"Does Bruce know?"

"Not yet." The light radiating off her faltered for a moment, and she stared at the ground. "I uh... I wanted to wait until after I had my first appointment and had a due date and everything. And I want the announcement to be special. So... can I ask a favor?"

"Sure, anything."

We stopped to wait for a light to change so we could cross Trident Avenue, and she turned to face me.

"Will you come to dinner at our house tomorrow? That way... you can be there when I tell him."

I stared at her. She chewed her bottom lip and kept clasping and unclasping her gloved hands. She wasn't saying it—because she would never say it—but she was nervous. She hadn't forgotten the early years of her marriage any more than I had, and this was the closest she'd ever get to admitting that sometimes... her husband still scared her.

"I'd love to," I said. "Now come on. I can't think of anything more worthy of celebrating than this. Bruce doesn't get off work for a little while, right? Let me take you out to lunch."

Bethany grinned and looped her arm through mine. "Thanks, that sounds really nice. You sure you don't mind paying, though? After all, I'm eating for two."

I laughed. "I have the feeling that's going to be your favorite joke for the next nine months."

"Eight, actually. October will be here before you know it."

"Wait a minute." I counted back the days to the last time I'd seen her, at Tavern. "Weren't you drinking a cocktail the other day?"

A triumphant grin spread across her face. "I beat you to the bar on purpose so I could order a virgin cosmo."

"You tricky woman. Well, come on, then. We have to start thinking about a baby shower."

We changed course, and I steered us to an Italian deli down the street. Bethany leaned her head on my shoulder as we walked, and I tilted my own toward hers.

"You're going to be an awesome aunt, Tess," she said.

You're damn right I am, I thought. *I'm going to make sure Bruce never has a chance to hurt you or your baby.*

Tess vs. Mob Mentality 18

Founders Square, the sunken plaza between City Hall and police headquarters, was packed. Thousands of voices echoed off the stone walls and pillars of our city's oldest and grandest buildings, creating the illusion that there were ten times as many people in attendance than there really were. And easily five thousand people had actually shown up.

As I stood on the stairs and looked over the sea of bodies, a strange feeling came over me. My entire life, I'd never done anything that mattered. I'd never been a part of something amazing. But here I was, about to join in an event that would go down in history: the first-ever rally in support of a real-life superhero. And nobody in this entire crowd but me knew the real score. The Fox wasn't just some vigilante. He had super-powers, and so did I. My chest swelled up like a balloon.

I was going to be a part of something great today.

It would probably be remembered as the strangest looking rally ever, as well. It looked more like Comic Con than anything else. I saw people dressed as superheroes from every comic book I'd ever read. Masks and capes abounded, but the most common costume was a simple set of furry, white-tipped fox ears.

"Oh, my God," I told Angie. "Where did everybody get those ears? I need some!"

She scanned the square, then pointed to a spot on the opposite side. Between two food trucks, a tall banner displayed a blown-up picture of the ears. It was too far away for me to read any of the words above them, but it looked like our best bet.

Angie grabbed my hand and dragged me through the crowd. It hadn't seemed possible—there were no gaps in the crush of bodies—but Angie called out, "Pardon me. Excuse me. Coming through!" in an authoritative voice and people made way. A few minutes later, we were close enough to read the sign.

"Forty dollars!" shouted Angie. "Greedy Ferengi!"

"I don't care. I'm getting those ears."

I wasn't alone in my mad desire to dress like The Fox for the day. The line was long, and I amused myself by watching the people around us. Many people had brought protest signs, and words in support of The Fox were all around me. GO FOX GO, THE FOX IS FOXY, HEROES ARE AMONG US. I hugged my own sign tighter to my chest. I'd hurriedly made it after work, and couldn't wait to unroll the poster board to show my solidarity.

"Did you notice the other group?" Angie asked as we waited.

"What other group?"

She pointed to a large cluster of people on the edge of the square. None of them were in costume, and their posters were entirely different in tone.

TAKE OFF YOUR MASK YOU COWARD.

LEAVE IT TO THE POLICE.

CAN'T FOOL US.

There were also several with a picture of a fox behind a red circle and a slash, and one that made me dig my nails into my flesh: ANIMALS BELONG BEHIND BARS.

"Wow," I said. "I didn't think anybody would be rallying *against* The Fox."

"Yeah. Just goes to show everything is divisive these days. Oh well—they're crazy outnumbered."

She was right. The anti-Fox crowd took up less than a fourth of the plaza. The cheering, costumed supporters of the vigilante were the clear majority, whether you measured by numbers or by volume.

We finally reached the booth, and I saw that in addition to the fox ears, they were selling matching tails. I chewed my lip for a fraction of a second before forking over eighty bucks for the full set. I clipped the ears into my hair, and Angie helped fasten the puffy tail to the back of my jeans. She wolf-whistled as I tried walking.

"Holy crap, girl. You should see the way your butt looks with that thing sashaying behind you. I think you should start wearing a tail all the time."

I laughed. "I don't think I could get away with it at work, Ang. But thank you."

"Come on." She took my hand again and pulled me back into the crowd. "Let's see how close we can get."

With Angie using her Moses powers to part the protesters, we were somehow able to get within a few dozen feet of the podium in front of City Hall. When we could push forward no farther, I unrolled my cream-colored poster board and held my sign above my head. I'd recreated my sketch of The Fox's face in four square feet of full-color glory. Above him, block letters read THE FOX ROCKS.

Around us, a lot of people were wearing bright orange T-shirts with the words "Fox Coalition" printed on them in black ink. In the days since the original security camera footage had started to go viral, a vigilante fan club had sprung up. Banners and signs everywhere encouraged the rally attendees to sign up for Fox Flash, an electronic alert system created by the Fox Coalition that let subscribers know when news or videos of The Fox surfaced. I wasted no time texting the number to sign up. No way was I going to be the last to hear about his adventures.

A tall man with thick, dark curls took the stage, wearing a pair of ears and a tail that matched mine. His thick, muscled arms stretched out from broad shoulders, and his large hands threatened to snap off the top of the podium. Something about him was familiar, and I squinted at his face, trying to dredge up a memory that was at least fifteen years old.

"Holy crap!" The words were louder than I'd intended, but nobody around me seemed to take any notice. They were too busy clapping and screaming support for the guy behind the microphone, the man who'd once been a hyper little Greek boy who'd chased me around my backyard when I was a child. My mouth hung open as I stared at the boy who'd been my first kiss, and who'd grown up to look... well, about as far from a tiny, wiry kid as I could imagine.

"Hello, Weyland!" His voice boomed out over the crowd, and he was greeted by another swell of cheers. "My name is Anatolya Katsaros, and I'm the founder of the Fox Coalition."

The orange-shirted throng around me screamed and stomped their feet in support of their leader. Their energy was contagious, and I throatily shouted along with them. After all, Anatolya had been my friend, and now here he was, leading the largest rally Weyland had probably ever seen.

"Look at all of you out here today! Thousands upon thousands of us stand with The Fox. They can't ignore us now!" He pointed behind the stage, toward police headquarters. "*They* say The Fox is a criminal. *They* say he's a danger, a threat, a menace to society. But we know better! He dares to do what the police can't, or maybe what they don't want to do. How quickly did they point the finger at The Fox and suggest he might be in bed with the criminals who terrorize our city? Too quickly, if you ask me!"

The crowd roared in agreement. Angie and I exchanged

glances. I knew in my heart The Fox wasn't a criminal, but I thought suggesting the cops were on the wrong side of the law was a bit... much.

"No matter what obstacles the police or City Hall throw at The Fox, we know his true colors. We know he fights for the weakest among us, that he is truly a hero. And with us behind him, they can't stop him. Keep fighting, Fox! We stand with you!"

His passion was contagious, and maybe my obsession with The Fox made me extra susceptible. But I wasn't alone; as I screamed my support, I heard a thousand voices screaming with me. I felt like part of one giant organism, one huge mass that wanted to make sure The Fox got to keep going. My emotions felt amplified. They felt powerful. They felt right.

I finally understood the draw of being part of an angry mob.

***

"That was amazing!" Angie's face was flushed, and she danced a jig down the sidewalk after we left the rally. "I feel so alive! Let's go kick some criminal ass, man!"

"Yeah, it was pretty mind-blowing to see so many people there," I said. "It was almost perfect."

Angie stopped dancing and started walking backward so she could face me. Her smile was a little too knowing, and I looked away from her, focusing instead on the traffic beside us.

"*Almost* perfect? I bet I know what was missing. It was that hottie Reed, right?" Angie heard some rhythm I couldn't, and began moonwalking down the pavement. "You were hoping for a passionate smooch in the middle of Founder's Square. Face it, Tess. You're a total romantic."

Damn. How did she know? The cold air around us pricked my cheeks, but they felt warm nevertheless.

"I'll tell you what would've made it perfect for me," she went on. "Can you imagine if The Fox had shown up, stood behind the podium, and ripped his mask off? Holy shit! I would've died on the spot!"

"What if he did show up? Except, you know, not in his usual costume." I wagged my butt back and forth, making my tail swing. "Maybe he bought one of these sets and just sort of blended in."

"Or maybe he has an ironic streak," she countered. "He could have been holding one of those 'the fox sucks' signs."

Laughing at the idea of the anti-vigilante crowd's numbers being boosted by the masked man himself, we stopped off at a bar for a nightcap. We got a couple of bottles of beer, sat on tall stools, and faced out the window, watching our fellow Fox supporters parade down the sidewalk toward the Fishbone. Some of them shared our idea of warming up with a drink, and before long the bar felt like a massive after-party.

"How's your mom doing?" I asked.

Angie shrugged. "Good, as usual. She's got the busiest restaurant in the whole Trident, and she loves it."

"I need to send her a card or a gift basket or something."

"For what?"

I lowered my chin, looking up at Angie with raised eyebrows. "Are you serious? She barely even knows me, but she's never hesitated to help me out, like having you take me to the hospital that day."

Angie dismissed my words with a wave of her beer. "That's just what she does. She's a natural-born mother hen. Trust me, as her only daughter I can speak with some authority on this subject. She's literally only happy when she's taking care of somebody."

"That doesn't mean I shouldn't thank her for it."

She shrugged. "So thank her. Get her a pedicure. The woman never sits down."

"Perfect." I clinked my bottle against hers. "To your mom."

"Hey, we're on the news!" someone shouted. "Turn it up!"

The crowd around us quieted, and we spun around on our stools to face the televisions that flanked the back wall. The bartender cranked the volume, and the voice of Jim Jenkins soon filled the room.

"...unprecedented numbers of protesters," he was saying. "People from all over Weyland and the surrounding area came out in support of The Fox."

Footage of the rally was playing, and the camera swept

slowly across a sea of fox-eared and caped people crammed into the square. The bar erupted into hoots and cheers, followed quickly by shushing before everyone quieted down again.

"That's me!" a woman shrieked. "Look, in the red costume!"

"Shut up!" a man yelled back at her.

The feed cut back to Jim Jenkins in the news studio. Beside him, a graphic featured a familiar drawing of The Fox.

"Holy moley. That's my protest sign," I said.

Angie squeezed my shoulder. "I told you it was the best one there!"

"...no effect on the manhunt for The Fox, however. Police Chief Steele released a statement to the press, asserting public opinion has, quote, 'No bearing on the legality of the vigilante's actions.'"

"Pfft," spat Angie. "Laws can be changed."

"Protest organizers were hoping a strong showing of support might be enough to entice the vigilante to make an appearance at the event," Jim Jenkins continued, "but The Fox appears to have been otherwise engaged. Police received an anonymous tip about a drug shipment arriving at Weyland Harbor this evening, but upon arriving at the docks, they discovered The Fox had beaten them there."

A patrolman appeared on screen. The faded blue and red hull of a large cargo ship was visible behind him. "All the suspects had already been subdued by the time our unit arrived on scene," the cop said. "According to witness statements, The Fox may have been involved. That's all the information we're prepared to release at this time."

"I guess we know why The Fox didn't show up at the rally."

"The rally and the drug bust come amid rising national attention on vigilantism," Jim Jenkins said. "Eight other individuals across the country appear to be following The Fox's lead, taking to the streets and fighting crime on their own terms. While most of them wear masks to hide their identity, one Chicago woman is crusading in the open."

A video that looked like it was shot with a front-facing camera on a smartphone began to play. A college-aged girl with angry red skin filmed herself, speaking directly into the camera like she was declaring a manifesto.

"My name is Maggie Long. The stars have given me a gift, and I'm not going to squander it. I may walk through fire, but none can harm me."

"She looks so familiar," Angie said, furrowing her brow. "Where have I seen her before?"

Jim Jenkins seemed to read her mind. "You may recognize Ms. Long from the media coverage last month surrounding the leaked identities of several Solstice Syndrome survivors in Chicago. Ms. Long and three other patients are in the process of suing the hospital for breaching their right to privacy, but her legal battles are nothing compared to what's keeping her occupied in the streets at night."

Another video played, showing a tall apartment building

on fire. A figure strode forward out of the nearly-collapsing structure, carrying a small child, seemingly untouched by the flames. My jaw fell into its now-comfortable position at my bellybutton.

"She's fireproof," I whispered.

Angie grinned and raised her beer. "What a time to be alive."

The train to the south side was nearly empty on Sunday morning. A large green tote bag sat on the seat beside me, holding potatoes and gravy packets. I was in charge of sides but didn't own so much as a single mixing bowl, so I was forced to do my cooking at Bethany's.

I scowled at my reflection in the train's glass window. The idea of a nice dinner with Bethany, who knew how to make all my mother's best dishes, had the potential to be amazing. Unfortunately, Bruce would be there.

Ugh.

That internal groan really summed him up. I cracked a smile as I imagined him finding out that when I thought of him, I didn't picture his aging face or hear his grating voice. I saw three letters, accompanied by the sound they spelled: U-G-H.

He'd probably be hurt. He was the kind of guy who imagined he was everyone's friend and couldn't fathom the idea of anyone not liking him. And now I was about to be forced to spend an entire evening in his company, biting my tongue at every crude remark he made and pretending I didn't hate him, all for Bethany's sake.

It was just about the last thing I wanted to spend my Sunday doing.

My first choice would be hopping on a plane, flying to Chicago, and tracking down Maggie Long. Our similarities were too large to discount as coincidences. She was a Solstice Syndrome survivor. She had superpowers. It proved my theory that those two things were related. How many other people had survived the Syndrome and gained extraordinary abilities? How many other people had watched the video of Maggie walking out of a burning building and thought, "She's just like me?"

I would've given anything to be able to sit down with her and figure out what was going on with us. Well, almost anything. Bethany needed me to be there for her tonight, so Chicago would have to wait until morning.

A pink and purple wreath made out of construction-paper hearts covered so much of Bethany's front door that I had to lift it to knock. Then I stood back and waited, hoping against hope that Bruce might still be sleeping off a Saturday night bender so Bethany and I could have some time alone together while we cooked.

Nobody answered.

Frowning, I knocked again, this time with more force. The door creaked open and a blast of cold air greeted me.

"Hello?" I called, stepping over the threshold and into their carpeted living room.

It looked like a hurricane had roared through the place.

The television set was laying on its face in front of their low entertainment center. Fashion and hunting magazines littered the floor. A tall brass lamp had been knocked over, and bits of glass from the lightbulb covered the carpet in a small burst.

My stomach hit the ground, and I ran into the kitchen. Everything was in disarray here too. The wooden chairs were all askew and one was upside down on the floor. One of its legs was missing. On the table, plates of lasagna sat uneaten. I touched the casserole dish; it was cold. The door to the screened-in back porch was hanging open, and frigid air from the waterfront was blowing into the house through the opening.

"Bethany!" I shouted.

A dog barked outside. I pushed open the screen door on the porch and dashed into the yard. Bear, Bruce's slobbering Doberman, was locked up in a chain link dog run next to the garage. His water dish had frozen, and his food bowl was empty. He whined at me through the fencing.

My left thigh throbbed, and I backed away from the fence as the memory of aunt Catherine's tiny, snarling dog played in my mind. Bear looked hungry and cold, but I thought the combination of those two things was likely to make him *more* aggressive toward me, not less.

I turned to go back into the house. I'd deal with the dog later.

Bear whined again. It was a strangely human sound, almost like a baby crying. I turned back to him, and he stared up at me. His wide, dark eyes were full of desperation, and he raised a single paw to touch the chain link. When he whined a third time, something inside me broke. I couldn't ignore him any more than I could ignore a crying child, cold and hungry and alone.

"Good boy, Bear." I inched toward the dog run. "Have you been out here all night?"

He barked and rushed the gate. He clearly wanted to get out of his cage, and his legs were shaking.

"Hold on," I told him. "I'll get a leash."

He barked, and I think he understood me, because when I turned back toward the house again he didn't whine. He sat down on the concrete and gave me those literal puppy-dog eyes again, as if to say, "I trust you, but please don't abandon me."

There wasn't a leash anywhere on the covered porch, so I crept up the stairs to the bedrooms. There was still a tiny chance nothing was wrong. Bruce and Bethany could both be asleep. But the bedrooms and the bathroom were empty; the Fabianos weren't home.

Maybe they ran to the store to get something for tonight's meal. It didn't make sense, not with the remains of last night's dinner still on the table. Bruce would never have stood for it. Despite never lifting a finger of his own, he demanded a clean house.

But I didn't even let myself think about the other possibilities, didn't let the words take shape in my mind for fear that the terrible images could become reality.

I grabbed a dog leash off the large dresser in the bedroom and headed back downstairs, trying to collect my thoughts. Had they had some huge fight? Maybe Bruce found out about the pregnancy last night, got pissed, and pitched a fit complete with throwing things and knocking over knick-knacks and table lamps. That could be where they were now —at the grocery store, buying some replacement light bulbs.

Or... *Don't think it. Don't think it.*

I thought it.

Or maybe Bruce finally crossed that line.

The sentence had barely finished forming in my mind when I stepped back into the kitchen and saw the blood. I'd been at the wrong angle to see it before, but a dark brown smear ran down the Formica counter and onto one of the white cabinets. It looked like somebody's face had been smashed into the counter, and they'd fallen to the floor.

My cell phone was in my hand, and I was dialing before I could even let myself wonder whose blood it was. I couldn't handle the thought, the possibility that...

Something had happened to Bethany.

Bear sat beside me and whined. I stared at him, marveling at myself. Here I was, sitting within arm's reach of a giant dog, and I wasn't even scared. I didn't have room to be afraid of Bear. I was too busy feeling terrified for Bethany.

Officers from the Weyland Police Department scoured her house, collecting evidence. From my spot in one of the wicker chairs on the screened-in porch, I saw a man scrape some of the dried blood from the countertop into a tiny vial. My stomach turned. Who did the blood belong to? Bethany? Bruce?

I had to look away. As I watched the cold winter breeze shake the frail, bare limbs of the Catalpa trees that lined the Fabianos' back fence, my mind churned. Where could Bethany be? I hoped she was someplace warm. I hoped she was somewhere safe.

Bruce had to have that much sense in his pea brain.

When I closed my eyes, I could picture the scene: Bethany pulls her famous lasagna from the oven and sets it down on the table. Steam rises up from the creamy dish. As she spoons the meal onto Bruce's plate, she smiles and tells him she had an "interesting" day. She sets his plate down in front of him and decides to break the big news early. She's pregnant.

That's when he loses it. He smacks her around, bashes her face into the countertop, then hauls her out the back door to his truck and drives her off to God-knows-where.

My mouth tasted sour; bile had crept up my throat while I imagined what had happened. I swallowed it back down. There was enough of a mess to clean up already without me barfing all over the sunroom.

"Miss McBray?" A tall, broad-shouldered police officer with a bushy black mustache took a seat across from me in the same wicker chair where I'd last seen Bruce. "I'm Detective Duffy. I need to ask you a few questions."

I nodded, not sure if I could speak without puking.

The detective pulled a pen and pad out of the inside pocket of his suit jacket. "You're Mrs. Fabiano's sister, correct?"

Another nod.

"And what brought you to the house today?"

Body language wouldn't work on that one. I swallowed, then croaked, "Sunday dinner."

"What did you find when you arrived?"

I walked him through everything I'd noticed when I got to the house. The front door left ajar. The living room and kitchen in shambles. The blood on the kitchen counter.

"And that's when you called the police?"

"Yes."

"Tell me, what's their relationship like? Any domestic issues?"

I frowned. "You don't know? I'm sure there's a file on them already." I paused, hating that my next words were even true. "He beats her."

Detective Duffy raised a heavy eyebrow. "We'll pull that record. Do you know of anywhere they might have gone? Any other properties or friends they might be staying with?"

I thought about it. They didn't have the money for some kind of vacation home. "Our parents live in Florida, but I doubt they'd have gone there."

Oh my God, I realized. *I have to call my parents.*

"Anything else you can tell us that might help?" the detective asked.

"She's pregnant."

The detective huffed into his mustache. He stared down at his shoes then knelt beside me. "Listen," he said. "I've been right where you are. My sister's married to a real lug down in Charlotte. The pair of 'em, they fight like cats and dogs, you know? There's always some kind of drama going on."

I stared at him. Why was he telling me about his sister? He should be out looking for Bruce *now*.

Detective Duffy gazed out the large screen windows

toward the woods at the back of the property line. "They used to live right around here, actually. Then they had a huge fight, and she showed up at my apartment, screaming and bawling about how they were finally through. I believed her, too. Got her all set up in my living room, told her we'd talk to a lawyer the next day. Then, in the middle of the night, she took off and went back to him. They ran off to Charlotte, and she didn't even bother saying goodbye. Had a couple of kids. I haven't even met them. Think she's embarrassed to bring them around, like she knows she made a bad decision or something."

He sighed and looked me in the eyes. "My point is, some people, they like the drama. They like to make big scenes in grocery stores then come home and make up, all lovey-dovey. Took me a long time to figure out she's as crazy as him."

My eyes narrowed, and ice crept into my voice. "My sister isn't crazy, Officer Duffy. And they didn't run off together. He *took* her."

"We're not discounting any possibilities at this point. I just want you to be prepared for what your sister might do in the future."

I stared at him. My sister was missing. She was off somewhere with her deranged, violent, and probably drunk husband. What the hell was this cop even talking about?

"But you're going to keep looking for her, right?" I asked.

"Of course. No matter the situation, whether your sister left with her husband voluntarily or not, there's clear evidence of battery here. We won't stop looking, okay?"

I nodded.

"Thank you, Miss McBray. You've been extremely helpful." He stood. "We'll be in touch. Officer Daniels will give you a ride home."

"No, thank you. I'll take the train."

Beside me, Bear barked. I looked down at him, and a thought struck me. "What's going to happen to the dog?"

"Well, if you or one of their neighbors isn't willing to look after it until we've found the Fabianos, we'll take it to Animal Control. They'll take care of him."

Bear whined, and he stared up at me with reddish-black eyes. The two rust-colored spots on his forehead looked like eyebrows, raised in a question. *Take care of him?* I wondered how long they'd do that before "taking care of him" for good.

A hard lump formed in my throat, and the words were out of my mouth before I could stop them. "I'll take him."

Bear nuzzled my hand; he seemed to know what was happening.

"I guess I'll be needing that ride after all," I said.

THE INSTANT I stepped into my apartment, my legs turned to jelly. I'd been struggling to hold myself together since seeing that bloody splotch on Bethany's counter, and now that I was in the privacy of my own home, my body broke down. I collapsed onto the couch, buried my face in the scratchy fabric of a throw pillow, and screamed until my throat was raw.

"What is going on with my life?" I whispered.

Two months ago, everything had been just hunky-dory. I'd had a steady job in Albany. I hadn't gotten sick yet, and I'd still been living under the delusion that my sister's troubles were behind her.

Now, probably because of that delusion, she was gone. He'd taken her somewhere. At least, I hoped he had. Because that was the best-case scenario, and I didn't even dare think of anything worse.

I screamed into the pillow again.

Something wet, warm, and stinky slid up my cheek. I lifted my face. Bear was panting happily next to me. As soon as my eyes met his, he barked right in my face. It startled me into a defensive crouch on my couch cushions. But rather than attack me, he ran to the cardboard box I'd brought home with us. He barked again and shoved the box with his nose.

"Oh, you're hungry." I heaved myself off the couch. "I'm sorry. I should've fed you right away."

In the kitchen, I unpacked the box, putting his stainless-steel food and water dishes on the floor beside my table. Bear nipped bits of kibble out of the stream that I poured into his bowl, then stood and wolfed down the rest.

"Yikes, take it easy, buddy." I'd heard stories about dog owners having to clean up canine puke in the middle of the night, and it wasn't a chore I relished doing. At least if it happened, it'd probably be on the kitchen tile. "You can stay here, but no way in hell are you sleeping on my bed."

As I watched the dog eat, I thought about calling my parents. What would I tell them? They'd never listen if I told them Bruce had done anything to hurt Bethany. They didn't believe me when I was in high school, and they wouldn't believe me now. Bruce was a smooth-talking salesman, and my parents were easily sold on the lie that Bruce was good for their daughter.

No, I needed to wait. If I called them now, even if they *did* believe me, what could they do about it? They couldn't afford to fly up to Weyland. That was why I hadn't told them I was in the hospital. It would've just worried them, and there was no way they could help—just like there wasn't anything I could do to help Bethany now.

I felt strangely envious of Bear. He was a creature bred to protect the people he cared about. His muscular legs and cropped ears told everyone that he wasn't to be trifled with.

From my fridge, Bethany grinned at me from a print of the selfie we'd taken at Tavern. She looked so happy, and the bar's lighting made her shimmer on the photo paper. Or maybe that was the early glow of her very new pregnancy. She looked bold and confident, like the camera had captured every ounce of her inner strength. From a piece of sketch paper beside her, The Fox stared down at me with shadowed eyes. He was like Bear. He just looked like somebody you didn't want to mess around with, somebody who could defend the people he cared about and stand up for what he believed in.

Then there was me. Small. Skinny. Weak. Sometimes at work, I had to get Angie to help me unscrew the caps on my soda bottles. I'd actually stopped buying my favorite brand of salsa because I could never get the damn thing open. I was useless at protecting Bethany.

I should've gotten her out of the house yesterday. I never should've let her go home to him alone. As soon as she gave me the news, I should've known this was coming.

I gripped the rough wood of my cheap kitchen table. I wished I was strong enough to smash it. Then, through the fog of grief and worry that had filled my mind since I'd gotten to Bethany's, I realized I was.

I *could* smash things. Maybe not with my bare hands, but I was capable of making them stronger.

Reaching down beside Bear, I pinched the rounded lip of his water bowl, pressing the cold metal between my thumb and forefinger. I didn't even have to close my eyes anymore; I just imagined the pulsing red glow and the change began to happen. I balled my hands into fists and waited a few seconds as they hardened into stainless steel. Then I raised my right arm above my head and brought it down onto the table as hard as I could.

The flimsy wood shattered beneath my metal fist. Bits of the light-brown material flew everywhere, and Bear yelped. My poor little table lay in a heap on the green linoleum floor of my kitchen. Compared to me, *it* was the weak one.

A slow smile spread across my face, splitting into a wide grin that probably looked a little manic. But I didn't care. I wasn't helpless. I was smart; I could find Bruce. I knew exactly what The Fox would do. He'd track Bruce down, figure out where he and Bethany were holed up, and make things right.

I knew how to do that now. I'd smash Bruce to bits, just like the table. He'd be the one getting beaten for once, and I wouldn't stop. Not even if Bethany begged me to.

I'd beat him right to death.

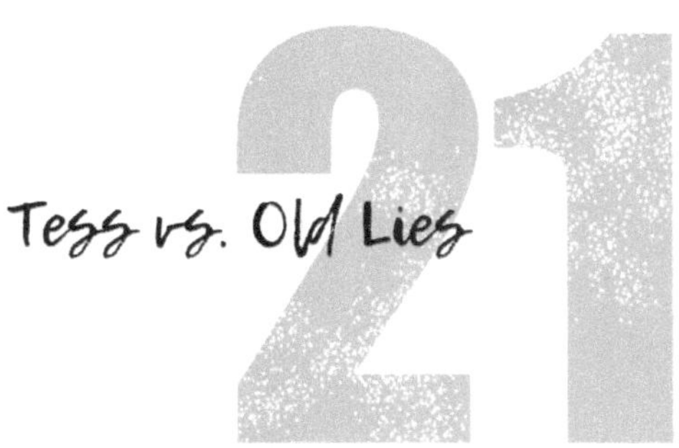

Tess vs. Old Lies

Belladonna Seafood was the largest employer on Weyland's west side. Their hulking factory took up fully one quarter of the area adjacent to the harbor, and they packaged what everyone—from large commercial fishermen to the smaller, two-man boats—managed to catch every day. Canned, frozen, or shrink wrapped—if you bought fish in a grocery store anywhere in the state, it probably came from Belladonna.

Monday morning, black smoke poured from the factory's tall stacks, and the stench of slurry filled the air. I descended the steps from the train platform and pulled my scarf up to my face, wrapping it around my head like a Bedouin in a sandstorm. It muffled the smell enough that I wouldn't have to hold my breath for the whole of the long walk to the facility's front doors.

I'd only just begun trekking across the large parking lot, past the pickup trucks and old sedans, when a voice called to me from behind.

"Hey! Miss!"

A tall guy was hustling toward me, holding onto a long black nightstick in one hand as he ran. He was wearing a brown uniform and a matching baseball cap. I stopped walking and waited for him to catch up to me.

"Can I help you?" I asked once he'd come to a stop beside me.

Hands on his knees, he panted for a few moments before speaking. "You can't just walk in here, lady. You need to sign in at the..." He raised his head, and his eyes lit up with recognition. "Oh! Tess!"

I knew at once who he was. It was the second time I'd seen him that week. "Anatolya!"

He straightened up and pulled me into a hug. "Tess McBray! I don't believe it. How long has it been, girl?"

"Since I've seen you, or since we talked? Because I saw you at The Fox rally the other day."

He let out a whoop of laughter. "Seriously? What a small world. I wish you'd said hi."

"It was a crazy day. You looked busy."

Just like at the rally, I was struck by how different he'd grown up to be than I'd assumed. I'd figured he'd look just like his dad—a tall beanpole of a man, slaving away in the kitchen at the family restaurant. Instead, I was standing in the shadow of a burly giant. And even if he hadn't been wearing the brown uniform of a security guard, I would've assumed that was his job. That or maybe a professional wrestler or a nightclub bouncer.

He pushed his cap back on his forehead and cast his eyes up and down my short frame. "It's been a long fifteen years, huh? What're you doing here now? Looking for a job? I could put in a word."

I shook my head. "No, I'm looking for Bruce Fabiano."

Anatolya furrowed his brow. "Bruce? He's your brother-in-law, right?"

Good. He knew him. That would make this easier. "Yeah, that's him."

"Why are you looking for him here?"

"Because he works here."

"No, he doesn't," Anatolya said, shaking his head. His brown hair, pulled back into a long ponytail, slapped each of his shoulders as he did so. "Not anymore, anyway."

Holy crap. He must've gotten fired since the last time I saw him. And when Bethany announced they have a baby on the way, the stress of not having a job and having to pay all those medical bills...

"When did he get fired?" I asked.

"Oh, he didn't get fired. He quit."

My eyebrows tried to join forces with my hairline. "He *quit*? When?"

"Gee, it must've been..." Anatolya looked up at the sky and pursed his lips. "About three years now."

I felt like the wind had been knocked out of me. Bruce

had told me explicitly that he still worked here. He'd even said he was a supervisor now. Why was he lying? Was he working at all? How were they affording their house payments?

"It was before I started," Anatolya went on, "but that guy is a legend around here. Everybody knows about him."

"Legend?"

"Yeah. I don't know whether to believe the stories or not, but everybody says he used to come into work drunk every day and stay out partying all night after his shift ended. Nobody knew when he slept, but somehow, he managed to keep up his production quotas. Guy was like a machine. That's what they call it now, when you finish a shift drunk and manage to hang on to your job. 'Pulling a Bruce.'"

I stared. Anatolya was talking about Bruce almost wistfully, his voice full of awe. Respect. Without intending to, I took a step back from him.

"Does that happen a lot?" I asked.

Anatolya shrugged. I found the gesture annoying, like he didn't think showing up to work when you're completely wasted was anything to get upset about.

"Happens enough to have a name, I guess," he said. "Anyway, everybody had all this money on Bruce, betting on when he'd finally do something unforgivable enough to get fired for, betting on *what* he'd do. I guess he got a DUI and they figured that'd be it, since you can't drive a forklift if you can't even be trusted to drive a car. But then he marched in and quit a few days later." Anatolya gave a low chuckle. "The chalkboard is still up in the break room off the main floor. Whoever was running that game hustled everyone good."

"Do you have any idea where he went after that?"

Anatolya shook his head again. "No idea. Somewhere close by, I think. I saw him last month, and—"

"Where?" I interrupted. "Where did you see him?"

"At Bilgewater," he said. "The bar on Blackfin Street. Pretty much everybody here goes there after the second shift."

"Okay. And you saw him there last month?"

Anatolya nodded. "He was buying rounds of shots for everybody. Wherever he went after this, seems like it pays him okay. I'm kind of jealous, actually."

Anatolya talked about Bruce like he was someone worth looking up to, and my jaw ached from clenching it.

"Do you think I could find him there?"

"Maybe. You'd probably have better luck catching him there than here." Anatolya shot me a grin. "And hey, if you're going to be there later tonight, maybe I could buy you a drink? For old time's sake?"

A tendril of dread crept into my stomach, surprising me. My mouth flapped open and closed a few times while I formulated a polite rejection.

"I'm actually going to head over there right now," I told him. "Just in case the bartender knows where to find him or something."

Inwardly, I cringed. It hadn't been a yes, but it hadn't been a no, either. Anatolya was apparently an optimist, because his expression relaxed into a lazy grin, and he shrugged again.

"Some other night, I guess."

"Yeah. Well, see you around."

Waving goodbye, I turned around and began walking back to the street. If Anatolya had noticed a difference between my warm hello and my frosty farewell, he didn't say anything.

How could he not notice? I thought, cringing on the outside this time. *You were a perfect ice queen. What'd he do to deserve that?*

I didn't have an answer. I'd always liked Anatolya when we were kids. Back then, I'd assumed we'd grow up and get married. I'd looked forward to the day when his Spiderman action figures would become *our* Spiderman action figures. But back then, I'd developed a crush on anyone I met.

Looking at him now, I felt no attraction whatsoever. It was a strange thing to realize, because not five minutes ago I'd been ogling his bodybuilder physique and thinking back to our childish romance beneath the trees. He'd grown up, that was for sure, but he wasn't as good-looking as, say, Reed.

Reed. I shook my head. I wanted to think about Reed, to dwell on the little electric shocks that seemed to accompany every touch we shared. But there was a face in my mind that pushed out everything else, and as I imagined her, I saw her crying out in pain, holding out one hand to ward off Bruce's attacks and using the other to protectively cradle the unborn child in her stomach.

My hands hardened back into fists of steel as I turned the corner onto Blackfin Street. I ached to find Bruce and show him what it felt like to be on the receiving end of a beating. Reed would just have to wait.

Tess vs. The Dive

The stale stench of day-old beer greeted me when I pulled open the quilted door of Bilgewater Lounge. Bruce's favorite haunt was a far different place from the chic, hipster-filled Tavern Bethany had dragged me to. Daylight filtered weakly through a few shallow windows near the ceiling, illuminating the mismatched selection of tables and chairs that filled the large room. Broken peanut shells littered the floor, crunching beneath my feet as I approached the bar. The place was next to empty on a Monday morning; only a few dedicated drunkards slumped against the scratched bar, clutching steins of flat ale.

There was no bartender in sight, so I chose a wobbly stool at the middle of the bar and waited. Two seats away, a man with red, piggish eyes lifted his head from between his folded arms and glanced at me. I must not have been the person he was expecting, because his eyes widened and he quickly lowered his head once more.

A soccer game was playing on a tiny television set, but the sound was muted. No music played. The whole place was eerily silent, and the thick layer of grime on the bar's top made me gag. I pulled out my mittens and put them on. The thought of accidentally absorbing anything in this place and letting it become my skin was too disgusting to risk.

A middle-aged woman in a black leather halter top emerged from a closed door behind the bar. She scowled and headed straight for me.

"I think you're in the wrong place, sweetheart." She had the voice of someone who'd been living on cigarettes and whiskey for the better part of three decades. "You gotta be twenty-one to drink here, and we don't have none of those fancy frozen cocktails."

I bristled. "Oh, I'm covered, *honey*." Reaching into my purse, I pulled out my driver's license and held it in front of her face. "Had my birthday six months ago. I'll take whatever you've got on tap."

She grunted, produced a cloudy stein from somewhere beneath the bar, and poured me a beer. I'm not exactly an expert, but even I noticed she held the stein perfectly upright so my beer was mostly head, and that the glass wasn't cloudy by design. *Ick.* Instead of commenting on it, I put enough cash to cover the drink and a healthy tip and said, "I'm looking for someone."

"Oh?" She raised a penciled-on eyebrow. "You won't find no sugar daddies here."

There was no question about it. She was trying to get a rise out of me. *What the hell have I done to her?* I wondered. *Besides being twenty years her junior?* I wanted to make a comment about her leathery skin, but decided to save that for after she'd given me what I needed.

"Bruce Fabiano," I told her. "Seen him lately?"

The bartender's eyes flashed, and I expected her to nod and tell me they were good friends or something. Instead, she shook her head and pulled out a bottle of whiskey and a shot glass. She poured herself a shot, tossed it back, and went back to glaring at me. "What's it to you?"

"I'm his sister-in-law." I decided to blur the truth a little bit. "I just moved back to Weyland, but I don't know where he and my sister are living, and I can't get ahold of them by phone. I remember him saying he likes to come here. Do you know where I can find him?"

Two stools down, Pig Eyes started coughing. He jerked his head up and barked into the air, not bothering to cover his mouth. Bits of spit erupted into the space above him, glistening in the weak light from the windows.

I scooted over a stool, not bothering to be subtle about creating more distance between myself and the viral volcano, and left my beer where it was.

Once his fit had subsided, he pulled out a white square of fabric and spat greenish mucous into it. With an apologetic wince at the bartender, he stuffed his handkerchief into his jacket pocket and lay his head back down.

The bartender poured herself another shot, apparently unconcerned by the billions of germs that were now floating down onto her collection of glassware. "Sorry, sister. Can't help you."

"Do you know anybody else I could ask? I'm really desperate."

She shook her head and crossed her arms over her chest.

"You don't know *anything* that could help me?" I pressed. "Who he drinks with when he's here?"

"Nope."

Her mouth was set in a hard line of finality. My tip apparently wasn't enough to get her on my side, and I regretted spending so much on my fox attire at the rally. If I were rich, I could've pulled twenties out of my pocket—one bill after the other—until she decided it was enough money to just tell me where that dick Bruce was hiding out.

I didn't get it. Was she playing dumb? She definitely knew who Bruce was. I could feel it. And this place was a dive; I didn't imagine hundreds of different faces passed through here every night.

There must be regulars, I thought. *Drunks like Pig Eyes down there who call this place home.*

That was it. I wasn't going to get anywhere with the cranky bartender, but maybe I could find somebody here when it was more crowded. Maybe one of Bruce's former co-workers would be here later, and I could get some information.

Not bothering to taste the germ-ridden beer fizzing away on the bar, I slid off the stool and headed for the door. *This isn't a dead end,* I told myself. *Tonight, I'll get some answers.*

———

THE DIFFERENCE between Bilgewater during the day and Bilgewater at night was... well, night and day. Heavy music poured out the open door of the bar so loudly that I could hear it before I even rounded the corner from the train station. The sidewalk in front of the bar was crowded with smokers, so I traded in the stink of the fish port for the burn of tobacco.

The bar was busy enough in the evening to need a bouncer, and he looked back and forth between my ID and my face fourteen times before letting me inside. I'd changed into the same low-cut blouse I'd bought for my ill-fated date with Will. I might not have enough money to bribe anyone into talking, but I was young and reasonably cute. That had to count for something, and I hoped somebody in there would get flirty enough to share some information with me.

Once the bouncer decided I was, in fact, the same Tess McBray who was listed as twenty-one on the ID card, he stepped aside so I could pass through the door and squeeze my way into the packed space. Behind him, the bar was full of dock workers and Belladonna employees, all looking to unwind after long shifts. Colorful spotlights played across a dance floor in front of a low stage, where a rock band was blaring something loud, fast, and full of shrill guitar solos.

I checked the bar and was relieved to see that the surly woman from earlier in the day was gone, replaced by a trio of paper-thin girls around my own age who probably made more in one night of tips than I did in an entire week at the call center. I chose one of the few empty seats at the bar, ordered a Stella—in a bottle, for safety—and took off my coat, hoping my exposed shoulders might act like some kind of beacon.

To my complete and utter shock, they did.

Moments after I took my first sip of the beer, a man squeezed between me and the crowd to my right. I glanced down at his gray twill shirt, which had Belladonna's blue fish logo and the name "Ian" embroidered over the pocket.

Bingo.

"Hey, gorgeous. Meeting somebody?" Ian shot me a lopsided grin and leered at me through heavily-lidded eyes. He was shouting, but I could barely hear him over the music.

I tilted my head and smiled at him. "Close," I shouted back. "Looking for somebody."

"I'll save you some time, sweetheart. Whoever he is, he ain't here. Now me, on the other hand..." He rested a hand on my knee.

My grip around my beer bottle tightened, and I gasped as I felt my fingertips begin to absorb the cold glass. I squeezed my eyes shut until the sensation subsided. The last thing I needed right now was to turn into something as fragile as that. The second-to-last thing I needed was this lecher misinterpreting my gasp for pleasure... which, of course, he did.

"Feeling okay, there?" he said, winking at me. "If you're tired, I know a place you could lay down."

Trying to play it casual, I crossed one leg over the other and dislodged his hand. Forcing a laugh, I waggled my fingers at him. "Oh, you dog."

"Seriously." Ian leaned toward me. His breath smelled like onion rings. "Why don't you and I get outta here?"

His hand found his way to my knee again, and I gritted my teeth. Losing all patience for playing some kind of coy long game, I cut to the chase.

"Actually, I have something I need to do first," I told him, allowing him to touch my leg for the time being. "Do you know Bruce Fabiano?"

He sneered and yanked his hand off me. "Don't tell me you're one of his girls."

One of his girls? What the hell does that mean?

I forced another laugh, hoping to cover my ignorance. "He's my brother-in-law. I can't seem to get a hold of the mutt. Know where I can find him?"

Ian narrowed his eyes. His gaze was suddenly sharp, and his sloppy drunk exterior was gone. "What do you want with him?"

"I want to see him. And my sister." I used the same white lie I'd told the bartender earlier. "I just moved back here and haven't been able to connect with them."

"Can't help you, kid. Now get out of here. This isn't your

scene." Ian pushed himself back from the bar and slipped into the crowd.

I stared after him. What had just happened? Like the bartender, he obviously knew Bruce but wasn't willing to share information about him, not even to family. Did they sense I was lying, or think I was lying about how I knew him?

Turning back to the bar, I sipped at my beer and mulled over everything I knew about Bruce. Aside from his drinking problems and the way he treated Bethany, it didn't add up to much. And speaking of math, how was he paying his bills without a job? Did he gamble? Maybe he owed somebody money, and that's who Ian and the bartender were afraid of. Watching myself in the mirror on the back-bar, I decided it wasn't likely. I looked like a little kid wearing her mommy's clothes and makeup. No way would anybody think I was tough enough to be working for a loan shark.

Whatever I was doing, it wasn't working. Not fast enough, anyway. While I sat here nursing a beer and trying to figure out how to flirt answers out of somebody, Bethany was in trouble. I didn't have the time for subtlety.

In the mirror's reflection, I scanned the crowd. I couldn't pick Ian out in the packed space, but there were a handful of guys wearing the same light gray work shirts, all sitting at a large table to one side of the stage. I watched the group until one of them got up and headed toward the restrooms.

Slipping off my barstool, I followed him down a long, narrow hallway. The music from the stage was muffled somewhat, but the pounding bass continued to rumble in my feet.

He stepped into the men's room, and I waited for him in the green light of a glowing EXIT sign halfway down the hall.

The song ended and I heard the singer mumble something to the crowd. Cheering. Laughter. Then, the band struck up again. I kept waiting, staring at the faded blue sign on the men's room door. That song ended, too, and the Belladonna employee still didn't come out of the bathroom.

What could be taking him so long? I wondered.

I crossed the hallway to the ladies' room and pushed open the door. It was a single-stall bathroom, the kind where the door opens right into the toilet and sink area. No stalls and minimal privacy.

The men's room is probably the same.

Checking over my shoulder to make sure nobody was about to catch me doing something very odd, I crept to the men's room door and rested my ear against it. It was hard to hear anything above the thumping rhythm of the live band. Frowning, I tried to force my ear to focus on the other side of the thin wooden door. I heard something—water?—or maybe it was nothing. Maybe the guy had eaten a whole plate of nachos and was paying the price. Maybe he'd be a half hour in there.

Just as I was about to retreat back to my barstool, someone grabbed my shoulder and spun me around. Ian was standing in front of me, digging his fingers into my collarbone. His black eyes were on fire, and two red spots burned on his cheeks.

"What the hell are you doing?" he growled.

"What?" My mind raced, grasping for any kind of plausible reason I could be mashing my face against the men's room door, but I came up empty. My mouth just opened and closed like a fish struggling to breathe out of water, and my shoulder ached where he gripped it.

"Come on."

Ian yanked me down the hall and shoved me through the door marked EMERGENCY EXIT ONLY. We spilled out into an alley that ran the length of the bar before dead-ending at a large green dumpster and a brick wall. At the far end, traffic passed by on Blackfin Street.

He pushed me up against the dumpster. "Time to cut the shit, little girl. Who are you, really? Bruce doesn't have a sister."

I tried to sidestep out from between him and the cold metal dumpster, but he kept a hold of the front of my blouse. I succeeded only in squirming. "I told you, I'm his sister-*in-law*."

"Is that a fact? He never mentioned you to me." Ian looked me up and down, then made a clucking sound. "And if I wasn't already pissed at that guy, I would be now. You're something else."

"Look, I don't know what you want, but I just need to find him, okay?"

"I told you before, kid. I can't help you. Bruce ran out on a debt, and if I knew where he was, I'd be there to collect it."

His grip was tightening on my shirt, and the fabric was

starting to strain around my ribcage. Between that and his bar breath, I was more than a little uncomfortable.

"If you don't know where he is," I said, "then what are we doing out here? Why don't I just go home?"

Ian shook his head slowly. "Too late, little girl. You should've left when I told you to. But you just had to stay and start poking around." He brought his face close to mine, so close that our noses nearly touched. "And you'll wish you'd gone home. Believe me. I won't hurt the merchandise, but once you've been sold, *they* will."

My eyes widened. Merchandise? They? I had no idea what he was talking about, and my gut told me I didn't want to know. My knees began to buckle, and I started sinking toward the ground.

Ian grabbed my hair with his other hand and jerked me upward. My scalp burned, and I cried out in pain. I'd never had my hair pulled that hard in my life. He spun me around and pushed me up against the dumpster again. He pressed his body into my back, and I felt his hot breath against my ear.

"Can't sell you 'til I've tested you first though, right? Gotta make sure you're quality."

He snaked a hand around my waist and tugged at my skirt, and my body locked up. His words snapped together in my mind like a jigsaw puzzle, and I finally saw the full picture. I knew what he was about to do. And after he was done, he was going to sell me. *Sell me,* like a collectible figurine.

For a moment, I saw myself as I'd been just weeks ago. Fragile. Tired. Scared. That version of me would give up. She'd go lay down in a clearing in the cold and wait for death to take her.

Maybe death did come, I thought. *Because I'm not that girl anymore.*

My bare hands were pressed against the dirty metal of the dumpster. Ignoring the feeling of Ian's hands on my body, I focused on the cold. It was sharp and unyielding, and I was close enough to it to smell the steel. I sucked the metal up into both of my hands, curling my fingers into tight fists before they hardened. I watched them turn the same faded green as the dumpster in front of me, and once they solidified, I moved.

I brought my hands downward and punched behind my back, blindly striking out toward where I thought his midsection might be. My left fist went wide, but my right connected with something soft, sinking into it. I heard Ian yelp, and his weight lifted from my body.

Spinning around to face him, I pulled my fists back again. My form was sloppy, and I had no idea what I was doing, but adrenaline had taken over. My heart screamed *"Punch!"* with every beat, and I obeyed, sending my fists toward him with wild abandon. Most of my punches sliced through the air between us, but several connected. His chest. His groin. And just as I'd managed to back him toward the bar's emergency exit door, my right fist—now a mound of cold, hard steel— slammed into his jaw. It cracked, loudly enough that I could hear it though the pumping rhythm of the music from inside the bar, and Ian stumbled backward before falling to the ground in a heap.

I stood over him and panted. My pulse roared in my ears and burned in my veins, and I pulled my right fist back again. He was down, but I could tell he wasn't out. He'd get up any second and come at me, and this real-life version of button mashing might not work twice.

"Hey!" a voice shouted from the Blackfin Street. "What's going on down there?"

I jerked my head up. A few dozen yards away, several smokers were walking down the alleyway toward me.

Shit. I backed away from Ian, toward the dumpster. How would this look? Would they believe I was just defending myself? There wasn't a scratch on me—he must've meant it when he said he wouldn't leave any marks—but he was bruised and bleeding. I glanced down at my hands and willed them to go back to normal. I couldn't afford to let anyone see me, not like this. In desperation, I scanned the alley, looking for anywhere to hide.

There was nothing. I was screwed.

"Head's up!" someone called from above.

I jerked my head upward just in time to see something thin and brown sailing toward my face. With a squeak of surprise, I dove to the side. A long piece of rope hung limply beside me. I followed it up the brick wall with my eyes; it went all the way to the roof.

"Grab it!" the voice yelled.

There was no time to think. The smokers were closing in on me; any second now, they'd be close enough to see my face. It was them or the roof. With a final glance at Ian's limp form on the ground, I wrapped the rope around my hands.

"Now what?" I called up to the roof.

"Hold on!"

I felt him pulling up on the rope and tightened my grip around it. As he hauled me upward, I tried to keep myself from scraping along the brick wall, but it was all I could do to hang on. This was testing muscles I hadn't used since the Flexed Arm Hang exercise in high school gym class, and I'd never been particularly good at that in the first place. I was traveling upward faster than I would've thought possible, and by the time the people below me reached Ian, I was being pulled onto the roof of the warehouse next to the bar, where I collapsed onto all fours.

A heavy hand rested on my shoulder. I lifted my head, and time seemed to stop.

I was face to face with The Fox.

23

After so many days of painting and drawing his face, it was surreal to be seeing it in real life. It almost felt wrong, like the versions I'd authored were the truth, and he was an imposter. But I knew that wasn't the case. He was real, and he was standing right in front of me.

As impressive as his costume had been in the grainy security camera footage, it was stunning in person. He was clad head to toe in some kind of black stretchy fabric that seemed to fade into the night sky behind him. And then there was the mask. Brown and black, it covered everything from his neck up and was topped by a pair of tall, pointed ears.

He tilted his head—*just* his head; the rest of his body stayed perfectly still—and narrowed his dark eyes. "Are you all right?"

For a moment, I forgot how to make words. The connection between my brain and my mouth had been severed the instant I'd realized his mask's ears had little tufts of black fur sticking out of them, and it took several seconds before I even remembered how to breathe.

Finally, the connection snapped back into place and my voice returned.

"I think so," I croaked. I struggled to my feet and checked myself. My short skirt had done nothing to protect my legs from the rough brick; I had long, ugly scrapes down my thighs and shins. My hands burned where the rope had pulled against them.

"Good. Come on. We need to get out of here."

The Fox took off running along the roof, heading away from Bilgewater and toward the waterfront. After a moment spent stupidly asking myself if this was really happening, then another moment deciding that it really was, I followed, stumbling along behind him as quickly as I could. The footing was difficult; the roof was flat, but it was covered in small pebbles, and my high heels kept catching on them.

I stripped them off and immediately regretted the decision. As I ran after The Fox, the rough stones dug into my feet. My heels stung; it felt like acupressure gone wrong.

My pace slowed down, and The Fox pulled away from me. After the distance between us had grown to several yards, he glanced back over his shoulder, skidded to a stop, and headed back toward me.

"You're sure you're all right?" he asked.

Without waiting for a response, he scooped me up into a

fireman's carry and began running again. His pace startled me. Even carrying me, he was moving much more quickly than he'd been before. The edge of the roof loomed, and lights of the wharf twinkled in the empty space beyond it.

We were running out of rooftop.

The Fox tightened his grip on me. "Hold on!"

He wasn't slowing down. If anything, he was speeding up, lengthening his stride with each step. Like a fool, I clutched at the sleek black fabric he was covered in, despite suddenly wanting very much for him to put me down. I knew what was coming, and I wanted no part of it.

The Fox stepped onto the raised lip at the edge of the roof, bent down, and sprung into the air. We sailed out into nothingness.

You guessed it. I screamed.

Then we landed. The Fox stumbled slightly, but he was still running as though jumping down two stories was nothing more than skipping the last two steps on a staircase. He kept going, racing down the backs of the shipping warehouses around us until we reached a tall box truck that was tucked into another alley. He stopped beside it and set me down on the concrete.

I leaned against the side of the truck and gulped in the salty sea air.

"Are you crying?" he asked.

"No."

But as I touched my face, I realized my cheeks were wet. I wasn't sure if my eyes were watering from the speed, or if I was so glad to be on solid ground and standing still again that I was weeping with joy. I started to laugh, and the noise echoed off the silent fronts of the warehouses and mingled with the sound of crashing waves.

"Maybe," I told him. "I don't know."

"Well, you can figure it out inside."

He slid up the cargo door on the back of the truck and helped me inside, where I promptly collapsed into an exhausted heap on the bare plywood floor. It was the kind of truck people might rent when they're moving into a new house, but this one opened up at the front to the cab. The Fox climbed in behind me, sliding the door closed. As soon as the latch clicked home, I was in darkness and silence.

I was alone, locked in the back of a truck with a stranger, and nobody knew where I was.

My heart began to pound. What had I done? I didn't know this guy. Maybe the police chief was right. Maybe The Fox wasn't anything more than a criminal himself. I'd barely managed to escape from Ian in the alley. Was I supposed to fight off The Fox, too?

He made no moves toward me, instead climbing into the driver's seat, starting the engine, and pulling slowly out into the street. I was puzzled by his low speed as we cruised through the shipping district. If I was behind the wheel, I would've driven as fast as possible to put as much distance between myself and Bilgewater as I could. I didn't ask any questions though. Instead, I sat in silence and turned my fists back into the green metal of the dumpster, just in case I needed them again.

The Fox drove us toward downtown, but instead of heading straight on to the commercial district he turned onto Triton, then onto Palaemon. He stopped the truck right in front of Helena's Place and turned off the ignition.

"Okay, Tess," he said, sliding out of the driver's seat and hunching to come back into the cargo space. "You're home."

My hackles sprang up, and I backed toward the rear of the truck. *How the hell does he know that?*

"How do you know my name?" I asked.

"Because we've met."

"We have?"

"You really don't know who I am?"

I shook my head, genuinely perplexed.

He raised a hand and pushed his mask up and over his head, revealing a square jaw and deep, chocolate brown eyes. It was a face I knew, one that'd been trying to force itself into my mind all day long. The second I saw it, the metal faded from my hands, leaving me clenching nothing more than ordinary fists.

"Reed?" I spoke his name in a whisper. "You're The Fox?"

He nodded.

"I don't... I can't believe it."

He gestured at his mask, now discarded on the floor in front of me. "Believe it."

"But you're..." I stared at him, unsure how to form the

question that had fascinated me even more than The Fox's identity. "Did you have the Solstice Syndrome?"

Reed sank down to sit cross-legged beside me on the plywood. "I knew you were smart. So you figured it out, huh?"

I nodded slowly. "It was the only thing that made sense. Then when I saw Maggie Long on the news, I knew I was right. How did *you* know?"

"When I saw your chart. And first, there was this."

He pulled off his gloves and picked up my right hand, pressing his palm against mine. Despite anticipating it, I was still startled by the jolt that burned through my skin where he touched it, as though he was made of something white-hot. I snatched my hand away and hugged my arms to my chest.

"And I've seen the way you can change," he said.

"How long were you watching me in that alley?" I said.

He shook his head. "That's not the first time I've seen it, Tess. I saw you on the train. The way your hand became like that metal stanchion."

I thought back to the day we'd met on the Fishbone. He'd seemed so absorbed in his phone; I'd been sure he hadn't seen me. But he had. He'd seen everything, yet said nothing.

"Why didn't you tell me?" I asked.

"You were spooked. I could tell. So..." He looked down at his own hands. "I followed you. Again."

"*Again?*"

"Yeah." He sighed. "Listen, I know this is a lot to take in. But just promise me you'll try to keep an open mind, okay?"

For the umpteenth time that night, I found myself without words. Reed apparently took my lack of an argument as a sign of my agreement, and the story began to tumble out of his mouth.

"That first day we met, in front of your apartment building? When you tripped and fell? You were right. I was following you."

The power of speech returned to me. "*Why*? How did you even know who I was?"

"I didn't. I was on my way to the train station on Triton, and I... I felt you. You were scared of something."

He stared at me like I was supposed to know what that meant. I didn't, so I stared right back.

"It's hard to explain. It's like..." He stared up at the truck's ceiling like he was hoping an explanation would handily appear there. He kept his eyes glued to the rivets in the metal above us while he spoke. "It's like people have a smell. Only not a smell, because it doesn't feel like it's my nose that picks up on it. It's almost a taste, or a reflex or... It's more just a gut feeling, I guess. And I know they need my help. But that wasn't the only thing I sensed in you. I felt... a sameness."

He locked eyes with me again, his face twisted into a pained expression.

"Is any of this making sense?" he asked.

"Honestly?"

His face fell, and I wished I'd been able to give him a different answer.

"I'm sorry," I said. "But for what it's worth, I don't think I could explain what I've been going through, either."

It was true. I hadn't even been able to put a name to it, and each time I made myself change, I felt like I was operating on mostly instinct. If I ever had to describe it out loud to someone, to tell them the way my skin burned and tugged when I absorbed something, the way it was my skin and not my skin all at the same time... I'd end up sounding a lot like Reed.

He leaned his head back again and groaned. "But I *want* to explain. I haven't been able to tell a single person about it because they'd think I was crazy, and they'd lock me up or something. And then I saw you on Palaemon Street, and you... you..." He swallowed. "You felt like me."

Something lurched in my stomach, and it took me a second to figure out why. I'd been assuming those little electric shocks I felt whenever Reed touched me were some kind of super-strong romantic spark. Instead, they were probably just the side effect of our shared weirdness, and he'd probably feel exactly those same sparks if he was touching Maggie Long or any other Solstice Syndrome survivor.

He lightly dragged a finger up the inside of my arm, and I shivered as tiny bursts of static electricity popped in the near-darkness.

"I've never felt that from anybody before. I had to know about you. So I followed you." He dropped my arm. "I'm so sorry. I know it's creepy."

It *was* creepy. Or, well, it would have been if the rest of the night hadn't been such a complete and utter dumpster fire. Compared to what Ian had tried to do to me in that alley, a little bit of light stalking was downright gentlemanly. And I couldn't fault Reed for following me. As soon as I saw The Fox and felt the smallest bit of kinship with him, I'd become a teensy bit obsessed.

Okay, a lot obsessed.

So I shrugged, reached forward as casually as I could manage, and picked up Reed's hand in both of mine. "It's okay. How about we call it even, since you saved my ass back there?"

He squeezed my hands. "Deal."

"Speaking of which, I feel disgusting. I can't wait to get into my apartment, rinse off, and crash."

Reed shook his head, his long light-brown hair swaying back and forth. "You can't stay here. It's not safe. That guy at Bilgewater could already be awake and giving a description of you to the cops."

"I don't think he'd go to the cops."

"What makes you say that?"

"Didn't you see what he tried to do to me?"

Reed's eyes narrowed and darkened, and his next words were nearly inaudible beneath the growl that accompanied them. "What did he do?"

I tried to relay everything I could remember about my encounter with Ian, from his lecherous knee-touching at the bar to his barely-veiled threats about selling me to the highest bidder. I wanted to keep it cold and impersonal, like I was talking about someone other than myself, and I desperately wanted to frame myself as anything other than the frightened girl I'd been back there in that alley.

But when I tried to talk about the way Ian had grabbed my hair, the way he'd pressed himself against me and slid his hands across my skin… my words shriveled up in my mouth, and I found myself hugging my knees to my chest, remembering the events without being able to recount them.

To my great relief, Reed didn't push me to finish my story. He supplied the ending for me.

"I saw you fight him off," he said. "You pack a hell of a punch, McBray."

His quiet compliment was enough to bring a shadow of a smile to my face, and I was able to lift my head and look into his eyes. He stood, reached out a hand, and helped me to my feet.

"Come on. I'm getting you somewhere safe, then I'm going back to Bilgewater. Somebody there knows more about this."

"Wait!" I reached up and encircled his wrist with both hands, ignoring the little jolt that hit me as I touched him. "You can't leave me out of this. Do you even know why I was at that dump tonight?"

"I overheard part of it. You're looking for some guy."

"Not just 'some guy.' My brother-in-law. And he has my sister. He's taken her somewhere, God only knows where, and he's hurting her. I know it."

He hesitated. "You're sure she's in danger?"

"When she's with Bruce, she's always in danger." It was a truth I wished I'd learned earlier, one that'd been staring me in the face since before they were even married, but I'd tuned it out. It was easier to believe Bethany's narrative, because if I believed it, I could at least run away from it myself. "And she's pregnant."

Reed looked away from me again and glared at the ceiling. He was silent for a long time. I hung onto his arm, afraid that if I broke contact, he'd tell me he was leaving me behind anyway. The initial spark I'd felt when I'd first grabbed him faded into a low, warm hum. As the seconds ticked by, I became more and more sure that if I could just keep touching him, he'd agree to help me.

I was right.

"All right," he said, sliding open the truck's cargo door. "But you need shoes. Let's go."

Tess vs. Interior Decorating

The second I opened my apartment door, Bear came bounding out of the kitchen and started barking. He sounded like an old man bellowing through a bullhorn, and I was sure he'd wake up the neighbors. The lean Doberman caught sight of Reed and raced straight for the door, knocking me into the frame as he shot past me.

"Bear! Down!" I told him.

"He'll never listen to you if you whisper at him like that," Reed said.

Bear was jumping up and down, pawing at Reed's chest. I wasn't sure if he was trying to lick him or bite him until his long black tongue shot out of his mouth and lapped up the side of Reed's face.

I felt helpless as I ineffectually patted at the dog's sleek back and said, "Down, boy!" in a perfectly loud voice.

Reed stared at me, eyebrows raised. "You don't actually expect that to work. How on earth did you manage to house-break him like that?"

"I didn't." I reached my arms around Bear's chest and pulled back. My attempt to yank him away from Reed failed, and he just kept lunging, trying to paw at Reed's face. "He's not my dog. He's my brother-in-law's."

"Ah." Reed gently cupped Bear's jaw in one hand and locked eyes with the dog. In a stern, commanding tone, he boomed, "Down."

My mouth fell open as Bear obediently sat back on his hind legs and looked up at Reed, panting while his tongue lolled out one side of his mouth. Reed took a knee in front of the animal and scratched him behind the ears with both hands.

"Good boy, Bear," he crooned. "Good boy."

Bear barked—a single, happy sound—and continued panting. When Reed stood and walked into my apartment, Bear leapt back up onto all four paws and padded after him. I clicked my jaw shut, wondering what I'd just witnessed. Was this another one of The Fox's powers? Or was this just how people who were used to dogs interacted with them? Shaking my head, I followed them, stepping through my apartment's open door.

And then I stopped, coming to a halt so quickly I nearly fell over. A horrified squeak escaped my throat, and I covered my mouth with both hands.

When I'd decided to obsessively wallpaper my entire apartment with images of The Fox, I'd never imagined he'd actually set foot in it someday. Unfortunately, in my adrenaline-fueled state, I'd forgotten all about my poor decorating choice until the moment I crossed my threshold and saw Reed staring across the room at forty different versions of himself.

While these walls weren't as thickly covered as the ones in my bedroom, there was still an unexplainably large number of drawings. There was no excuse for it, but that didn't stop my mind from running in circles and trying to come up with one: I was drawing a comic book about a character that looks suspiciously like—but definitely isn't—The Fox, or maybe I'd been commissioned by a local art gallery to do an exhibition on the local hero?

Stupid, stupid, stupid, I berated myself as I stared at the pencil sketches and—*dear God*—a large acrylic portrait on canvas leaning against my television.

Reed looked around the room, nodding at the ink-and-paper nightmare surrounding us. "Nice place," he said. "Lots of space."

I almost didn't dare look at him. When I was finally able to raise my head, his dark brown eyes seemed to promise, *Hey, I won't say anything if you won't.*

"I'll go change," I said.

In my bedroom, even more likenesses of The Fox stared down at me from every wall. I ran around the room and tore several of them down before realizing I didn't have time to take care of them all. I stuffed the ones I'd managed to rip down into the small wastebasket beneath my desk and started digging through my drawers, frantically looking for something stretchy and athletic. My run across the rooftop had quickly taught me the value of Spandex and shoes with good arch support.

A few minutes later, decked out in yoga pants, a black sweatshirt, and some Sketchers Sports that had never even seen the inside of a gym, I emerged from my bedroom. Reed had moved into my kitchen and was examining the photograph of Bethany and me that was taped to the fridge.

"I can see the resemblance." He pulled down the picture and tucked it into a pocket, saying nothing about the sketches of his own masked face that covered the rest of the space. "Are you ready to go?"

"I think so." I gestured down at my outfit. "Do you think this is okay?"

For the first time that night, Reed cracked a smile. It was a small one, just a tiny glimmer compared to the radiant and infectious grin he'd shown me when we'd run into one another on the train, but it was enough to break the tension.

"It's better than what you had on before, that's for sure. Your feet feeling all right?"

They weren't, but I wasn't about to say so and risk him making me stay here. The bottoms of my feet burned against my socks. They felt torn and raw, just like my hands had been after I'd tripped and fallen in the street in front of Reed.

I blinked, and the memory of my ripped-up hands swam before my eyes. Yes, they'd been shredded and bloody from the concrete. Until they'd *changed*. Once I'd gotten them to turn back into flesh and bone, they'd been fine. The skin had looked smooth and pink, like I'd just had them super exfoliated.

Realization slammed into me so hard I tipped backward, catching myself on the fridge before I could fall to the ground. They didn't just *look* like they'd healed. They really had. Somehow, the process of changing into another material and changing back had healed me.

Reed's tiny smile disappeared, and he softly grabbed my shoulders to steady me. "You're not all right, are you? Tess, I'm not bringing you along if—"

"I'm fine." I stared up at him with wide eyes. "Better than fine. Hang on."

Shaking his hands off my shoulders, I plunked down into a kitchen chair and tore off my socks and shoes. Reed grimaced when he caught sight of my feet; the soles were cut and bleeding, and my socks were already turning red.

"Tess—"

I held up a hand to silence him. "I told you, hang on a minute."

This was different than anything I'd done before, and I needed to concentrate. I'd gotten good at absorbing materials through my hands—it'd taken me less than a second to suck in the metal from the green dumpster so I could start swinging at Ian—but I'd never even dreamt of trying it with my feet before. I planted them firmly on the linoleum beneath my chair, closed my eyes, and tried to *feel* with them.

It happened more quickly than I was prepared for. The instant I began to tug at the thread of cold that ran up the length of my soles, my feet began to transform. My pale flesh took on the off-white, speckled coloring of the kitchen floor, and my skin became tight and unyielding. I allowed the linoleum to spread up as far as my ankles, then stopped pulling. I experimented with flexing my toes, but despite straining until my head ached, I couldn't budge them.

"Wow," Reed whispered.

I glanced up at him. "You're impressed by that? You jumped off a two-story building not an hour ago."

"I'm not denying I can do some cool stuff. But everything I can do just feels like... I don't know... an amplification of things I could do before. I was already pretty into fitness. But *this*"—he gestured down at my feet—"this is just insane. Can you walk around like that?"

"I don't know. I've never done this before."

"Well, try."

He reached out and pulled me up so I was standing in front of the table, then went into my living room to stand in front of my couch. Holding his arms out in front of him, he said, "Walk to me."

Feeling like a toddler who was attempting her first steps, I raised my arms for balance and took a tentative step forward. My feet were heavy and inflexible, and I couldn't bend my ankles. Raising my knees high and swinging each foot forward, I clomped into the living room.

"You look like Frankenstein's monster," Reed remarked when I reached him.

I raised an eyebrow at him. "That's the second joke I've ever heard you make."

"What was the first?"

"Tinfoil hat."

He shook his head. "You're so wrong on both counts, I almost feel bad for you. I really do have a tinfoil hat, and you really are walking like a stiff, reanimated giant."

Grinning, I held onto his hands while I let my feet return to normal. Looking over my shoulder, I bent my knee and raised a foot behind me to examine its underside. The cuts had healed, and my flesh was smooth and pink, like I'd just gotten a pedicure.

Reed reached behind me and caught my foot in one hand, running his thumb up the length of my sole. It tickled, and the little jolt of electricity that accompanied his every touch zipped up past my heel and along my calf.

"Strange," he said. "Your skin feels hot, like you're running an extremely high fever. Does it feel warm on the inside?"

"Not really." I flexed my toes, happy to be able to move them again, and tried to gauge the internal temperature of my feet. "They feel cold while I'm absorbing something. Icy."

Reed's eyes narrowed. "Interesting. Absorption. That's what it feels like to you?"

"Yeah... sort of like a sponge sucking up water, I guess. Why? What would you call it?"

"I don't know. From the outside, it doesn't look like you're soaking anything in. It looks more like camouflage. Like a chameleon." He tilted his head. "Or a butterfly."

For some reason, his last comparison made me blush, and I stepped away from him, allowing my hands to slip out from his.

"In any case," I said, ducking my head to hide my burning cheeks, "I can't run like that, which sucks. I was sort of hoping to never have to wear shoes again."

"We just need to find you something flexible but non-penetrable. Then you'll have built-in steel-toed boots." Reed smiled and tucked his hands into his pockets. "Maybe you're not a butterfly after all, but a tough little armadillo."

After returning to my bedroom for a fresh pair of socks, I sat back down in the kitchen to pull my sneakers back on, then returned to the living room. In my brief absence, Reed had sat down on my couch and was staring into Bear's eyes. It looked like they were having a silent conversation.

"I'm almost afraid to ask what you're doing." I sat down beside Reed and looked down at the dog.

Bear looked fierce. His mouth was closed, and he stared straight into Reed's eyes. Looking at the pair of them together, I was struck by their similarity. In the direct light of the lamp, Bear's eyes were a deep reddish brown, not very different from the velvety mocha shade of Reed's. They were each focused on the other, wearing expressions of grim determination.

"You're not..." The question sounded stupid in my mind, but I felt compelled to ask it anyway. "You're not part dog or something, are you?"

"What?" Reed broke eye contact with the dog and stared at me in surprise. "What makes you say that?"

I gestured at the two of them. "It looks like you're communicating telepathically. And you were able to get him to behave in the hallway."

Reed burst out laughing. It was the same deep, booming sound he'd made on the train the first night we'd really met. As much as I liked the sound, my shoulders rode up toward my ears, and I felt suddenly defensive.

"What's so funny?" I demanded. "I'm just asking a question."

He kept laughing. "Seriously? People can't talk to dogs, Tess. We're just having a staring contest. It's fun."

"Don't act like it's so ridiculous. I can turn into whatever I touch. You're crazy agile and have some kind of super sense."

His laughter slowed to a chuckle and then he cut himself off. It seemed to take some effort, as he kept sputtering a little as he spoke. "I'm sorry. You're right. There's no such thing as normal anymore. Nothing is too ridiculous." He cleared his throat and looked at me with round, serious eyes. "To answer your question, no. I'm not part dog. So far as I know, I'm completely human."

"So far as you know?"

He shrugged. "I mean, do you know where your powers came from? Because I don't."

"Well, no."

"So we could be mutants. Or aliens. Or science experiments." He shrugged again. "Who knows? But what I do know is this: our powers are a gift. We have to use them accordingly."

"What exactly *are* your powers?" As I asked the question, I felt a tinge of envy. It seemed like he could do so much more than me, and that his abilities were so much more applicable.

"Well..." He cupped his chin with one hand and rubbed it. "I guess if I had to break it down and label it, I'd call it extreme agility. One part of it, anyway. I'm way faster now than I thought any human could be, and I'm able to jump higher and farther than I thought possible. Sometimes it feels like I can fly, sort of. Just for a tiny distance."

"I know that feeling," I said dryly. "You flew me off the top of that warehouse. I thought I was going to die."

He laughed. "Sorry about that. To be honest with you, I love the rush. It's like a dream, except in real life."

"But you've got the other thing, right? Your super-sense?"

"Yeah. That's a little harder to describe." He looked down at Bear and scratched him behind both ears. "I guess it's almost like a dog whistle. Something only I can pick up on. That's one of the reasons I decided to use the image of a fox as my disguise. They're really quick and nimble, and they're related to dogs. They have great senses and make good hunters."

I grinned at him. "Perfect. Let's go hunting, then. How do we do it? How can we find Bruce?"

Reed stood up and whistled. Bear leapt to his feet and stood at attention, as though waiting for a command.

"We use our four-legged friend," Reed said.

Tess vs. The Hunt

Bethany's house loomed in the starlight. One of her neighbors must've been a thoughtful person, because her storm shutters were firmly closed, protecting the windows from the fierce winds that would often come up off the sea during the winter. One sickly yellow bulb burned on the covered porch at the front of the house.

We skirted the silent structure and headed around to the back. I hoped none of her neighbors saw us creeping around in the hours before sunrise, because they'd probably call the cops. In the backyard, the door to Bear's fenced dog run hung open. Reed allowed the Doberman to go inside, where Bear happily sniffed at the blankets in his kennel and lapped at the ice in his silver water dish.

"Wait here," Reed told me.

"Where are you going?"

"Inside." He inclined his head to one side, and the tall fox ears that sat atop his mask pointed to the house. "I need to grab a few things."

"And you don't want me to come with you?"

"Do you *want* to come with me?"

Twisting around, I eyed the building. The knowledge that Bethany wasn't inside—cutting fashion ideas or recipes out of lifestyle magazines—made the place seem cold and uninviting. And who knew if the police or that same thoughtful neighbor had cleaned up the chaos in the living room and the kitchen. Or if anyone had cleaned up the red smear on the countertop.

I turned my back on the empty house. "I'll wait here."

Reed nodded and disappeared behind me. I stood in the chilly yard, letting the scents of salt and fish from the harbor wash over me, and watched Bear bound around the dormant lawn chasing errant leaves that had escaped Bethany's rake. Smiling, I pictured her working industriously in the yard, planting annuals and turning her flower bed into a note-perfect recreation of something out of *Better Homes and Gardens*. She was always happiest when she was making something.

I'm going to talk her into that photography class when I get her back, I decided. She had an artistic eye; she could make a living with it.

A few minutes later, Reed appeared back at my side.

"Did you get what you needed?" I asked.

In answer, he held up a crumpled black and green

bowling shirt. He held it up to my face, and I leaned away from it. I didn't want Bruce's dirty laundry anywhere near my nose.

Reed cracked a smile. "Good instincts. This thing is pungent, which is just what we need."

He put two fingers in his mouth and whistled sharply. Bear stopped trying to dig up a power line and darted over, sitting at Reed's feet in a perfect stance of attention. Reed took up the dog's leash and let him sniff the shirt.

"Get the scent, Bear," he muttered. "Find your master."

Bear's ears stood up straight, and he jerked his head toward the woods.

"Smell him?" Reed whispered.

The dog barked a single shrill yip that seemed incongruous with his size and coloring.

"Then take me to him."

With another bark, Bear took off running. If Reed was anything less than inhumanly fast, he wouldn't have been able to keep up with the dog. As it was, the two of them kept an equal pace, leaving me to huff and puff behind them.

Bear led us down the slope, into the dense stand of trees lining the back of the housing development. Before long, the two of them pulled out of my line of sight, and I had to track them by the noise they made as they crashed through the trees.

A grim thought formed at the back of my mind as I ran. What could Bruce be doing in the woods after dark, two days after he and Bethany disappeared? I'd never heard of them going camping, and the woods weren't big enough to get lost in. If he was back here, would Bethany be with him?

The worst question of all was one I didn't want to think—I *hated* to think—but despite my efforts to fight it off, it came anyway.

If they're back here, will they even be alive?

The thought set off a cascade of others. Maybe Bruce hadn't snatched Bethany. Maybe the destruction in their house wasn't the result of them fighting. Maybe someone or some*thing* had come into their house and dragged them out. I'd never heard of bears or cougars coming into people's homes around here before, but when the weather got strange, anything could happen.

The sounds of Bear and Reed running through the woods came to an abrupt stop.

"Reed?" I called.

Silence.

"Bear?"

From my left, Reed appeared from between the trees and held a single finger up to his lips. "Shhhh," he whispered. "We found something."

My heart stopped. "What is it?"

He beckoned for me to follow him and led me a little ways farther down the hill to a tiny clearing in the pines. I looked around in earnest, but didn't see anything except dead leaves and patchy weeds on the ground.

"What am I supposed to be looking at?" I hissed.

"Here."

Reed crept forward and knelt down in the middle of the clearing. He swept the ground with one hand, revealing a dark sheet of metal. A few sweeps later, I could see a handle and a pair of rusty hinges.

A door was set into the ground. Reed raised his eyebrows at me, and I realized he was silently asking if I was ready to see what was inside. I clenched my fists into tight balls at my sides and took a deep breath. If Bear found this place, Bruce must be inside. And if he was able to get into an underground shelter, he hadn't been mauled to death by some animal.

That meant my initial instincts about this whole thing had been right. Bruce had taken Bethany, and she was under my feet right now, being held in that shelter against her will.

I nodded, and Reed pulled open the door.

At the bottom of the wooden stairs that led down from the clearing, a heavy metal door blocked our way. Reed rested his ear on it for a few minutes as Bear panted quietly beside him. Then he took two steps back and kicked the door right above the handle, making it burst open.

Through the open doorway, I could see a cramped, low-ceilinged room. Against one wall, stacks of gray plastic tubs lined the concrete slab. Against the other, a long narrow cot covered with tattered green canvas barely hovered above the floor. The place stunk of human waste, and even in the dim light of the camping lantern that hung from the ceiling, it didn't take long to see why. A five-gallon bucket that had been fitted with a toilet seat sat in one corner of the room. It had been used. A lot.

In the opposite corner, Bruce stood with his back against the wall and his hands above his head, squinting into the darkness that still shrouded Reed and me.

He was alone. The low, wide plastic tubs in the bomb shelter weren't large enough to hide Bethany. Wherever she was, it wasn't here.

"Look, Ian, I was about to come see you." Bruce lowered one hand to cover a cough then raised it again. "I swear."

He doesn't know it's me, I realized.

I wondered briefly how I could use that to my advantage. But before I could come up with anything, Bear spoiled the moment by bursting through door and running toward Bruce.

"Bear!" Bruce gasped. "What are you doing here?"

At first, I thought Bear meant to jump onto Bruce's chest and lick him, the way he had when he'd first met Reed in the hallway outside my apartment. But as the dog leapt through the air, he let out a low growl that grew into a shrill bark. Bear knocked Bruce backward, slamming the man's head into the cinderblock wall, and began biting and tearing at his face.

I stood, awestruck, in the doorway. Part of me was terrified, and the old injury in my thigh wanted to throb and complain and make me cower in fear of the big, bad dog.

But the louder part of me was envious. Bear was doing exactly what I wanted to do. *I* wanted to tear into Bruce. *I* wanted to beat some answers out of him. That louder part took me over, and a fraction of a second later I was crossing the small concrete room, brushing a finger against the camping lantern on the low ceiling and preparing to turn everything from my fingertips to my elbows into metal.

A deafening whistle split the air, stopping me before I could even pull back my arm for that first delicious punch. Ahead of me, Bear pushed off Bruce's chest and padded back to my side, where he struck up a defensive stance and snarled at the heap of a man he'd left in the corner.

"Ugh!" Bruce squinted up into the light again as blood poured down his face. "Bear, what the hell?"

"He's not your dog anymore," Reed said from the doorway. "He answers to us now. An animal like you doesn't deserve Bear's loyalty."

"Who is that? Who's there?" Bruce lifted a hand to block out the lantern's light. When his eyes met mine, they widened. "Tess?"

For the first time since the day Bethany had brought him home, he said my name with no trace of saccharine coating, no flirtatious undertone, no cackling laugh. I knew it was likely fear of his former dog that made his voice shake, but it brought a smile to my face nonetheless.

Reed took a position on my other side then, stooping so he could fit inside the low room. Bruce's eyes bugged out of his face.

"What the hell is this?" He shrank away from us, deeper into his corner. "You know The Fox?"

I didn't answer. Reed was tense beside me, poised like a fox about to leap after its prey, and I could tell he was about to take control of the situation. In that instant, a surge of envy shot through me, and I realized how much I hated the thought of standing here and watching Reed beat some answers out of Bruce.

It wasn't that I didn't have the stomach for it.

I just wanted to be more than a spectator.

I wanted to be the hammer that made Bruce talk. I owed him that much, for the bruise on Bethany's cheek on my first day back in town. For the black eye on my sixteenth birthday. For all the other things he'd done that Bethany had successfully hidden from me.

Before Reed could step forward, I flung my arm out in front of his chest and pushed him backward. He looked down at me, eyebrows raised, and I mouthed a question at him.

"Can I?" I silently asked.

He nodded, relaxing his posture and taking a step back. I took a deep breath and tried to calm my features, then stepped directly in front of my brother-in-law. Bruce was bleeding from a large gash on his cheek, and one sleeve of his shirt had been torn to shreds.

"Hello, Bruce," I said in a quiet voice.

"Tess?" Bruce struggled to his feet and took a step toward me. "What are you doing here?"

"Stay where you are," I barked. I didn't want him getting anywhere near me. He stunk of sweat and feces, and I didn't trust myself not to tear his jaw clean off his face if he got within an arm's reach of me. As it was, I ached to pull on the memory of touching the metal lantern and let my fists do the talking. "Where is she?"

"Where is... who?" He seemed genuinely confused.

I was dumbstruck for an entire second. Could he really not know the only reason I would ever come looking for him? I sputtered for a second to get my mouth going again. "My si-... your w-... *Where is Bethany?*"

Bruce's eyes widened. "You mean she's not with you?"

"With me? Why would she be with me?"

All color drained out of Bruce's normally ruddy face, and the busted veins on his nose contrasted sharply with his sudden pallor. He stumbled forward, pushing past me and sinking down onto the low cot to cover his bleeding face with his hands.

"No," he murmured against his palms. And then it seemed that was all he was capable of saying. "No, no, no, no!"

Reed and I exchanged glances. This wasn't how I'd thought this would go.

I tried again. "Bruce, where is Bethany?"

His voice was barely audible and cracked heavily. "She's supposed to be staying with you. I knew they were coming. I told her to go. She didn't want to leave me, but I knew..." He trailed off, raking his hands through his wavy hair.

"Who was coming?" I demanded. "Bruce, what happened?"

"I couldn't tell her why she needed to leave, I just told her she had to go. She was crying, begging me to stay. And then we were fighting. I... I was throwing things, you know, just little stuff, trying to make my point." He fingered a cut on his forehead. "Got myself pretty good with a piece of glass. I bled all over the countertop."

The breath I was holding let out a fraction of a percent. So it hadn't been Bethany's blood. It was a small relief, but I still felt miles away from finding her. I needed Bruce to get to the point.

"And she left?" I prodded.

He gulped. "Eventually. She took my car—said she was driving to your place—and I was cleaning up the living room when I saw the van pull up. A black van."

He stared at me like I was supposed to know what that meant.

"I don't understand."

"My employers. My real ones. I lied to you, okay? I didn't get a promotion. I haven't worked for Belladonna in years."

I knew that already but didn't bother to interrupt him. He was finally talking, but still not fast enough, and I was already struggling not to reach down his throat and yank the words out myself. So I simply stared at him, unblinking, and willed him to go on.

He complied. "Ian and Jared Nyx."

The muscles in my neck throbbed involuntarily where they'd been squeezed in the alley. What were the chances it was the same Ian? Weyland wasn't a big enough town for coincidences. It had to be the same one.

"Where did you meet them? At Belladonna?"

Bruce nodded. "Yeah. They own it."

"And what do you do for them?"

"I run security. For their… side business."

"Cut the crap, Bruce," I said. "Tell me exactly what you do for them."

"I make sure the right cops get their payments. So they don't sniff around too much, you know? And I look after some of their call girls. The ones they keep in town, anyway. They've got a lot of fingers in a lot of pies, none of them legal. Gambling. Drugs. People call them the Nightshades."

A low growl came from my left. Reed was standing beside me, arms crossed over his chest, digging his fingers into his biceps. I'd been so intent on Bruce's story that I'd forgotten he was there.

"So." The light from the lantern burned in Reed's over-large pupils. "Those are their real names. Jared and Ian Nyx."

"You've heard of them?" I asked. "The Nightshades?"

He gave a single, terse nod. "It's a name I keep running into, but that's all I had—just the alias. I didn't know who was behind it. I just knew that name was connected to all the recent kidnappings."

What little color that remained in Bruce's face drained away. "You know about those?"

In two short steps, Reed crossed the room and grabbed Bruce's thinning hair, yanking the other man's head back with one hand and grabbing him by the throat with the other.

Bruce cried out—a short, sharp choking sound—as he was hoisted up off the cot.

"Yes," Reed hissed into Bruce's face. "I know about it. I've known for weeks, and I've spent *every moment* trying to track down the monsters who are ripping those girls away from their families, the scum who are sentencing those girls to live in Hell for the rest of their now-shortened lives."

His gloved fingers tightened around Bruce's neck. Bruce gasped for air, and his legs kicked uselessly beneath him.

"How long have *you* known, Bruce? Three years? Is that how long you've been running security for the Nightshades?"

Bruce clawed at Reed as his face slowly started to turn blue.

"Stop!" I tugged down on Reed's arm, trying and failing to loosen his grip. "You'll kill him!"

"It's no less than he deserves," Reed snarled.

"My sister! If you kill him, we might never find her!"

His lip curled backward, but he released Bruce back down onto the cot. "Fine. He's all yours."

I waited for a few minutes while Bruce wheezed and coughed into a thin, filthy pillow. When he seemed to have gained most of his breath back, I finally spoke.

"You thought she was with me. Well, she isn't. So do you think they have her? Would they have taken her?"

"Maybe." He stared down at the floor. "They'd consider her collateral. Against my gambling debts."

I ground my teeth together. Collateral? How could he sit

there and talk about his wife like that, like she was just a thing?

As I tried to decide how long I might go to prison for murdering the sack of crap who sat in front of me, Reed roamed around the cramped space, checking in the plastic totes and unscrewing the top of a large water bottle. After picking up a long metal bar and twirling it in one hand, he turned back to Bruce.

"You've got plenty of food and water to last you at least a week," he said. "I'm leaving you down here until I've taken care of the Nightshades."

"W-what?" Bruce spluttered. "You're going after them?"

"Do you expect me to leave those women in their hands? I'm not a *coward*." Reed spat out the last word like it had a foul taste.

"You can't leave me down here!" Bruce jumped off the cot and clutched at my arm. "Tess, please!"

"It's better than you deserve." I yanked my sleeve out of his grip, and Reed, Bear, and I walked out of the room.

"They'll kill you!" he screamed after us. "You're leaving me to die!"

Without responding, I closed the heavy door on Bruce behind us. We climbed the wooden stairs back up to the clearing, and Reed slid the metal bar through a pair of handles on the trapdoor set into the ground. Bruce was locked in his hideaway.

"What if he's right?" I asked. "If they kill us, what'll happen to Bruce?"

Reed shrugged. "He'll share our fate, I guess. Does that bother you?"

I saw Bethany's bruised face in my mind's eye and thought about the women Bruce had let the Nightshade Brothers steal from the alleys of the Trident and the other slums over the years.

"Not one bit," I said.

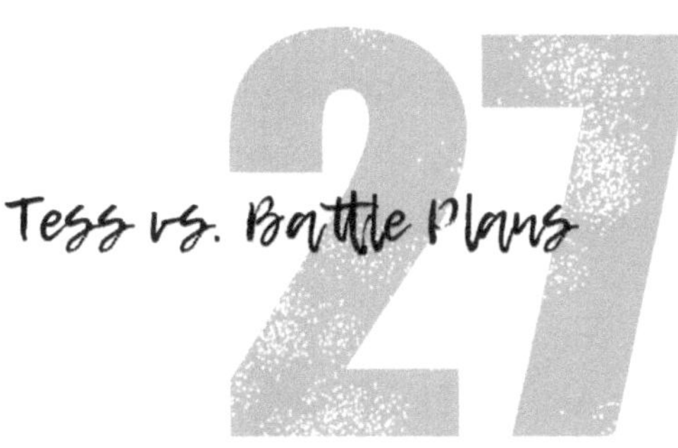

Tess vs. Battle Plans

Reed was quiet on the drive back to Bilgewater. He'd briefly sketched out his plan to me on the walk back through the woods, but now he sat in silence and concentrated on the road. The sun was rising over the harbor, turning the ocean a brilliant shade of orange. Bear sat in the back of the truck, his tongue lolling happily out of his mouth as he watched us.

"Are you sure this is a good idea?" I asked him. "Won't there be like, I don't know, guys with machine guns? Guard dogs? Dangerous stuff?"

He glanced over at me, then turned his attention back to the road. "I'm curious," he said. "What exactly are you picturing?"

"Well, it's a warehouse, right? So, I guess lots of levels and ramps, and about a hundred guys with guns standing between us and my sister."

He snorted, managing to pack a whole lot of judgment into one little piggy noise.

"You watch too many action movies. Sure, these guys are going to have a lot of muscle, but we're not going to rush in there, guns blazing. The Nightshades have gotten spoiled. They're used to operating in the open. They have so much money and so many cops on their payroll, they don't feel like they have to hide."

"How can you even know that? You didn't even know their real names until half an hour ago."

"That was the *only* thing I didn't know. I've been learning a lot of about them, about the shady underbelly in the south side. I used to think life was simple—go to work, have fun on the weekends, pay the bills. But there's a whole other world out there—a world where people don't play by the same rules normal people do. And now we're a part of that world."

"'We?'" I repeated. "Uh, newsflash: you and I aren't exactly in the same league here. For one thing, you've got a costume."

"You really don't think we're the same? You decided to take the search for your sister into your own hands. The second you walked into Bilgewater with your insane plan to flirt information out of somebody, you became a vigilante."

I folded my arms across my chest. "I don't think that word applies to what I'm doing at all."

"Did you or did you not beat the holy hell out of Ian Nyx in an alley last night?"

"That was self-defense."

"Okay, sure. I agree that if you hadn't started throwing punches, you would've gotten hurt. Well, in a hypothetical alternate past when I wasn't just about to dive off the building and strangle that guy to death."

"You were watching?"

"Not all of it. It took me a few minutes to get out the front door of the bar, get into my costume, and circle around the block to climb onto the roof of that warehouse."

"You were in the *bar?*" My voice was shriller than I would've liked it to be.

"I told you, I was watching you. Which is why I know you followed a Belladonna worker down the hall to the men's room. What exactly were you planning to do to that poor guy? Turn your hands into steel and beat some answers out of him?"

I stared at him, aghast. "No! I was... Well, I'm not sure what I was going to do. You said it earlier. Flirt for information."

"Right. Come on, Tess. If flirting didn't work, and you were alone with that guy in the bathroom with your sister's safety on the line...?" He trailed off, leaving the question hanging in the air, but didn't push me to answer it.

And I was glad. I really didn't know what I was capable of, which was exactly why I wasn't so hot on the idea of going into someplace where there were a whole lot of people who *did* know what they were capable of. The only stuff I knew about fighting came from comic books, and there tended to be a lot of "POW!" and "OOMPH!" callouts over the important stuff.

But what was my alternative? Go home, feed Bear, and read about characters who were way braver than I dared to be? Wait for the cops to work it all out? Officer Duffy clearly thought Bethany and Bruce had just run off somewhere to work out their problems. And now that I knew about this other world, where women could just disappear and people could pay off cops to look the other way, I couldn't go back to a regular life. I couldn't pretend I hadn't seen behind the curtain.

But I could follow Reed. I watched him, his stark features drawn together as he concentrated on the road over the dashboard, and something he said in the bunker came back to me.

"Hey, was it true what you said back there? You've been searching for the missing girls for weeks?"

"Yeah, why?"

I chewed my lip, not sure I wanted to know the answer to the next question. But I needed to know. "Did you... did someone you care about go missing?"

He flicked his eyes over at me for a brief second. "Not exactly."

I'm embarrassed to admit I was relieved. The teensiest part of me had been scared his wife or girlfriend had been taken.

"Why, then?" I pushed. "Are you really just that noble?"

"Would you find it hard to believe if I was?"

Shrugging, I flicked a piece of lint off my armrest. "Not

really. I could see it. But it makes me feel like a jackass. I've known about my powers for a couple weeks, and it didn't occur to me to use them to find these girls until my sister became one of them, you know?"

"My motives weren't as noble as you might think." He paused and pursed his lips. "The cops brought me in for questioning on the disappearances last month."

My jaw hit my shoes. "Seriously? Why?"

"Three of the girls came through the ER the week before they went missing, and I administered their x-rays. They all came in for different reasons and saw different doctors, so I was the only connection the detectives could find."

"Are you still a suspect?"

"Technically, yes. No alibi. So I started looking for the girls to clear my name. I don't think I'm really a main suspect or anything because the cops haven't come back to question me, but..."

"Now it feels like the right thing to do," I finished for him.

"Yeah." He glanced over at me again. "Make you feel better?"

"Depends. Are you going to let me keep working with you?"

He drove in silence for a few minutes, staring out at the road ahead of us. At last, he simply nodded.

"Good," I said. "So what makes you think we'll find more answers at Bilgewater? It was a pretty solid dead-end for me last night."

"You said the worker you followed never came out of the

bathroom, right? What if it's not a bathroom? What if it's an entrance to a whole separate kind of club?"

Remembering what Ian had threatened to do to me in that alley, I shuddered. "Definitely possible."

"There's a warehouse immediately behind Bilgewater that has signage claiming to be backup storage for Belladonna Seafood, which the Nyx brothers own, right? What if they're keeping more than canned crab in there?"

"You think that's where all the kidnapped women are?"

A pained look flashed across Reed's face. "Not all of them. I think it's a holding facility. At best, they probably keep their victims there a few days before shipping them off."

The bottom dropped out of my gut, and a hollowness filled the space where my stomach should've been. "A few days?"

Bethany had been missing for two days. Reed knew it, and I could see the warning in his eyes. There was a chance we were already too late.

I swallowed, forcing the sudden rush of grief back down. *She could still be there. We have to try.*

"What do I need to do?"

"I wish we had more time to prepare you, to teach you how to fight. But we need to get in there tonight, before... Well, before we lose any more time. So we need to work with what you've got. I saw what you did to Ian Nyx."

"Yeah, but that was pure adrenaline."

He quirked an eyebrow. "Do you think you'll be calm when we're facing down the Nightshades and their men?"

Fair point. "Okay. So I just... let my instincts take over? Start throwing punches?"

"No, I'm not saying that either. You have to think about your abilities. Don't use your bare fists. You can absorb anything, right?"

"Yeah, I think so. I mean, everything's worked so far."

"We'll be in a warehouse. There should be plenty of good, hard materials for you to morph into. Steel. Brick. Wood. Stay behind me. Follow my lead. We have the advantage of surprise. If we're stealthy enough, nobody even has to get hurt."

He sounded so confident. I almost forgot that until the meteor shower, he'd just been a regular guy working a regular job in a hospital. Which Reed was the real version now? The one who wore scrubs or the one who ran around in a fox mask?

For Bethany's sake, I had to trust that it was the latter. After all, my powers had changed me. I was no longer the scared, dying girl who checked herself out of the Hudson Research Center. I was someone brave enough—or maybe stupid enough—to break into a warehouse in broad daylight hoping the local mafia was using it as a front for their illegal activities.

Reed turned onto Blackfin Street, then pulled the truck into a space behind a stack of storage pods in a parking lot. He reached behind my seat, rummaged around in a box, and handed me a wad of black fabric.

"Here," he said. "It's not much, but you need to hide your face, just in case they have cameras."

I pulled the fabric apart and realized it was a thinly knit ski mask with holes for my eyes, but none for my mouth. I frowned and wrinkled my nose.

"I know, I know. It's not as fashionable as mine." Reed put on his own stylized mask with its tall fox ears. "But the important thing is nobody can track this back to us if we manage to make it out of there."

He made a valid point. I didn't want the Nyx brothers coming after me. I pulled on the mask, trying to ignore the way it scratched at my face and made my breath feel too hot and too close.

Reed cut the engine and slid out of the truck. "Let's go get your sister."

Tess vs. Self-Restraint

The Bilgewater Lounge looked sad and desolate in the misty air of the morning. It'd been hours since last call. The loud music of the night before had been silenced, and the only sounds around us were the squawking of seagulls and the belch of a truck engine from down the street. Even Bear was quiet as he padded along beside me, his posture as protective as it'd been in Bruce's bomb shelter.

It was surreal, walking down the same alley where Ian Nyx had attacked me not even twelve hours before. It seemed like six lifetimes had happened since he'd pressed me against that green dumpster. I went down to the end of the alley to give the metal behemoth a pat.

"Friend of yours?" Reed muttered.

"You might say that." I felt indebted to its rusty metal body for helping me save my fragile hide. I eyed the heavy metal door beside us, which had only a large deadbolt in place of a knob. "Are you going to pick the lock or something?"

"No," he said. "I noticed they have an alarm system when we were here yesterday. You can usually spot them—blinking red light on the wall opposite any staff door like this."

I thought back to the long minutes I'd spent in the hallway by the bathrooms, waiting for the Belladonna worker to re-emerge. I hadn't even noticed a light.

"What, then?"

"Your old pal Oscar the Grouch is going to give us a boost."

"Oscar the Grouch *lived in* a garbage can. He wasn't a dumpster."

"Close enough. Come here."

He crouched down slightly, interlacing his fingers to make a foothold for me, and helped me clamber onto the dumpster's sloping plastic lid. Beside me, the narrow window from the men's room at Bilgewater hung slightly open, the pane of glass angled upward away from the building. Even in the still morning air, a terrible odor wafted out from the toilet below us. The stench of the aftermath of bar nachos and beer —ejected from both ends of drunk dock and cannery workers —managed to squeeze its way through the thin layer of polyester that protected my mouth and nose. I retched and reflexively pulled on my little black knit gloves.

"Good idea." Reed lifted his own gloved hands and flexed his fingers. "No prints."

"Gross," I said. "I was picturing it being a hallway or something, not an actual, working bathroom."

"Not every guy who comes in is going to the brothel or whatever they've got back there. They need a place for the legit customers to..." He rolled a hand in the air. "Well, you know."

"Reed, we're about to commit a felony here. There's no need for euphemisms."

I suspected he wanted to laugh at me, but he didn't say anything. Instead, he leapt into the air and landed softly on the dumpster lid beside me. Then he leaned down and pushed hard on the window frame, snapping it clean off at the hinges. He carefully lowered the window down to the ground, then looked at Bear.

"Stay here, buddy. Howl if you see anyone, then run back to the truck, okay?"

Bear stared up at him, panting softly. I didn't know how the dog could understand a command that complicated, but Reed seemed to think his message had been received and noted.

Reed turned back to me. "Ladies first."

As he grabbed my hands to lower me through the window, and his fingers grazed my exposed wrists, I focused on the pleasing electric pulse passing between us so I wouldn't have to think about the fact that I was putting my brand-new shoes onto the seat of a toilet where guys like Bruce would rest their cans. Reed came in after me. Feet first, he slipped through the window, twisting in mid-drop to let each of his shoulders through the small opening. He landed lightly, his combat boots barely slapping the wet floor. Then he pulled open the stall door, and we stepped into the men's room.

It looked like a normal bathroom to me, with two wide stalls across from a row of three urinals. I found it disgusting that there was no sink, but didn't think there was anything suspicious about the place. Reed had keener observational skills than me and kicked in the door to the second stall, which sat in the corner of the room. A narrow wooden door marked "Private" was set into the yellow-tiled wall, next to the toilet paper dispenser.

Reed raised an eyebrow at me. "Does that look like a normal place to put a storage closet or something?"

I shook my head. He pressed his ear against the door, closed his eyes, and listened for a few moments. He tried the doorknob.

"Locked," he whispered.

"What do we do now?"

"Stay here."

He slipped out of the stall and out the bathroom door, leaving me to hover uncertainly in the men's restroom by myself. I alternated between holding my breath and filtering air through my gloved fingers and wondered what normal people like Angie were doing right then. Eating breakfast and getting ready for a grueling day at the call center, probably. I couldn't decide if I was envious or not.

Reed returned a few minutes later with a small keyring.

"Found the office," he whispered. "Hopefully one of these works."

The fifth key he tried clicked into the lock, and the handle twisted in Reed's hand. He pushed the door open, revealing a long hallway lined with closed doors. To our right stood a wooden podium that reminded me of a waiting area at a family restaurant. It even had little menus sticking out of the basket on its side. I pulled one out and skimmed it over.

"'Full body massage,'" I read aloud, keeping my voice low. "'Hot mud treatment.' They're all just spa services. There's even a section for facials." I handed him the menu. "Holy cow, check out these prices. Five hundred for a massage."

"Clever," whispered Reed. "I bet every service on this card is a code for something else. Come on. We need to check these rooms."

Now I knew why the Belladonna employee never emerged; he was probably treating himself to a little after-work rub down. Gross.

Repeating his process from the door in the bathroom, Reed listened at the first room on our right before slowly twisting the knob and pushing open the door. The room was empty except for a long massage table and a small cluster of oil bottles on the floor. It smelled strongly of vanilla and sweat.

Door after door, we found empty massage rooms with no signs of life. I got the feeling they'd been recently used though; the scents of the oils seemed too strong to be anything but fresh.

By the time we searched the last room, which was just as empty as the first, my patience had run out.

"Dammit!" I kicked over a few plastic oil bottles and stormed back into the hall. "I thought she'd be here!"

Reed crossed his arms and stared down the row of open doors. "Me too. I thought this would connect to the warehouse."

"Aren't we in the warehouse now? There's got to be a door somewhere." I brought up my right fist and allowed it to harden into steel beneath my knit glove. "I'll check."

He grabbed my wrist and yanked me back away from the wall, then held a finger up to his lips. "Jesus, Tess!" he whispered, lowering his hand. "You don't think a noise like that will attract attention? Keep it together."

"Okay, okay."

Reed released me, and I walked halfway down the hall, back toward the bathroom. He followed, and I let him pass me by. Then I turned on my heel and bolted back toward the blank, dead-end wall, letting the cold steel spread from my hands all the way up to my shoulder joint.

"Stop!" Reed shouted behind me.

He was faster than me, and I knew it. But I was only inches from my goal, and not even someone with super-human speed could have stopped me in that moment. I crashed right through the sheetrock and wall studs. Dust swirled around me, and I skidded to a stop at the edge of a cavernous warehouse.

Morning sunlight shone through high, narrow windows

along the roofline two stories above me, illuminating several rows of filthy mattresses on the concrete floor. There wasn't anyone there—no guards, no women, nobody. The space was littered with clothing, empty soda cans, and discarded candy wrappers. I let my arm return to normal and searched the room, kicking garbage out of the way as I ran from mattress to mattress, sweeping aside thin blankets and scanning for any sign of Bethany.

Then I found them—a half-dozen long, shimmering strands of blonde hair resting on a stained pillow. I bent down and scooped them up, and then rough hands grabbed me from behind and dragged me backward.

Tess vs. Tess

"**G**et off me!" Whoever had me was strong and had caught me completely off-guard. Struggling felt useless, but I did it anyway.

He spun me around to face him, and I found myself mask-to-mask with Reed. His mouth was set into a hard line, and his brown eyes burned with furious anger. Without saying a word, he dragged me back through the warehouse, down the vanilla-soaked massage parlor hallway, and shoved me up and through the window in Bilgewater's bathroom. I turned around, expecting him to climb up after me, but instead he crossed his arms and stared up at me through the window for several seconds.

When he finally spoke, his words were a low growl. "You're on guard duty with Bear. Whistle if you see anyone."

"But I can't—"

He walked out of view before I could inform him of the

major flaw in his plan. I'd never been able to whistle; I just looked like I was trying to cool down some soup every time I tried. I put one foot through the window in an attempt to lower myself back into the bathroom, remembered the rage in Reed's eyes, and decided it might be better to follow his orders.

I slid down the top of the dumpster and landed beside Bear. The dog glanced up at me and bumped his head against my hand before turning his attention back to Blackfin Street. The minutes ticked by, and as I sat and stared at the morning traffic at the far end of the alley, a little knot of shame and embarrassment began to grow inside me.

Was I too impulsive? Looking back on my life, I'd never been big on planning. I'd bolted out of Weyland on a whim, preferring to upend my life over having yet another difficult conversation with my family about Bruce, then reversed that course with little more than an hour's consideration. How much better would my life be right now if I took the time to think things through? I had a feeling I wouldn't be sitting in an alley wondering what Reed was doing. Maybe I'd be working for a comic book company somewhere with a decent income and a real future ahead of me.

But where would that leave Bethany? Bruce got into bed with the Nyx brothers before I even graduated high school. Whatever path my life might have taken, Bruce was already firmly on his road to ruin with Bethany riding shotgun. If I wasn't so quick to action, I might not even know she was missing right now. If I bothered to think about things logically, I might have waited too long to start looking for her.

If I'm not too late already.

The image of all those vacant mattresses haunted me. I clutched the golden strands of hair I'd found on the pillow, and I had to believe they belonged to Bethany. She'd slept on that mattress. She was close, and I wasn't going to give up on finding her. Not ever.

A high whistle sounded, and Bear stood up and began padding out to Blackfin Street.

"Hey!" I whisper-shouted. "Come back here!"

But it was just as ineffective as when I'd tried to order him to stop jumping on Reed. Bear ignored me, leaving me no choice but to stand up and follow him. Just before we reached the sidewalk, Reed pulled up to the curb in his white box truck. Bear and I climbed inside, and I took my place in the passenger seat.

"What did you find?" I asked.

"That depends." Reed didn't look at me as he pulled away from the curb. "Are you ready to start listening to me? Or are you going to just keep doing whatever you feel like doing?"

Grateful for the time I'd had to myself in the alley, I was able to answer him calmly. "I'm really sorry. I couldn't shake the feeling that Bethany was on the other side of that wall... I was sure I'd find her if I could just get over there."

"Well, you're damn lucky you didn't find her. Because she wouldn't have been alone. I told you our *only advantages* are stealth and surprise, Tess. You can't just go barreling into an unknown situation." He looked over at me then, and I was shocked to see sadness in his dark eyes. "You could've died."

"I know. It won't happen again."

Reed shook his head and turned back to the road. "You don't know that. I don't know that. If I'm distracted trying to protect you, I won't be able to protect myself. Or your sister, when we find her."

"You think we can still find her?"

"I think I know where they went after they cleared out of the warehouse. After your run-in with Ian in that alley, he probably got spooked. That move wasn't planned. The warehouse would've been spotless if they hadn't left in a hurry."

"So they had to go somewhere close, right? Somewhere they already had access to?"

"That's what I'm thinking. And I have a hunch it's going to be another warehouse." He pulled the truck over and gestured.

I stared out the windshield. "You think they're here?"

Ahead of us, the enormous, smoke stacked headquarters of the Belladonna Seafood processing plant loomed.

He nodded. "We just need to figure out a way to break in."

Tess vs. Two Strikes

Reed and I hadn't settled on a plan to break into Belladonna, but we agreed on one aspect: Bear couldn't come with us.

"I'm sorry, buddy," Reed told the dog as we sat in the truck outside my apartment building. "You're a brave guy, but it's too dangerous. You need to stay here."

Bear stared back and forth between us beseechingly, whining quietly. His classic puppy-dog eyes worked, and I threw my arms around him.

"Can't he come?" I asked Reed. "If he stays quiet in the truck?"

Reed shook his head, but he was smiling. "Tess McBray, don't make me be the bad guy."

Bear whined again, turning his head toward mine, and ran his tongue up the side of my face.

"Bear is special," I said. "He knows how to be quiet, don't you boy?"

Bear squeezed his eyes shut and seemed to smile up at me, but Reed's face turned serious.

"He can't come. It's too much of a risk—for us and for him. He'll be fine in your apartment, trust me."

It wasn't Bear I was worried about. Truth be told, I'd grown to love him. His presence made me feel safe, and I hated the idea of going into a proverbial lion's den without my guard dog by my side. Even if Reed would be there with me, I wanted all the backup I could get.

Reed seemed to read my mind. "We'll be fine, too."

"Promise?" I whispered.

He hesitated, and my heart sank. Of course he couldn't promise that. It'd been a stupid question.

"Never mind." I slid the truck's door open and hopped out onto the sidewalk. "Come on, Bear."

The dog followed me up to my apartment, and I made sure he had enough kibble and water to last him for a few days, just in case I couldn't come back right away.

"But I will be coming back," I told him. It made me feel better to say it out loud.

I also made sure the door to my balcony was open so he could access the puppy training pads I'd set out for him. I hated to admit it, but this wasn't a good situation for a dog. I'd been so wrapped up in my search for Bethany, I hadn't really thought about what it must be like for a giant Doberman to be cooped up in my tiny one-bedroom.

"Don't worry, buddy," I said. "I'll find someone to walk you."

After leaving my building, I detoured to Helena's Place to see if she'd be willing to take my secret dog for a walk. Given how much she seemed to love helping people, I had no doubt that she wouldn't mind helping a big, furry, four-legged animal. A large CLOSED sign hung in the window, but when I tested the door it opened. I went inside and weaved between vacant clusters of tables and chairs toward the door leading to the back office.

"Hello?" I called.

No one answered.

I pushed open the office door and found Helena slumped in her computer chair, clutching a tissue box and staring off into space. Her brown eyes were bloodshot and puffy, and her black curls stuck out wildly in every direction. There was no trace of the strong, collected woman I'd met on my first day back in town. A pang of worry shot through me; whatever had happened to cause this transformation, it was serious.

"Helena, what's wrong?" I pulled up another chair and sat down across from her.

She simply shook her head and kept staring at the corner.

"I'm going to call Angie, okay?" I pulled my cell phone out of my pocket and dialed Angie's number. She'd know if this was a normal thing for her mom to do, and would want to come over to help her mom deal with whatever was happening.

A second after I hit the "Call" button, I heard a muted vibration coming from Helena's lap. I realized the tissue box wasn't the only thing she was holding. Behind it, she hugged a spaceship-shaped backpack to her chest. I sat there for a moment, staring at the backpack until Angie's voicemail picked up and the buzzing stopped.

"Hi, this is Angie!" the recording chirped. "If you're hearing this, I must be on an away mission. Wish me luck, 'cause I'm just a red shirt. Leave a message, and I'll get back to you later!"

I tapped the button to end the call and dropped the phone to my side. "Helena," I whispered, "where is Angie?"

At the name, Helena's shoulders began to shake. Sobs racked her body, and she clutched the backpack tighter.

I felt very cold. "Helena? Can you tell me where she is?"

After several long seconds, she finally answered, her voice so quiet I had to strain to hear her. "They took her."

She didn't need to specify who "they" were. I knew at once that even if Helena didn't know their names, she meant the Nightshades. I stumbled backward, bumping into the doorframe behind me. There was no way this was a coincidence. They had to have taken Angie because of me, because of what I'd done to Ian in that alley.

No, that doesn't make any sense. I shook my head, trying to straighten out the twisted lines of logic that were tangled up in my brain. Ian Nyx could easily figure out who I was, especially since I'd told him the truth about my relationship to Bruce. But how would they know about Angie? We didn't live together. I hadn't even seen her since we'd spent the day together at the rally. Had they taken her Saturday night, or sometime since then?

"When?" I asked through gritted teeth.

"Last night. She helped me close up and headed home..." Her voice choked off, and she shook her head. "I'm so sorry."

"It's okay," I lied. "Everything is going to be okay. Have you talked to the police?"

She nodded. "They came in this morning, just as the rush was starting. They found this"—she lifted the backpack for a moment before hugging it close again—"under the stairs to the Fishbone station by her apartment."

Furious rage boiled up inside me, and it was a struggle not to stand up and punch a hole through Helena's wall to match the one in my apartment. But that wouldn't do Helena or Angie any good. I needed to keep my cool.

"It's going to be all right," I said. "I'm going to find her."

Helena shook her head. "What's going on, Tess? My baby girl!"

She began to wail, and the sound was filled with so much sorrow it cut into me like a knife. Just then, the door opened, and one of the diner's regulars—one of the men with an untamed beard who'd helped me into Angie's car when I was injured—stepped into the office. He nodded to me, then leaned down and helped Helena to her feet.

"Come on, Helena," he soothed in a deep, gravelly voice. "I'm gonna take you to your sister's, all right? Let's go, now."

She stood on wobbly legs and started shuffling out of the room. As she passed me, she reached out a hand and dug her nails into my shoulder. "Find my baby," she said. "Please."

Her eyes were wild, and I wasn't sure if she knew she was talking to me or if she thought the police were here again. But I nodded, and her grip relaxed. She released me as her friend pulled her out of the office. I stood up and followed them outside, watching as he settled her into a low sedan before returning to lock up the restaurant. My emotions had frozen, along with my legs.

This can't be happening, I thought. That single sentence ran laps around my mind like the chorus of a very uninspired song. What was going on? Was I cursed? Every person I got close to—everyone I loved—was being snatched away from me. My thought from inside Helena's office echoed in my mind: it couldn't be coincidence. I wondered what I'd done to make the universe hate me so much that it punished the people around me just for being in my life.

Several minutes after Helena and her friend drove away, my knees unlocked, and I was able to move again. I turned my back on the restaurant and climbed into Reed's passenger seat.

His face paled when he saw my expression. "What's wrong?"

As I relayed what Helena had told me, two red spots of anger grew on Reed's cheeks. When I got to the part about the police finding Angie's backpack near her apartment downtown, he slammed his fist into the edge of the steering wheel so hard it bent a little.

"Dammit!" he shouted. "They've never taken someone from that far north before. They targeted her, and we need to find out why."

"Because of me," I said. "They took her because she knows me."

"They couldn't possibly have put that together. You met Ian Nyx less than twelve hours ago."

I didn't respond, because I didn't have any answers, but I couldn't shake the feeling that somehow Angie was in danger because she was my friend.

Reed chewed his lip, and I stared at him, wishing I was as strong as he was. I could see the wheels turning in his head. He was putting together a plan—a plan he'd be able to execute because he'd been gifted before he'd gotten his powers. He'd already been smart. He'd already been driven by compassion. Now he was super strong, super-fast, and he could sense when people needed his help.

What could I do? I could toughen my skin into steel, but that was just armor. I wasn't clever like Reed or brave like Bear. I wasn't well-connected; literally the only two people I thought of as friends had been snatched up by the Nightshades. I was, in a word, worthless. I could tag along as Reed's little sidekick, but I'd never be a hero like him, the kind of person who helped so many people that he had his own fan club.

Fan club.

"Holy crap!" I shouted.

Reed stared at me. "What is it?"

"I have an idea, and I think it's a good one."

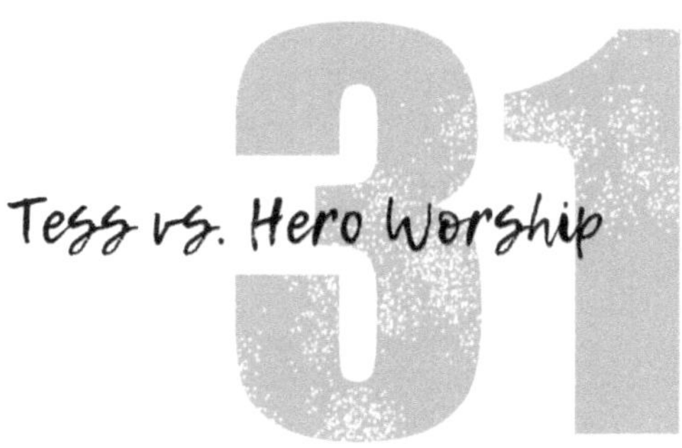

Tess vs. Hero Worship

My heart raced as I climbed the stairs to the train platform. In just a few minutes, I was going to make contact with someone who could be our man on the inside, someone who might be able to help us get to Bethany and Angie much more quickly than we could manage on our own. That is, if luck was on our side.

I wasn't comfortable with relying on good fortune. But I'd found myself arguing on the side of rolling the dice just minutes before when Reed had expressed the exact same concerns about the fickle nature of Lady Luck.

"I don't like it," he'd said, glaring out the windshield at the Fishbone station off Trident Avenue. A light rain pitter-pattered on the roof of the truck. "He works for the Nightshades."

"No, he doesn't. He works for the Nyx brothers at the processing plant. His job is legit."

"How do you know that's his only gig? That's a pretty convenient position if he wanted to moonlight as security for their other interests."

I shook my head. "He wouldn't do that."

Reed's scowl deepened. "You're basing that on the person you knew when you were five."

"Seven," I corrected.

"Whatever. That's a long time, and people change. Are you the same little girl who ran around with him in your parents' backyard?"

I folded my arms across my chest. "Yes."

Okay, I was being a teensy bit petulant at this point. But every question Reed asked chipped away at my confidence in my plan, and I'd been on shaky ground to start. I needed to feel like I was making the right call, or else I wouldn't be brave enough to go through with it.

And Bethany didn't have time for me to be anything less than fearless.

"Look," I said. "You weren't at the rally to support your own alter-ego, but I was. So only one person in this truck heard Anatolya's speech about you. He's on our side, Reed. I could feel his conviction in the way he spoke. He wasn't faking it."

"You're right, I wasn't there. I was putting a stop to a drug shipment. I've dealt with way more criminals than you have, Tess. So of the two people in this truck, I'm the one who's better qualified to decide if we can trust this guy."

"Which is exactly why we're going to vet him." I glanced

down at the clock on the dashboard. "The train will be here in like five minutes, and we're not exactly swimming in other options here. Either I need to get up there, or we need to pull the plug. Your call."

We glared at each other over the center console. The sound of the rain on the roof was like the ticking of a clock, counting down to the point of no return.

"Fine." Reed clicked a button, unlocking my door. "But if I get the slightest feeling that something is off with this guy, even if it's just because he smells funny, I'm calling it. We'll find another way in."

"Agreed."

Now I stood next to a poster of a grinning Jim Jenkins on the train platform, tapping my foot and praying I wasn't wrong about Anatolya. A train pulled into the station, and I watched for him among the lunchtime commuters streaming onto the platform. He was easy to spot since he was twice as broad as everyone else. I waved to him but didn't wait for him to come to me. Instead, I hurried over to his side and grabbed his arm.

"Hey—what?"

Without answering, I pulled him back onto the train. The doors closed behind us.

"What's going on?" he asked.

The car was only half full, and I glanced around to make sure we were out of earshot of the other passengers. Everyone else was at least a few rows away from us, so I decided it was safe enough for a whispered conversation.

"Look, first I have to apologize. I sort of lied about why I wanted you to meet me."

His face fell. "I knew it. This isn't a date."

I raised an eyebrow. "You thought this was a date?"

"You asked me to lunch."

"Yeah, as *friends*. I meant that I wanted to catch up with you, not... you know."

"Oh. Wait—so what part of that was a lie, exactly?"

"I said I *sort of* lied. I really do want to catch up with you. But I need to take a raincheck on the whole lunch part. And the whole talking-about-what-we've-been-up-to part."

"Okay, so just everything was a lie then." He shot me a weak smile, and guilt compressed my chest. I reached out and grabbed his hand, giving it a reassuring squeeze.

"Listen, I wouldn't drag you out on a mysterious not-date like this for anything less than a really, really good reason."

He pulled his hand out from mine. "Okay, I'm listening."

I glanced around again, then stood on my tiptoes to bring my lips to his ear. "I'm taking you to meet The Fox."

———

AFTER CHANGING trains and heading into West Weyland, where the airport and the state penitentiary took up most of the real estate, Anatolya and I finally left the Fishbone and took a shuttle to an airport parking garage. There, in the open air of the top floor, we found Reed waiting for us.

More specifically, we found The Fox waiting for us. In

full costume. On top of a black Hummer. Standing with his fists on his hips like some kind of 1930's comic book character, except without the cape.

I had to stifle a laugh.

Anatolya, on the other hand, was awestruck. He pointed up at The Fox with one wagging finger like a fangirl at Comic Con who just spotted her favorite actor.

"That's... that's... " he sputtered.

"I told you I was taking you to see him."

He turned to me, his blue eyes misting over. "I didn't think it could be true."

The Fox leapt off the tall SUV, managing a flip before landing lightly in front of Anatolya. I made a mental note to never, ever stop giving him shit about how thick he was laying this on. There was no way he wasn't enjoying it just a tiny bit.

"I hear you're the founder of the Fox Coalition," he said, his voice deeper and rougher than normal. I coughed to mask a snort. "Thank you for rallying so many people to my cause."

Anatolya managed a squeak that sounded like, "Thank welcome."

"What inspired you to do it?"

"I-I-I don't know." Anatolya, who was just as tall as Reed and even a little more muscular, seemed cowed in the other man's presence. He slumped slightly and stared up into The Fox's eyes.

"Sure you do," The Fox urged, resting a hand on Anatolya's shoulder. "That's a big undertaking, and it's not something most people would have the guts to do. So, what was it that gave you the idea?"

That mild bit of flattery did the trick, and Anatolya straightened up. "I, uh—" He cleared his throat. "I guess I just thought it was about time somebody really did something. All the crime, and all those girls going missing... I hated reading it in the news every day. Then you showed up, and I realized even if I can't do what you do, I might be able to help you keep doing it."

The Fox nodded. "Good answer. And I appreciate it. Really."

I caught his eye and asked a question with my eyebrows. He inclined his head, so I took a deep breath and turned to Anatolya. "Okay, so here's the deal. I didn't just bring you here to thank you for the rally and everything. We actually need your help."

"'We?'" Anatolya repeated. "You work with The Fox?"

I hesitated and glanced at Reed, who nodded again. "Yeah. I'm sort of his... sidekick, I guess. But I'm not, you know, super-powered like him," I rushed to clarify.

"That is so freaking cool," he breathed.

"Um... thanks. Well, anyway, we need to get into the storage warehouses at Belladonna. And probably into the shipyard, as well."

"At Belladonna?" Anatolya crinkled his nose and frowned. "Why?"

I hesitated. I trusted Anatolya enough that he wouldn't tell his bosses we were coming, but did I really trust that he wasn't a part of the Nightshades' side businesses? I stared into his eyes, trying to decide if I saw anything there that pays remotely like Ian Nyx or Bruce Fabiano.

All I saw was my old friend, the grown-up version of the little boy who'd played tag with me in the woods behind my house. Then I remembered: he wasn't just *my* friend. He'd known Bethany, too. She'd babysat the pair of us on countless Friday nights. The three of us had built forts out of cardboard boxes in the summertime, playing in them until the fall rainstorms melted them away. As I looked at him, fifteen years disappeared from his face, and I saw him as he was back then—a kid with nothing more to worry about than math worksheets and spelling bees. That little boy was still in those deep blue eyes, and it was the kind of childlike innocence Bruce and Ian had poisoned out of themselves long ago.

"It's Bethany," I said. "She's missing, and Ian Nyx has her. Don't ask me how I know; I just do."

Anatolya blinked at me slowly. "Bethany? She's gone missing? I haven't seen it on the news."

I shook my head. "The police don't think it's related to the disappearances in the Trident. She was taken from her house on the south side, and the cop I talked to is convinced she and Bruce just ran off somewhere together. But they didn't."

"And you think... you think Ian is involved? C'mon, he's my boss. He's a good guy."

"What makes you think he's so good? Because he pays

you on time? Maybe gives you a bottle of whiskey at Christmas?"

He was silent.

"That's not 'goodness,'" I said. "There's a difference. He might wear a mask of common decency, but he's pure evil under there." I paused. "I've seen it myself."

Anatolya stared at me then, and I had the strangest sense. It was like déjà vu, but through a mirror. I felt Anatolya searching my eyes for exactly what I'd been looking for just a moment ago: a reason to trust me.

He must've found one, because he nodded tersely and looked back and forth between The Fox and me. "Okay. I can get you in. Bring a van or a box truck so we can pass you off as an office supply delivery, okay?"

Reed finally spoke. "When?"

"My shift starts in a few hours. Come to the main entry gate at four o'clock."

Four o'clock. The words sent a jolt of pain through my body. I ached for sleep; I didn't even dare count the number of hours since the last time I'd closed my eyes. And even my last night's sleep had been fitful, because I'd been plagued by nightmares of what I imagined Bruce doing to Bethany. In my mind, I knew I should be grateful we wouldn't have to wait long to continue the search for Bethany, but my body screamed for some rest.

The Fox thanked Anatolya and the two men shook hands before I walked our new accomplice back to the shuttle stop at the base of the parking garage. Then I stood there for a few minutes, watching as the bus took him to the Fishbone station before heading back to Reed. My feet moved slowly; I wanted to run to Reed so we could start preparing, but I was quickly running out of energy. Even the thought of walking the hundred or so yards to the open-air lot where we'd stashed the truck was draining.

Yet again, Reed came to my rescue. Before I'd gone more than fifty feet, he pulled up next to me and leaned across the seat to open the passenger door. I pulled myself into the truck, sighing back into the upholstery and wondering if he'd mind if I slept on the way back to the docks. To my surprise, instead of leaving the lot, he pulled into a space and shut off the engine.

"What are you doing?" I asked.

"It's the long-term parking, so I've already paid for the day."

He stood and pulled me to my feet, practically dragging me into the truck's cargo area. At some point since I'd left the truck to meet Anatolya, Reed had put together a makeshift bed from piles of mismatched blankets and two small pillows. He pulled out his cell phone and checked the time.

"We have just under four hours before we need to be at the Belladonna gate. There's nothing worse than trying to fight when you're fatigued, so... we need to take a nap." He hesitated. "Unless you're not comfortable with that?"

In answer, I sank to my knees and crawled into the bed. The floor of the truck was nowhere near as soft as my mattress at home, but in that moment, it felt like a cloud.

Reed lay down beside me, somehow arranging himself so we weren't touching, but there was little more than an inch between our bodies. I started to think about that, getting so far as to wish he'd put his arm around me, and then gave into my fatigue and slept.

Tess vs. The Sea Beside The Sea

One Friday night when I was sixteen, I snuck out of my bedroom to go to a party. It was after my curfew, and I remember feeling guilty as I climbed down the trellis from my window and dropped onto the wet grass. But that was nothing compared to what I felt hours later. When I arrived home and had to climb back up again, I stood on the lawn and stared up at my lighted window, paralyzed with fear.

I couldn't remember if I'd left my light on. There were two possibilities: either I'd left it on and everything was fine, or my parents were sitting on my bed and plotting my punishment in the lamplight. As long as I stayed on the grass, I wasn't in trouble, and I preferred that state of limbo to the possibility of getting grounded. Eventually, I swallowed my fear and scaled the trellis to find that I had, in fact, left the light on when I'd left. My parents never even knew I was gone.

A similar feeling of dread squeezed at my guts as I pulled the truck up to the security kiosk in front of Belladonna Seafood, but much stronger. Since Anatolya already knew I was involved, we decided I'd do the driving. Reed crouched behind the driver's seat to remain out of sight of any cameras, and I was glad he couldn't see my face. I simultaneously felt the need to vomit and to use the restroom. I could probably manage the first—Reed had to have a bucket or an old fast food bag somewhere in the back of the truck—but the second would be impossible. I could hardly walk into the Belladonna lobby, use their bathroom, and then break into their storage facility ten minutes later. I might as well just waltz into Ian Nyx's office and start punching his teeth in while his security team watched.

The truck idled next to the open, empty window of the kiosk while my colon clenched and unclenched. I'd expected Anatolya to lean out right away, but there didn't seem to be anyone in there at all. Had his shift changed? Were they onto us? Did he turn traitor? Was he being tortured somewhere right now, spilling everything he knew? Stomach acid crept up my esophagus, and I switched from wishing for a bucket to wishing for some Tums.

"Something's wrong." The words burned in my throat. "He should be here. We're so screwed."

"Calm down," Reed muttered from behind me. "Give it a minute."

The seconds ticked by. I dug my nails into my biceps, trying not to let the fear that was growing in my stomach take over to the point where I might flee out the back of the truck. I closed my eyes and thought of Bethany and Angie, picturing the three of us eating dinner in Helena's diner, talking about baby names and making plans for Bethany's shower. They'd be great friends; I just knew it.

The sound of a window opening to my left made my eyelids snap up. Anatolya was there, holding a clipboard and staring at me with raised eyebrows.

"Uh, hi," I managed lamely.

"Purpose of visit?" Anatolya's voice was sharp and professional.

"Delivery. Office supplies."

"Purchase order?"

"Uh..." Panic exploded in my chest. *We didn't talk about this!*

Anatolya handed me a pink sheet of paper. It had the blue Belladonna logo on top and listed four cartons of copy paper and a case of packing tape. The words "PO Approved" were stamped at the bottom.

"Perfect, ma'am, that's all in order," he said. "Go on through. Warehouse is to your left and all the way back."

Before I could thank him—and I really, really wanted to gush those words about five thousand times—he slid the kiosk window shut with a firm *click*. I sat there stupidly for a second before pressing down on the gas.

"We're clear," I whispered to Reed.

"Good. What the hell was that about a purchase order?"

I passed the pink paper back to him. "Anatolya gave me this. He was really prepared."

"Hmm. If this all goes well, we owe him big time."

If. If, if, if, if, if— The word flashed in my mind like a neon sign. One hurdle down and untold numbers more to go.

The Belladonna campus was enormous. It took several agonizing minutes just to cruise through their expansive parking lot, which stretched all the way down their main processing plant. Ahead of us, the ocean drew nearer, marked by the tall watchtowers at Belladonna's private docks. At last the massive plant ended, and I turned the corner to behold a small sea of flat-roofed storage buildings. Row after row, they stretched all the way to the harbor. I cursed.

"What is it?" Reed asked.

"There's not *a* warehouse. There's like thirty."

He stuck his face between the two front seats and surveyed the expanse of buildings. I kept the truck creeping forward, but I had no idea where to go from here. The sheer number of warehouses we needed to search overwhelmed me, pressing me downward until I could hardly see above the dashboard.

"It's going to be okay." Reed climbed up into the passenger seat. "Keep driving."

I shot him a look that clearly communicated my opinion that this was utterly hopeless and that I'd completely failed my sister and my friend, but he couldn't see it. He'd squeezed his eyes shut so tightly it looked like it hurt, and his head was tilted to one side.

"Keep going... keep going..." Despite sitting next to me, his voice sounded distant, like his focus was way outside of the truck. "I think... yeah. Left. Go left."

I turned the wheel, taking us down a row of warehouses that looked identical to the one we'd just left. He pursed his lips into a grim smile.

"This is definitely it. I can feel them."

"Feel who?"

"The missing girls. They're alive, and I can sense their fear. Their pain." He opened his eyes and stared through the windshield, raising a hand to point at the warehouse at the end of the row, on the waterline. "And they're in there."

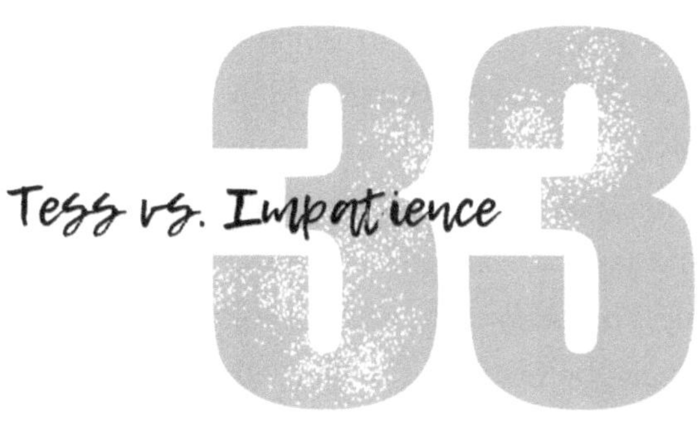

"How many people do you think are in there?" I whispered.

We crouched between two stacks of moldy wooden pallets that sat between the warehouse and the sea. A frigid wind from the harbor whipped around us, and I was grateful for the black ski mask that covered my face. Unlike the rest of the buildings in the area, this one had an air of neglect. The windows along the roofline were all boarded up, and bits of garbage had collected along the lines where the building's sheet metal siding met the asphalt. If I'd been alone, I would've driven right past it. It just felt like... nowhere.

But Reed wasn't fooled. Of the two gifts the meteor shower had given him, his ability to sense people in distress seemed the handiest. He stared at a spot on the warehouse's exterior, his eyes so focused I was surprised lasers didn't shoot out of them and cut us a new doorway.

"I can't tell. I think they must be close together. Maybe they're keeping them all in one room or something. I just know this feels a lot stronger than anything I've ever felt before, even from patients at the hospital when they're in a lot of pain." He shook his head, squeezing his eyes shut once again. "I'd say there are at least four."

Four. The odds were good that Bethany and Angie were in there, maybe even just on the other side of this wall. But the thought that they were in so much agony that Reed had been able to feel their anguish from twelve warehouses away... it sickened me. I reached out and touched the wall, letting the brown-painted steel chase an icy shiver into my fingertips and up my arm.

"Easy there." Reed pulled me away from the building. "This can't be like back at Bilgewater. You can't just barrel through the wall and start throwing punches. We need a plan."

"Hey, I'm in control. See?" I raised my hand, letting my skin return to normal. "Just getting material for later."

"Good. Because I'm going to need you to sit tight for a minute. I'll be right back."

"Where are you going?"

"To get a better idea of where they are. This building is too big. I don't want to have to worry about the whole thing."

I opened my mouth to object, then snapped it shut again

and settled for a terse nod. I wasn't super excited to sit here alone just inches away from the viper's nest, but arguing would just waste valuable time. I had no idea how long Bethany and Angie had or what would be waiting for them when their time ran out.

Reed donned his mask and crept down the edge of the building, managing to stay lower to the ground than I could possibly accomplish without falling over. He disappeared around the corner, and I shrank deeper into the crevice between the pallets. After more minutes than I was happy about, Reed re-appeared from the other side of the warehouse, his body just inches above the asphalt as he came back to me.

And then he was gone again, leaping to the top of one of the stacks of pallets as lightly as a cat. He covered the distance to the roof in another single, silent bound. I saw him crouching on the edge of the roof for an instant before he moved inward, and I waited impatiently for him to come back into sight.

A light *thump* above me signaled his return. He dropped down into the space beside me and pushed his mask up onto his forehead, looking pleased.

"I've got them," he said. "They're in the far corner, closest to the harbor."

"You're sure?"

"Positive. Their emotions are like a radio signal, and I got crystal-clear reception from that side." The little bit of happiness faded from his eyes, and a shadow crossed his face. "I can almost hear their voices in my head, calling for help."

I swallowed. One of those voices belonged to Bethany. I didn't have Reed's powers, but I could feel it. If she wasn't still alive, I'd know. And since Angie had been missing for less than twenty-four hours, the odds were good that she was in there, too. That knowledge stoked the flames inside of me until I felt my skin burning with anger.

They were in there.

They were hurting.

And I was going to do something about it.

"So what's the plan?" I asked.

Reed's mouth twitched, and then he pulled his mask back down over his face. "We're doing it your way, McBray. We're going to smash our way in."

We crept around the building, and I struggled to move a fraction as stealthily as Reed. His footfalls made no sound at all, but my sneakers crunched on everything from stray pebbles to bits of garbage. I cringed with every step, convinced I was giving away the game. But nobody burst out from any of the warehouse exits, and when we reached the far corner Reed stopped and looked at me.

"Whenever you're ready," he said.

I touched the aluminum siding of the warehouse again. As I tugged on the thread of cold inside both of my arms, calling the metal into me, I stopped. Could I punch through this metal sheet with hands made of the same material? Or would I need something stronger?

"What's wrong?" Reed whispered.

"I need something tougher than this wall to be sure I can break through it."

He raised an eyebrow. "Well, I don't have my toolbox handy. You'll need to improvise."

Scanning the wall in front of us, I noticed discolored little circles at regular intervals along the edge of the siding. *Nails,* I realized. Whatever they were made of, it was strong enough to puncture the aluminum and hold it tight to the building's frame. I rested the tips of my forefingers on two of the nails and pulled the material into myself. An instant later, my fists had hardened into little round sledgehammers.

I smiled, remembering the way I'd destroyed my kitchen table, and started throwing punches. I'll admit; it felt pretty damn good. Ever get so pissed, you just want to break something? This was cathartic. Therapeutic, even. With each punch, I felt my grin grow a little bit wider.

The warehouse wall didn't last long.

When the dust cleared, I could see straight into the building. A familiar face stared back at me.

"Angie!" I sidestepped through the narrow doorway I'd created and ran across the room to her.

She was on her hands and knees inside a metal cage about the size of a dog kennel. Her normally sleek curls were matted with dirt, and her clothing was torn. Her fingers poked out through the black metal grid that made up her prison. I shoved my mask up with one hand so it was more like a beanie, revealing my face.

"Tess!" Her voice was hoarse and strained.

"I'm here." I let my skin return to normal, covered her hand with one of my own and forced a smile. "You're going to be okay."

As Reed stepped into the room behind me, I swept my head side to side, taking in the rest of the space. We stood in the corner of a room so large my entire childhood home could've easily fit inside. Half-walls blocked this part of the warehouse from the rest. Above us, a rickety catwalk ran the length of the building, disappearing out of sight over the partial walls, and the wind from outside whistled through a crack in one of the boarded-up windows near the ceiling.

Angie's cage was in the middle of a long line of a dozen identical cells, half of them filled. The anguished faces of several of the missing girls stared out at me, their eyes wide. I looked for Bethany but didn't see her, and my heart thumped to a standstill. Then I realized the empty cells weren't all actually empty; their occupants had just crumpled to the ground. Bethany's blonde head rested on the floor of her cage.

"Oh, my God!" I rushed to her cage and tried to fit a hand through the grid to touch her, but the metal bars were too close together. I pressed an ear against the cage near her face and heard low, ragged breathing. "Quick! She needs help!"

Reed hurried over, knelt down, and stared at her. "She looks severely dehydrated. We need to get her out of here."

"Okay—*how?*"

"We have to find a key. Fast. I don't know how much time we have before somebody figures out we're here."

A high, falsetto laugh tinkled from the catwalk above us. "Oh, little fox. We already have."

Tess vs. The Impossible

My head snapped back, and I stared in horror at the man standing above us. His gray hair made him look middle-aged, but he was as lean as Reed and was dressed in a sleek black suit and tie. He leaned on the catwalk's railing, his face stretched into a wide smile that seemed to show every tooth in his mouth. He reminded me of a shark.

"You know," he said in a sing-song voice, "I was starting to think you'd never come."

Run! my instincts screamed, and I was just about to obey them when I heard a gunshot. The sound hadn't even finished tearing through my eardrums before the pain hit. My left leg collapsed under me, and I shrieked in agony. My scream was echoed by the girls in the cages. My foot was on fire, and the pain radiated all the way up through my hips. I glanced down at my sneaker and saw a small black hole, which was rapidly filling with blood. My vision fuzzed just as it had at the meteor shower.

I was passing out.

"Tess!" Reed's voice rang out through the clouds. "Stay with me! You're okay!"

The blackness lightened into a dull gray, and then my vision cleared enough to see his face across the room.

"Breathe. In, out. *Breathe.*"

I grabbed onto his words, catching my breath. The gray fog lifted a little with each inhale, and then I could see clearly once more.

And what I saw sent me into hyperventilation all over again.

Ian Nyx stood beside The Fox, holding a small black pistol against Reed's masked temple. He was dressed exactly the same as he'd been at Bilgewater—in a tight-fitting button-down shirt with the Belladonna logo embroidered on it. One eye was swollen closed, and both were ringed in angry black bruises. His nose was bandaged, and he sported a long row of stitches down his right cheek. I felt a twinge of satisfaction. I'd changed his face forever.

Reed's hands were high in the air, but his voice was calm. His eyes were fixed on mine. "You're okay," he repeated. "You're strong. Hang in there."

"Yeah, hang in there, little brat," Ian said. "The foot was just the beginning. I want you wide awake for what I'm going to do to you next."

"Easy, Ian," the black-suited man called. He climbed

down a narrow ladder that hung from the catwalk, skipping the last few rungs and landing lightly on the concrete floor. "First things first."

"Fine." Ian pushed the gun into Reed's skull, making him tilt his head sharply away from it. "First things first, says the man. And what the man wants, he gets."

"That's right. And who's the man, Ian?"

Ian's one good eye narrowed. "You are, Jared."

"Well, well. Turns out you *can* listen, after all." Jared glanced down at me and tsked. "So this is the one you let get away."

"She's more dangerous than she looks."

"No doubt. But this is no way to treat a guest. Stand up, my dear."

He offered me his hand. I looked past him at Reed, who gave me a tiny nod. The meaning was clear. *Do what they say, or we're both dead.*

I reached up with both hands and allowed Jared to help me to my feet. A wave of dizziness slammed into me as soon as I stupidly tried to put pressure on my left foot, and I tipped to the side. He clucked like an old Southern woman and straightened me up again. I sucked in air and lifted my injured foot off the ground, relying on my right leg to hold all my weight. I wished I'd bothered to take more than two yoga classes so I could've gotten crazy good at the Tree Pose.

Jared leaned in so his face was right next to mine, then inhaled deeply through his nose. "Ahh. That's the scent I've been looking for. You're going to make me a very rich man."

A shudder ran through my body. Had he just *smelled* me? I guess I shouldn't have been surprised a human trafficker would do something so creepy.

"What a pair the two of you are," he said. "Do you have any idea the trouble we've had trying to track you two down? And now here you are! It's like a miracle."

He leaned away from me and smiled, the way your hairstylist might smile after getting your haircut *just* right. I winced, trying to keep my balance.

"So tell me... Were you two doing it on purpose?" he asked.

"Doing what?"

He waved a hand. "Diluting the water, so to speak. Using the old 'I'm Spartacus' trick to make everyone smell like you."

I glanced past him at Reed, who lifted his shoulders in a shrug and shook his head. Ian pushed the gun harder against his head and sneered.

"I have no idea what you're talking about," I told Jared.

"Ha!" The sudden spike in Jared's volume made me stumble backward, and he straightened me up again. "I knew it. Ian said it was on purpose, but then, he's an idiot. I was sure you couldn't control it, but I had no way to test my theory. I can't smell my own scent, you see."

My head was starting to feel cloudy, and my foot was throbbing. But the tangled threads that'd been twisting around in my brain since that morning in Helena's office were starting to braid together into a shape that made sense.

"You have powers?"

He tapped the end of his nose lightly with one finger. "Oh, I see that crinkle. Don't like having something in common with me, hmm? Well, too bad. I had to suffer through that goddamn syndrome just like you, and this gift is my reward. It's come in pretty handy, too. Do you have any idea how much someone with powers can go for on the black market? A million, easy." He huffed out through his nose. "Which is why it was so frustrating to keep sensing you two, snatching up girls who smelled like you, only to find out they were just carrying some kind of phantom scent."

Reed made a strangled sound. I knew exactly what he was thinking, because the same thought was stabbing into my own heart: *It was my fault.*

Everyone Reed treated must've picked up a trace of whatever it was that Jared Nyx could sense. And if they crossed his path... they were targeted. Angie and Bethany were the only two people I spent a lot of time with, and I'd rubbed off on them. I'd been right; they'd been taken because they were close to me.

"But you're here now, and time is money, so..." Jared turned sharply on his heel and strode toward Reed. He pulled a gun from his jacket, rested the muzzle in the center of Reed's forehead and jerked his head in my direction. "See to her."

Ian let his gun arm fall to his side and took his brother's place in front of me.

Jared dusted off his jacket sleeve with his free hand.

"Now, I'm a gentleman, understand? I hate to let a lady see me when I'm angry. Move."

Reed hesitated, and Jared cocked his head to one side.

"I'm afraid I'm not expressing myself quite clearly enough. Let me try again." Jared's voice suddenly deepened into a low growl. "Move your ass or your little piece gets it."

"Don't do it!" I started to move toward him, and Ian snapped his gun up into my face. He mimicked his brother's tsking sound.

"Did he tell you to move?" he whispered. "I don't think so."

I stared helplessly as Jared marched Reed toward an empty cage.

"Get in," he said.

"And if I don't?"

"Ian," Jared called.

While I was still watching Jared and Reed, Ian landed a kick straight into my stomach that sent me reeling backward.

"Tess!" Reed shouted again.

A metal door slammed to my left, and I raised my head to see Ian's fist coming toward my face. I raised my hands to block it, but he punched right through my defenses and connected squarely with my nose. Bone crunched and searing pain spiked through to the back of my skull. As I sagged there, fighting for breath, he shoved me into an empty cage at the end of the row and slammed the door shut on top of me. The space was cramped, and I had to hunker on my hands and knees like an animal.

"Watch them," Jared told his brother. "I'll be in my office."

He climbed back up the stairs to the catwalk and disappeared over the wall. I turned my head, trying to see where Reed had ended up, and caught a glimpse of his dark mask a few cages down from me.

"There," Ian snarled, gripping the bars of my cage from the outside. "Consider that a little bit of payback."

It took me a few minutes to catch my breath and formulate a response through the waves of pain that were tearing through my head. "You deserve every bruise," I finally spat back at him. "You're a monster."

"Sweetheart, you don't even know what I am. I'm the most powerful man in Weyland."

My foot ached, my heart was pounding, and the small part of my brain that wasn't reminding me how much my nose hurt was split between worrying about my sister and worrying about my friends. So I fell back on old faithful: being a smartass.

"Funny," I said. "Looked to me like your brother holds that title."

He snorted. "I might not have his little *gift,* but I'm twice the man he is."

I closed my eyes, unable to keep looking at his sneering face. Despite the pain in my nose and foot, I still retained a firm grasp on the obvious. Reed, Bethany, Angie, and I were all now locked in cages. The details of anything close to a plan eluded me, but I knew step one of getting us all out of here was getting back into fighting condition. If I could heal scrapes and bruises... could I heal a gunshot wound?

There was only one way to find out.

Ian had apparently lost interest in me and was strolling up and down the row of cages with one hand in his pocket, leering at the girls inside and occasionally kicking at the metal grids that covered them. I took advantage of his inattention and focused on the way my sock felt around my left foot. I could feel the fibers against my flesh and found the frigid undercurrent that now seemed to run through my entire body. With one little mental tug, the skin of my foot became knit cotton.

At once, the burning sensation ceased. But the aching pain was still there. I tested the foot, pressing it against the back of my cage, and nearly yelped. The outside was healed, but the inside was still damaged. I twisted my neck to look back at my foot, trying to picture what was going on beneath my shoe. I wanted to pull it off and poke at my wound, but I'd have to contort myself to accomplish that in this low little cage. As distracted as Ian was by the captive women in front of him, I knew he'd notice me doing anything other than sitting still.

So I was left with my own imagination. If my skin was healed, I wasn't bleeding anymore. I slotted that fact into a little "Plus" column in my mind. On the downside, the bullet was probably inside me now. I didn't see it on the floor where I'd been standing, and it had to be somewhere. What was it doing to my body? Wreaking havoc on my little foot bones and my muscle tissue?

I shuddered. I didn't even like the thought of getting my ears pierced, and now I had a little metal bullet inside me. Maybe forever, unless I wanted to cut my foot open again and fish it out.

Shaking my head, I dismissed the thought. Right now, I needed to figure out a way to heal my foot all the way through. I wondered if it was possible to suck that cold feeling deeper into my body. Could I heal my own bones? Reconnect severed blood vessels?

Or... would my body stop working? When my skin turned to steel, it was just as solid as the metal object I pulled from. I couldn't flex my fingers or bend my knees when I'd transformed. So if I pulled that power any deeper into myself... would my blood turn into strands of cotton? Would my veins carry the change back to my heart?

I swallowed. That was a chance I couldn't afford to take. I was no use to anyone if I was dead.

"Shame." Ian stopped in front of Angie's cage and clucked his tongue. "Lotta good talent here. I wish I could keep you around, but business is business, you know?"

Angie's voice was defiant. "What are you going to do with us?"

"It's been done, sweetheart. You'll stay in your fish box until your buyers come for you. You've been sold. Normies to the regular traders, carriers to the breeders. And this one"—

he stopped mid-step and spun around to face me again—"will go to auction."

I stared at him in shock. I'd never heard someone talk so casually about selling human beings like used cars, and half of what he said didn't make any sense to me. "What's a carrier?" I asked.

"People like the blonde back there. Ones who got the sniffles at the solstice but didn't get the full-blown ride."

He's talking about Bethany, I realized. "How do you know she got sick?"

He shrugged. "Jared can smell it, same as he can smell your powers."

"So she carries the virus?"

"Virus?" Ian laughed. "We all carry the virus now, idiot. It's like the cold. It'll always be around."

"What, then?" If something was wrong with Bethany, I needed to know, even more than I needed to know what was going on with my own body.

Ian leaned in close to my bars and flashed his teeth. "She's got the gene. That little babymaker just turned into a moneymaker. And you know what the best part is? She's already preggers. She sold for four times what we got for the others."

My right hand shot out, and I grabbed at the metal grid that separated us, trying to rip my cage apart. I wanted to rip *him* apart, too. He danced backward, laughing, and brandished his gun.

"Nice try, little girl. But I can't let something like that slide. Why don't we make that hand match your foot?"

"Leave her alone!" shouted Angie from down the row.

"Oh, you've got something to add to this, huh?" Ian stomped off down the line to her cage. "I've always loved curly hair. Maybe it's time I took you for a test drive."

Through the rows of metal bars and the filthy, matted heads of the girls between us, I saw him unlock Angie's cage and pull her up out of it by her hair. He dragged her across the floor to the door and yanked her out of the room.

From the other side of the wall, she screamed. The sound was like a siren in my head. It blocked out all thought, and suddenly there was only action. I was blinded by a single, driving desire.

I needed to kill Ian Nyx.

"Tess," Reed hissed. "Are you okay?

"No, I'm not okay." Flipping over onto my back so I could reach my feet, I gritted my teeth and pulled off my shoes, including the bloodied one. It hurt like hell, but Angie's screams from the other room demolished my own need to cry out.

"What are you doing?"

"Trying to get out of this damn cage," I hissed back. "What are *you* doing?"

"Same. They seem pretty solid, but I think I can pick this lock with enough time."

Time was something we didn't have, not with Angie out there, alone with Ian Nyx. I heard the sound of metal clinking on metal coming from Reed's cage, but tuned it out and concentrated on getting my socks off. Once my feet were free, I planted them on the crisscrossing bars that made up the back of my cage, gripped the grids at my sides, and sucked with all four of my limbs.

I pulled *hard*, focusing on dragging the cold metal bone-deep in my injured foot. I let my skin harden all the way up my thighs and from my fingertips to my shoulder blades. It was more than I'd ever attempted before, and it was agony.

As I'd feared, the blood in my left foot solidified. I couldn't feel any sensation there at all. But the feeling, or lack thereof, didn't spread any further than that. I tried not to wonder if it was doing something horrible and I just couldn't feel it, and focused instead on hardening the skin across my body. Almost every inch, from my fingertips all the way up to my earlobes, turned to steel. I even let it creep across my forehead and my cheekbones like war paint, but left my eyes, mouth, and broken nose alone.

I was like a metal statue. My body exactly matched the cage that surrounded me. I attempted to flex, to bend my elbows, but I'd been immobilized by my new armor.

Time to take it down a notch.

First, I let my feet return to normal. My left foot felt like it'd fallen asleep, but it no longer hurt. I'd take the oncoming pins and needles over the pain of torn muscle tissue and tiny broken bones.

Next, I closed my eyes and pictured the little anatomy doll on my drafting table at home. While most of the miniature human figure was made of rough, wooden geometrical shapes, its joints were made of smooth, polished half-moons connected by metal pins. I imagined my own body was like that anatomy doll, except most of me was made of metal and my joints were made of regular, human flesh. I felt a slight warming sensation in my elbows, knees, and other bendy places. When I opened my eyes again, I could move. Not quickly, and not easily. I was too heavy, and I'd never realized how much my torso normally turned and shifted when I so much as crouched down or lifted my arms. But I was mobile. And I was protected.

I'd turned myself into a walking suit of armor.

From beyond the door, Angie's screams grew louder. It had only taken me a few seconds to transform my body, but it already felt like way too long. Without even pausing for breath, I pulled back my arms and punched at the bars around me with all my might.

The cage exploded with a clang and a clatter. As I stood up and walked out onto the floor, testing my ability to walk without falling over in this heavier state, Ian burst back into the room. When he saw me, he clenched his jaw and his eyes flashed.

"Oh, you little bitch." He drew his gun from the back of his pants. "I don't know what you're playing at, but the game's over now."

He leveled his weapon at me, aiming straight for my chest. Only a few yards separated us, and I knew he wouldn't miss.

Bang!

The shot rang out. But... I felt no pain. The bullet ricocheted off my chest, going wild and lodging in the wall behind Ian. He stared at me, his mouth hanging open in shock.

As for me? I grinned.

And then I charged.

I had no plan. None of Reed's fancy fighting skills. I was just an angry, five-foot-five-inch, adrenaline-fueled tank barreling across the room at the scum-sucking lowlife who'd managed to hurt every single person I cared about in this world.

Ian Nyx didn't stand a chance.

My metal fist connected with his face a millisecond before the rest of me slammed into him, knocking him backward. His gun went flying, and he landed in a heap a few feet in front of me. I leapt on top of him, straddled his prone body, and lost myself in the rhythm of my punches. I saw nothing. I heard nothing.

I was nothing.

At least, I wasn't me. There was no Tess McBray. There was only Vengeance, pummeling Evil's face into the cold stone floor.

I didn't know if I would stop.

And it scared me that I didn't know if I cared.

"Tess!"

A pair of strong hands gripped my shoulders from behind and yanked me off Ian. I blinked, and the room slowly came back into focus. To my left stood the row of cages, full of wide-eyed women who regarded me with as much fear as they'd shown the Nyx brothers. In front of me lay Ian, surrounded by blood and broken bits of concrete. His chest was moving. He was alive.

I stared at his face, surprised he had one to stare at after what I'd done to him. Shaking, I raised my hands. They weren't metal anymore. None of me was. At some point, I'd lost the cold thread that kept my skin transformed.

I was me again.

The shaking spread from my hands to the rest of my body, and I stood there trembling and staring at Ian's unconscious form on the ground. *I could've killed him.*

"Ian!" Jared's voice echoed across the room.

My head jerked up, and I spotted him standing atop the catwalk. Our eyes met.

"I'll kill you!" he screamed.

And then a black blur flew in front of me, darting up the stairs just as Jared drew his gun. Before the older man could get off a shot, Reed was on him. Jared's ability to smell other powered people was nothing compared to the increased agility The Fox boasted; their scuffle lasted less than three seconds before Jared lay unconscious at the top of the stairs.

"Tess." Reed jumped back down to me and pulled me into a tight hug. "Are you all right?"

Am I?

I didn't know. I didn't care about me. I only cared about...

"Bethany!" I pulled out of Reed's arms and sprinted for her cage.

She still lay on the floor of the shallow space, her fine blonde hair matted to her forehead with sweat. I knelt down beside her and reached my fingers through the bars, barely managing to touch her forehead. She was still going—still fighting—but she looked so frail, so weak. It chilled me to my core. Were we too late?

"We need to call an ambulance."

"On it," Angie said from behind me. She'd come back into the room and was rifling through Ian's pockets. She pulled out a cell phone and a set of keys, tossing the latter to Reed.

Reed unlocked the top door of Bethany's cage and lifted it off. The front and back panels fell open, creating a little tunnel. I climbed half inside, cradled Bethany's head in my lap, and cried until I heard the sirens in the distance.

Sunlight spilled through the wide windows of Bethany's hospital room, covering her in warm light. She looked like she was posing for a recreation of one of those Renaissance paintings of the Virgin Mary holding the baby Jesus, with a shining, golden halo surrounding her and a look of motherly bliss on her narrow face.

She smiled down at her newborn daughter, just back from getting all of the not-so-picture-perfect afterbirth muck washed off her tiny body, then grinned up at me with tired eyes.

"Isn't she amazing?" she whispered.

I reached down and squeezed Bethany's ankle, since her hands were otherwise engaged.

"She's perfect."

Bethany went back to staring at her baby in wonder, which is exactly what I imagined every other mother in the maternity ward was doing just then, and I decided to take advantage of the good lighting. I sat down in a surprisingly comfortable chair beside the window, pulled out my sketch-pad, and started roughing out a portrait of my sister and my tiny niece, Hope.

Prior to this, I'd always found it strange when people named their children after feelings. I thought it put an awful lot of pressure on the kid to turn out bright, happy, and bubbly. That, or to change their name to Raven when they hit their goth phase. But now... I got it.

It'd been eight months since the events at the warehouse. While I'd been sitting on the floor of Bethany's cage, waiting for the ambulance to arrive, I wasn't sure if she'd ever open her eyes again. Or if she'd ever get to meet her baby.

But despite her tiny frame, Bethany fought through. She spent a couple of weeks in the hospital regaining her strength, then moved in with me. I had a feeling that even if Bruce wasn't currently in Weyland Penitentiary awaiting sentencing for his involvement in the Nightshade Brothers' human trafficking operation, she still would've kicked him to the curb. Her baby gave her the courage to look out for herself and gave her hope that everything might work out okay in the end.

"Knock, knock," came a singsong voice from the door.

It swung open, and Angie and Helena stepped into the room. Bethany's eyes lit up when she saw them, and she held out a hand to Helena. After Bethany had moved into my apartment, Helena made it her personal mission to make sure

Bethany got enough to eat and even threw her an enormous baby shower right in the restaurant.

Angie said Helena did it to thank me for helping rescue her, but from the way Helena took care of everyone in the Trident, I'm pretty sure she would've done all that anyway. But she did give me extra hash browns every time I came in and never charged me a dime for any of the meals I had in her place.

The three women now in this room were the only people who knew about my involvement in the rescue. As soon as Reed had finished cleaning up anywhere his or my blood had landed, we fled the scene. Angie and the rest of the women identified us to the authorities only as The Fox and The Butterfly.

Helena brought the tips of her fingers up to her mouth. "Ohh, Mama. She is a vision."

"Would you like to hold her?" Bethany asked.

In answer, Helena leaned over the bed and picked up little Hope. I jumped out of my chair and offered it to her.

"Thank you, dear," she said.

I picked up the new Nikon camera I'd given Bethany at the baby shower and took a few pictures of Helena holding Hope and of Angie perched on the windowsill. Bethany had started Hope's first scrapbook the day she got the first ultrasound photos, and I knew she'd want to include pictures of her new "extended family." After my stint as official photographer, I sat down on the bed next to Bethany. Helena cooed at Hope while Angie asked Bethany for all the gory details of the birth. A few minutes into a fiery recount of Bethany's pre-epidural experience, my phone buzzed with a message from Reed.

"Gotta go." I leaned over and kissed Bethany's forehead.

"Be careful," she called.

"Always."

Leaving behind four of the most important girls in my life, I left to meet the two men who dominated my life these days. I took the Fishbone to Blackfin Street, where Reed's truck was parked in its usual place overlooking the docks. I pulled open the heavy sliding door and found him sitting inside, scratching Bear behind the ears and looking at something on a tablet that Anatolya was holding.

"There she is." Reed shifted over, making room for me to sit between the two men.

"Are we all set?" I asked.

Anatolya nodded. "Plane's chartered. We have to be to the hanger in a little over an hour. We're just killing time."

On the tablet, they were watching a live stream of the nightly news. Jim Jenkins sat behind the news desk, his eyebrows high on his forehead.

"Hometown heroes or ticking time-bombs?" the aging newsman said. "We talk to local citizens about their thoughts on the vigilante presence in Weyland and the hundreds of powered individuals who are popping up across the globe."

"Ugh," I groaned. "Do we have to watch this?"

Anatolya laughed. "Nobody listens to this guy. The Fox Coalition is literally a hundred times bigger than it was in

February, and money is pouring into our crowdfunding campaign. Trust me, Jim Jenkins is in the minority."

I thought back to the crowd of people at the "Support The Fox" rally Angie and I had gone to. If Anatolya's group had grown a hundredfold, the group of anti-Fox protesters had probably grown, too.

It worried me that Maggie Long and a handful of other Solstice Syndrome survivors were operating in the open. If someone really wanted to, they could find out where Maggie lived. Where her family lived.

So far, the only people targeted for having superpowers had been Reed and me. But the Nightshades hadn't been after us because they hated us. How long before the old human habit of attacking someone just for being different kicked in, and super-powered people became the "other?"

Reed didn't seem worried. He just switched off the tablet and shot me a smile. "Yep. So no sense watching him. You all packed?"

In answer, I started to lift up my shirt.

"Hey, whoa!" Anatolya covered his eyes. "Not in front of me, you guys."

"Very funny," I said. I wasn't showing any skin. When I peeled off my t-shirt, the gray fabric of my costume shimmered in the light. Reed had custom-ordered it for me after the warehouse, and it covered me from head to toe in a tough but stretchy material. In keeping with my new moniker, I'd drawn stylized butterflies on the pants and sleeves. Around my waist, he'd created a belt that had dozens of different types of material embedded into it. Now I had whatever I needed, whenever I needed it. Stone. Steel. Even diamond.

One of these days, I hoped to have an excuse to use that last one.

"That's it?" Reed teased. "Not going to show me the bottom half?"

I grinned at him, playing along. "You sure Anatolya won't mind?"

"We can kick him out of the truck for a while."

"That is *it*." Anatolya threw up his hands in mock defeat. "I quit. You two lovebirds can run your own fan site and keep track of the money. I'll go back to working security."

"You'd miss us too much," Reed told him.

"No way—you guys are the worst." Anatolya cocked his head to one side. "I would miss Bear, though. I'll admit it."

"Oh, crap. We have to get him back to my place."

Anatolya drove us through the city to my apartment, where we dropped off Bear. He couldn't come where we were going. Then we headed to the airport, where a private plane was waiting to take us to Chicago. Maggie Long, the fireproof Solstice Syndrome survivor who was brave enough to let the world know her real identity, had called a meeting. It was going to be the first real-life assembly of people with superpowers, another thing I'd always thought was only possible in comic books.

I grinned as I stepped onto the tarmac. The world had changed. But I didn't mind.

I'd gotten to change right along with it.

Thank you for reading *Superhero Syndrome*! I sincerely hope you enjoyed getting to know Tess with me. If you did, I would deeply appreciate a short review on Amazon, Goodreads, or your favorite book website. Reviews are crucial for any author, and even a line or two can help another reader discover this book.

Want to know when the next story is on the way and other big news? Join my email list and get a free ebook!

http://carynlarrinaga.com/free-ebook

Join me on Facebook and Twitter to chat about books, cats, horror, and anything else that strikes your fancy!

https://www.facebook.com/carynwrites
https://twitter.com/carynlarrinaga

SNEAK PEAK: DONN'S HILL (THE SOUL SEARCHERS MYSTERIES, BOOK ONE)

Turn the page to sample the first chapter in Caryn Larrinaga's award-winning debut novel, DONN'S HILL

Ghosts. Psychics. Murder. Just another day in DONN'S HILL.

The pickup hit a pothole and bounced me up into the air. Not high enough to send me over the tailgate and into the highway, but enough to get me to flail my arms and make an ass out of myself. When I landed back down on the cold metal truck bed, the battered paperback copy of Kurt Vonnegut's *Welcome to the Monkey House* flew out of my hands.

"No!"

I hurled myself after it, managing to grab it out of the air before the wind carried it away. Cradling the book, I flipped backward through the pages and checked for damage until I reached the inscription on the inside front cover: *Happy birthday Mackenzie! Love, Dad.*

The book was irreplaceable. It'd been stupid to try to read it in the back of a pickup truck while we were speeding along the highway, but I didn't have anyone to talk to on the hour-long drive from Moyard to Donn's Hill. Boredom had gotten the best of me.

You'll just have to live with being bored, I told myself, tucking the book into the bright yellow hiking backpack that held all my worldly possessions. *It's not worth the risk.*

It was just as well that I stopped reading; the truck was slowing down. I craned my neck to see over the tall cab to make sure the driver was taking me where I'd asked to go, and that he wasn't making a detour to a cabin full of his deranged cousins or something.

The prospect of being killed on the way to my new life was why I'd been nervous to hitch a ride with a stranger. I thought it was pretty ironic that the driver had made me sit in the open truck bed instead of in the cab with him as though he was in danger from *me*. Me, the tiny twenty-seven-year-old girl who sometimes still had to buy clothes in the juniors' section at Kohl's.

My fears were put to rest when I saw a weather-beaten sign at the side of the road reading E-Z SLEEP MOTEL. The pickup truck pulled into the motel's parking lot, coming to a stop under the awning that sheltered the front office. I hopped out with my pack on my back.

"Thanks for the lift," I told the driver.

He leaned out his open window and tugged on the brim of his baseball cap. "You sure you want to stay here? There's better places in town. My sister runs a B&B right on Main."

I'd priced that B&B and all the other lodging options within Donn's Hill's city limits. The rates were outrageous;

all of them were five times as much as a room at the E-Z Sleep.

I shook my head. "Thanks, but I'm good here."

He cast a doubtful eye over the structure. The motel was older, built in the seventies, with a row of small rooms strung side by side on a single floor. The building sat sideways, perpendicular to the highway to maximize the number of rooms that got to enjoy the breathtaking view of the weathered paint and broken windows of the abandoned lumber mill next door. Despite the low room prices, there wasn't a single other car in the weedy parking lot.

"If you're sure…"

"I'm sure. Thanks again."

He shrugged and pulled away, heading back down the highway toward Donn's Hill. I put both hands on the small of my back and pushed it forward, stretching out my spine. It ached from the long bus ride to Moyard and then the pickup truck. I couldn't wait to relax in my room, maybe even draw a bath and soak for a while.

I tugged open the door to the motel's lobby. The scent of stale cigarettes made my nose crinkle, and a sallow-faced clerk stared at me from behind a Plexiglas window.

"Can I help you?" He punctuated the question with a spit that he shot into a narrow-necked beer bottle with the label torn off, adding a bit more to the pool of murky brown saliva that filled it.

"Um, yes. I have a reservation."

He chewed in silence for a moment before responding. "Name?"

"Mackenzie Clair."

The clerk rifled through a small pile of papers in a tray on the desk. Beside me, a baseball game played on a flat-screen television mounted on the wall. The technology felt out of place among the lobby's ripped vinyl furniture and the motel's outdated filing system. I wondered if my online reservation was the first they'd ever gotten.

At last, the clerk found my reservation receipt. "Okay, looks like you already paid. Just gonna need to scan your ID."

I unslung the backpack from my shoulders and dug out my wallet, handing over my driver's license. A pang of sadness hit me as I realized that the address it listed wasn't mine anymore. I didn't even know what it was going to be replaced with. For some reason, the prospect of having to register for a new ID card in this new state made my decision to pick up stakes and move to Donn's Hill more real than packing my bag had done.

The clerk heaved himself out of his little desk chair and crossed the office to make a copy of my ID. "So what brings you to town? Hope it's not for the festival. You're two weeks too early."

He chuckled, as though he'd made a good joke, and then returned to his desk and spat into the bottle again. My stomach turned. I was grateful the Plexiglas window was blocking whatever smell was probably wafting up from the clerk's bottle every time he added to it.

I swallowed back the bile that threatened to fill my mouth. "Personal business. How far is it to town, anyway? Could I walk there in the morning?"

"I'm sure you can manage it. It's just a few miles."

He took a sip from a bottle. For one hideous instant, I thought he was drinking his tobacco spit back down. Then I realized the label on the second bottle was intact.

He passed me a receipt, a small bronze key, and a television remote control. "Sign this. And don't go walkin' off with that controller, or it's a $30 charge to your card."

"All right. Thanks." I pushed the receipt back to him, took my key and remote, and left the lobby.

"Have a good night," he called. I heard him laughing as the door swung shut behind me.

<hr>

My room felt... sleazy. It was the kind of place I imagined Josh and his *other* girlfriend had had all their secret rendezvous. That is, when I'd been in town. When I'd been out of town, like for my father's funeral, he'd just brought her home to our bed.

The wound was still fresh. It took all of two nanoseconds for my anger to bubble up to the surface, and I hurled my backpack into the corner of the room. I had to remind myself to breathe.

Simmer down, I thought. *You left him behind. Let him go.*

I turned my focus to inspecting the room. It was

reasonably clean, but there was no getting rid of the lingering odor of stale cigarettes that had followed me from the lobby. The only attempt at decorating was a sad watercolor of a storm-tossed sailboat, which hung above the queen bed. Nothing from the dusty brass fixtures to the peeling floral wallpaper looked as though it had been replaced since the motel opened.

My visions of soaking in a bubble bath evaporated the second I opened the bathroom door. A clear shower curtain hung limply from its rod, revealing a cramped stall and a worryingly small shower head. Everything was made from one giant piece of molded plastic, presumably so it could be thoroughly cleaned with a power washer. It was the kind of modern efficiency I imagined a serial killer in the movies would appreciate.

Rubbing the small of my back, I meandered back over to the bed and collapsed onto the rough comforter. I lay there for a while, staring at the heavy curtains that covered the window and wondering, not for the first time, if I'd made the right decision.

I unplugged the alarm clock and switched off the lamp. Tomorrow, my new life would begin.

Ghosts. Psychics. Murder. Just another day in Donn's Hill.

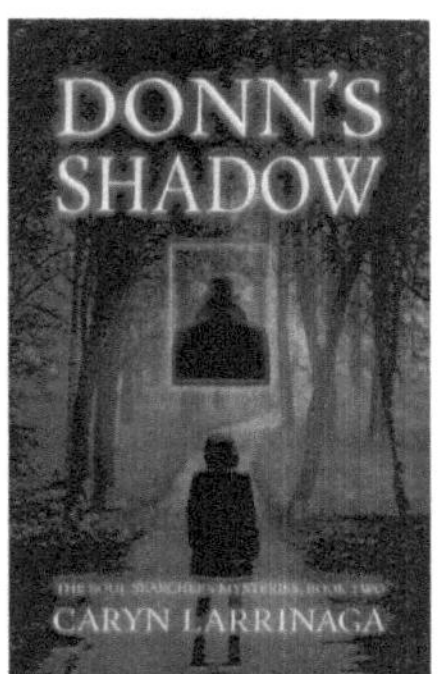

Return to the most haunted small town in America in DONN'S SHADOW.

How do you catch a killer who moves like a ghost? Find out in DONN'S LEGACY.

ACKNOWLEDGMENTS

To all the superheroes in my life:

My husband Kelly, who has an inhumanly high tolerance for my nonsense and a telepathic ability to know exactly when I'm most in need of a hug and a peanut butter cup;

My brother Robert, who protected me when I was just a tiny nerd and continues to come to my rescue on a regular basis;

My parents, who made me everything that I am today and—despite facing incredible challenges of their own—never fail to make me feel loved;

My editor Kelley, who used her laser vision to see through the issues in my first draft and, as always, helped me make better choices;

My beta readers Brandy, Rachel, Sarah, and Shannon, all of whom deserve capes and wonderful toys;

And all my friends, family, and readers who supported me so much during and after the release of my last book that they emboldened me to do it all over again...

THANK YOU. I love you all.

ABOUT THE AUTHOR

Caryn Larrinaga is an award-winning mystery, horror, and urban fantasy writer. Her debut novel, *Donn's Hill*, was awarded the League of Utah Writers 2017 Silver Quill in the adult novel category and was a 2017 Dragon Award finalist.

Watching scary movies through split fingers terrified Caryn as a child, and those nightmares inspire her to write now. Her 90-year-old house has a colorful history, and the creaking walls and narrow hallways send her running (never walking) up the stairs. Exploring her fears through writing makes Caryn feel a little less foolish for wanting a buddy to accompany her into the tool shed.

Caryn lives near Salt Lake City, Utah, with her husband and their clowder of cats. Visit www.carynlarrinaga.com for free short fiction and true tales of haunted places.

facebook.com/carynwrites

twitter.com/carynlarrinaga

instagram.com/carynlarrinaga

amazon.com/author/carynlarrinaga

goodreads.com/carynlarrinaga

DONN'S HILL

"A genre-bending gem of a book, cozy meets horror meets cat fancier in a unique town of psychic tourism and ghostly secrets."

JOHNNY WORTHEN, AWARD WINNING AUTHOR OF THE FINGER TRAP, THE BRAND DEMAND AND WHAT IMMORTAL HAND

Return to the most haunted small town in America in DONN'S SHADOW.

How do you catch a killer who moves like a ghost? Find out in DONN'S LEGACY.

A woman struggles to outsmart the demon who bargained for her father's soul. An elderly shut-in with a monstrous secret is tormented by a door-to-door salesman. Six-eyed creatures congregate on the ceiling of a remote bungalow, puzzling a newly rescued tabby cat. An imp's loyalties are torn between a vulnerable child and the god of dreams.

In her debut horror collection, award-winning author Caryn Larrinaga spreads her nightmares under your feet. Fed by the dread her anxiety brings her, each of these eleven tales is a journey into an unsettling universe just parallel to our own—one populated by haunted objects, unwanted urges, and creatures from beyond human understanding. Dread softly.

Agatha isn't looking forward to Christmas. While other eight-year-olds are hoping for a pile of presents, she just wants her evil stepsisters to leave her alone. Summer and Rain have a cruel idea of what passes for fun, and it always involves tormenting Agatha.

When the three of them get stuck inside their house on Christmas Eve, the twins force Agatha to play a twisted version of Hide and Seek. But they aren't the only things hiding in the house, and someone is about to get more than they bargained for beneath the tree...

Dive into stories about love, loss, greed, and revenge. Meet creatures like the mischievous *Galtzagorriak*, the deadly *Gaueko*, the beautiful *Lamiak*, the legendary *Erensuge*, and the wicked *Sorginak*.

The captivating tales in *Galtzagorriak and Other Creatures* are lovingly illustrated by artist Carina Barajas, and are sure to delight the whole family. Whether you're already familiar with the Basque Country or this is your first introduction, you don't want to miss this collection.